This no longer seemed like a good idea

At the sound of the bell over the door ringing, Molly swiveled in her seat. The new arrival was Richard Ward himself, tall, imposingly handsome, glancing around the sandwich shop until he spotted her at the table in the back corner. And, damn it, there was that loose-hipped walk that always stirred something in her.

She'd been the one to suggest they meet for lunch, completely separate from their kids.

"The waitress left you a menu," she said inanely.

He nodded and pulled out a chair next to her. He took up way more than his fair share of space, and that, too, unsettled Molly; she was a big enough woman, she was taller than most men with whom she dealt.

Oh, get a grip! You're not an adolescent. But feeling a lot like one right now.

"Mr. Ward, thank you for coming." *This is Trevor's father. Trevor's father, Trevor's father.* She'd chant it as many times as she had to.

This was not a date.

Dear Reader,

I love to put heroes and heroines through horrific tribulations I've never experienced (and never want to, thanks anyway). I've got to admit, *No Matter What* hit way closer to home for me than my usual stories do. For one thing, once upon a time I was a teenage girl who had passing thoughts about what a pregnancy would do to my life. The idea of telling my parents any such thing was unthinkable. Wow.

I'm not sure my father ever took seriously the idea that his little girl ever *had* sex, even after I was married and produced two children. As it happens, both those children were girls. Who became teenagers. Who dated. My youngest had a boyfriend who drove a fancy pickup truck. He'd bring her home and they'd sit out there in the driveway forever and ever. Half an hour would pass. I can't tell you how desperate I was to march out there and shine a flashlight in the window. What stopped me (besides my desire not to utterly humiliate my daughter) was the common sense realization that they had already been gone all evening, doing heaven knows what. If they were going to do *that,* it probably wouldn't be when parked in front of her house with her mother pacing inside.

We survived those teenage years, and I'm proud to report that both my girls graduated from high school and college *without getting pregnant.*

Fact is, pregnancy is an ever-present terror for any mother of a teenage girl. This book was triggered when it occurred to me that a teenage pregnancy wouldn't be any picnic for the parent of the boy who is responsible, either. Hmm...

And I've got to tell you, I love teenagers in all their sulkiness, defiance and amazing leaps to maturity. So enjoy meeting Caitlyn and her mom, and Trevor and his dad!

Janice Kay Johnson

PS—I enjoy hearing from readers! Please contact me c/o Harlequin Books, 225 Duncan Mill Road, Toronto, ON M3B 3K9 Canada.

No Matter What

JANICE KAY JOHNSON

HARLEQUIN®
entertain, enrich, inspire™

Recycling programs
for this product may
not exist in your area.

ISBN-13: 978-0-373-71807-8

NO MATTER WHAT

Copyright © 2012 by Janice Kay Johnson

www.Harlequin.com

Printed in U.S.A.

ABOUT THE AUTHOR

The author of more than sixty books for children and adults, Janice Kay Johnson writes Harlequin Superromance novels about love and family—about the way generations connect and the power our earliest experiences have on us throughout life. Her 2007 novel *Snowbound* won a RITA® Award from Romance Writers of America for Best Contemporary Series Romance. A former librarian, Janice raised two daughters in a small rural town north of Seattle, Washington. She loves to read and is an active volunteer and board member for Purrfect Pals, a no-kill cat shelter.

Books by Janice Kay Johnson

HARLEQUIN SUPERROMANCE

SIGNATURE SELECT SAGA

*The Russell Twins
**A Brother's Word

Other titles by this author available in ebook format.

CHAPTER ONE

MOLLY CALLAHAN STUDIED the boy slumped sullenly in a straight chair facing her desk and wished desperately she could hand off dealing with him to someone else. Anyone else.

She liked her job most of the time, although discipline was her least favorite facet of it. No choice, though. The high school was small enough that she was the only vice principal. She gave brief, wistful thought to steering Trevor Ward and his father, when he arrived for an emergency conference, into Principal Marta Brightwell's office. Unfortunately, Marta's strength was making everyone feel really optimistic about whatever was under discussion, at least as long as they remained in her presence. A fine quality, but one that failed to solve all those everyday problems that were Molly's bailiwick.

Even so...that's what she *should* do. Her feelings toward this particular boy—belligerent, defiant, aggressive—were not dispassionate. Considering the fight she and her daughter, Cait, had had only last night over Trevor, Molly could admit, if only to herself, that she wished he had never transferred to her school. It would be really good if he slouched out beside his father and never came back. She didn't exactly wish him ill. She'd be satisfied if Daddy decided to transfer him to a private school or ship him home to Mom. But she wanted him gone. Gone from her life, and especially gone from Caitlyn's.

She should be trying to understand what was throwing him into turmoil, but she couldn't make herself care. Knots were climbing atop knots in her neck, her head throbbed, she expected Trevor's father to arrive any minute and she had not the slightest idea what she was going to say to him.

Trevor held an ice pack over one eye, but the trickle of blood emerging from a nostril was turning into a stream. Molly sighed, snatched a handful of tissues from a box and went around the desk to thrust them into his hand.

"Your nose is bleeding again."

He grunted and pressed the wad of tissues to his nose.

"If it gets any worse I'll need to send you to the nurse's office." Which she had not done, because the victim of Trevor's rage was currently occupying one of the cubicles there, waiting for *his* mother to pick him up. Aaron Latter was in considerably worse shape than Trevor. Molly could only be glad he'd gotten a few blows in, at least.

Which was unworthy of her, she reflected, surreptitiously massaging her temple. That said, she'd be talking to Aaron's parents later, too. One more thing to look forward to.

"Trevor, I'm going to ask you to wait out in front. I'll need to speak to your dad privately. Mrs. Cruz will help you if you get to feeling worse."

The stare he gave her from the one eye that wasn't swollen shut chilled her. It was almost emotionless, and yet…full of something. She had never before been afraid of a student, but at that moment she came close.

And her daughter had a massive crush on this boy.

Boy? As he rose slowly to his feet, she realized part of the problem. Seventeen years old, a senior, he didn't look like a boy. He looked like a man. He was already six foot three. Although he hadn't yet achieved his full bulk, he had broad shoulders and more muscles than most of the male teachers had ever dreamed of possessing. He must shave daily and at two o'clock in the afternoon already had a dark shadow on his jaw. His eyes were so dark, brown iris melted into pupil. When he gave someone a black look, it *was* black.

He was also, unfortunately, exceedingly handsome. The minute he'd walked in the front doors the first day of school, he'd turned every female head in the building. Molly had seen even a couple of the younger women teachers flush at the sight of him. With his physique, dark good looks and sullen temperament, he was the Heathcliff of West Fork High School.

Didn't it figure that his brooding stare had turned to Cait, Molly's bright, perky, academically advanced, sunny-tempered, beautiful, fifteen-year-old daughter.

Molly realized that she was grinding her teeth together as she escorted Trevor out of her office. No wonder her head was throbbing.

Once he lowered himself to one of the visitors' chairs, she took the tissues from his hand and inspected his nose. "It seems to have let up," she said briskly. "Mrs. Cruz, please call Jeannie if Trevor's nosebleed worsens."

"Of course, Ms. Callahan." The school secretary looked past Molly. "Ah…Trevor's father is here."

Molly turned, and felt her heart sink. If it got any lower, she thought grimly, her stomach would start digesting it. A distinct possibility, since she'd missed lunch.

Trevor's father, striding down the hall toward her, looked like Trevor would when he finished maturing. If he was lucky. Mr. Ward also didn't appear to be any happier than his son, and it was Molly who was the target of that angry, frustrated stare, not the son who deserved it.

Her favorite kind of parent—the "my son can't possibly be responsible" variety. The "I am pissed at you for interrupting my day and attempting to hold my kid accountable" variety.

She stiffened. How fortunate that she was in the mood to deal with him.

"Mr. Ward," she said, holding out her hand. "I'm Vice Principal Molly Callahan. Thank you for coming."

BARELY THREE WEEKS into the school year, and he'd already been yanked from his day to sit down with the vice principal to discuss Trevor's behavioral shortcomings. As if he hadn't noticed them.

Richard had become reacquainted with his son precisely four weeks ago, when he picked him up at the airport after a hysterical call from Trevor's mother, Alexa, who'd told him he "had" to take Trevor because she'd had enough. Richard's eyebrows had risen over that. Trevor's grades were top-notch, he was a superb athlete and this past summer he'd worked with kids at the Boys & Girls Club while coaching summer basketball. He was an all-around high achiever.

Richard would have loved to raise both his kids. He'd missed having them this summer. One of the worst days of his life had been when Alexa broke it to him that she and husband number two were moving to California.

At least he'd have Trevor for this last year, before he headed off to college.

Yet shipping him back to his mother was looking better by the day, he thought grimly.

With one swift, encompassing glance, he took in his son, who held an ice pack to one eye and sat slumped low in the chair. His head was bowed. He didn't raise it to look at his father, not even when the woman standing beside him said, "Mr. Ward."

Son of a bitch, Richard thought, ashamed to feel ready to kill the messenger as well as the creature that inhabited his son's body, but unable to smile at her and say, "Great to meet you."

Unlocking his jaw took some effort. "Ms. Callahan."

Her voice was familiar; they'd spoken on the phone briefly last week after Trevor's first fight. She had a hell of a voice, with a husky timbre that would stir any man's interest. Beyond that initial reaction, he hadn't given it much thought. Ms. Callahan—the *Ms.* was said with militant emphasis—was likely a rigid, cast-iron bitch. On the phone she'd been terse and had nothing helpful to say. He'd been able to tell she was disappointed to have to admit that she had as yet been unable to assign responsibility for the fight to either boy.

"However," she had declared, "unless a fight begins with a clearly one-sided assault, both students need to be penalized. We have zero tolerance for fighting." That time, she'd suspended Trevor and the other boy each for two days.

If she expelled Trevor now, what the hell was he supposed to do with him?

They were in her office before he really saw her and then it was a mild shock. Molly Callahan was young to be in administration—surely not older than her mid-thirties. She was also...okay, not beautiful, but *something*. Sexy, he decided, if you discounted the steely glint in her gray eyes. Tall for a woman, maybe five-ten. Possibly a little plump by current standards, which weren't his. Generous hips, even more generous breasts, sensational legs that weren't stick-thin and wavy hair of a particularly deep shade of auburn. Natural, if her creamy skin was any indication.

She circled around her desk and gestured toward a chair. "Please, have a seat, Mr. Ward."

He stiffened at her tone of voice. He was not one of her students.

"I gather Trevor was involved in another fight," he said curtly.

"Trevor unquestionably started this one. For no apparent reason. The other young man accidentally jostled Trevor in a crowded hallway. He turned around swinging. One of our teachers observed the entire altercation and described the 'flare of rage' on Trevor's face as frightening. Perhaps you can explain what's going on with your son."

His jaw had gone into lockdown again as she spoke. For the first time it occurred to him that he might be ill equipped to be a full-time parent. He had never, not once, gone to a parent-teacher conference. Yeah, he admired report cards, but he hadn't been there to set rules for homework, to do flash cards, to fold his arms and say, "You knew what you had to do this week to earn that trip to the zoo, and you blew it, buddy."

Not my fault.

No, it wasn't, but resentment that he hadn't had the

chance welled up in him until he was all but choking on it.

Ms. Callahan's ill-disguised disdain and dislike rubbed him the wrong way.

"Trevor is a seventeen-year-old boy. If you've looked at his records, you'll find that at his previous high school—an urban high school with a significantly larger class than here in West Fork—he was in the running to become valedictorian. Colleges were scouting him for both football *and* basketball. Here he's transferred for his senior year, and it appears West Fork High School is already failing him." Richard knew he wasn't being fair, but right this minute he didn't damn well care. He didn't appreciate anything about *Ms.* Callahan's attitude.

Her back was so stiff he could tell it wasn't meeting her cushioned office chair. Her lips thinned. "Trevor has been uncooperative and unpleasant since the day he started class. I need to know if he was angry at having to leave his former school to come here. Was he, for example, sent to live with you as a disciplinary measure, Mr. Ward?"

"No," he said shortly, if not altogether honestly. "His mother has recently separated from her current husband." Her third. "I believe Trevor was reasonably fond of him, but hadn't lived with him so many years the attachment was deep. I'm aware that moving to a new school for your senior year is hardly ideal, but he didn't object."

They glared at each other. Her eyes, Richard decided, were closer to gunmetal gray.

"In other words," she said icily, "you'd like to blame the teachers and students here for somehow, in a startlingly swift few weeks, driving your son to rage that inspires him to attack another boy without provocation."

At his sides, Richard's hands flexed briefly into fists that he forced himself to relax. *I'm not handling this well.* But goddamn it, couldn't she say something helpful? Offer some guidance? Where was the school psychologist? Or didn't they have one?

"No," he said reluctantly. "Of course I don't. Trevor's attitude hasn't been great at home, either." Major understatement. "All I can tell you is that I'm trying to get to the root of it. I'd appreciate some sense that you and his teachers care about Trevor rather than seeing him as nothing but a disciplinary problem."

Fire lit her face. She planted her hands on her desk and half rose from her chair to lean toward him, apparently calling on the greater height to emphasize her authority. "Perhaps it hasn't occurred to you, Mr. Ward, that there were two boys involved a week ago. Two boys today, one of whom is likely on his way, as we speak, to the emergency room. I care about my students. Trevor was the aggressor today." She straightened, on her feet, and held up a hand to silence him when he opened his mouth. "My first obligation is the safety of *all* students at this school. Do I care? Yes. I also care about the boy Trevor battered bloody this afternoon. I am this close—" she pinched her thumb and forefinger nearly together " —to expelling Trevor. Because I *care,* I am only suspending him for the remainder of the week. However, let me make clear to you, as I did to Trevor, that if there is any repeat of his aggression, I will have no choice but to expel him from this school. Do I make myself clear?"

Somewhere midspeech he'd risen to his feet, too, so that *he* could tower over *her*.

"Yeah," he said, "you do. Thank you for your consideration, *Ms.* Callahan. I'm moved by your obvious concern for my son. So moved, I'll be sure to mention it to the principal. Possibly the superintendent, too. John is a friend of mine."

His threats, issued in a gritty voice, affected her not at all. She continued to gaze stonily at him. He nodded and walked out. This time his son let the hand holding the ice pack drop and looked at his dad. If there was something worried or even childish on his face, it was fleeting and replaced by his now-current sullenness.

"We're going home," Richard said, and kept walking, leaving Trevor to fall in behind him or not.

Good. Great. His meeting with Vice Principal Callahan had made *him* sullen, too, and about as mature, behaving like the average middle schooler, forget high school.

And now he had to figure out how to be the parent.

CAITLYN SNATCHED A carrot that her mother had just peeled and crunched into it. Molly pretended to slap at her hand but then took another carrot from the crisper and began to peel. She watched with pleasure as Cait plopped her book bag on the breakfast bar, hopped on a stool and hooked her feet on it. Orange bits flew as she chewed and talked.

"Wow, I don't know what *his* problem is, but today Mr. Sanchez was a total—" She grinned at her mother's raised eyebrow. They'd agreed years ago that she could express honest opinions of her teachers but not use profanity or obscenities to do so. "Jerk. He was a jerk today.

He was in some kind of snit because nobody, like nobody, passed his stupid quiz. Of course it's *our* fault. Did it occur to him that maybe he failed to successfully teach a concept? I mean, *duh*." Another enthusiastic crunch. "So he tried again, and I still don't get it. Who needs advanced algebra anyway?"

"Engineers, I'd guess. Mathematicians, computer geeks, scientists."

"You know this for a fact."

Molly laughed. "Well, no. I confess I got an A in second-year algebra and can no longer remember a single thing I learned. I thank God on my knees daily that you haven't needed my help."

"About that." Cait reached for the zipper of her backpack. "See, there's this thing I don't get…" She giggled at her mother's expression. "I'll figure it out myself, thank you."

She rambled on for several minutes. Molly would have basked in the pleasure of having Cait talking to her, really talking, if she didn't know that soon—any minute—she herself would have to drop a bomb on the mood. Obviously, Cait and Trevor had not spoken since he'd slunk out at his father's side without finishing the day.

She would have waited until after dinner if it weren't for the possibility of the phone ringing any minute. Unless Richard Ward had suspended his son's phone privileges? *Yeah, sure.*

Cait finished telling Molly about a friend who was being such an idiot about this guy who treated her like garbage, and why would she put up with that?

Usually Molly would have commented. Instead, she

took a minute to look at her daughter and think, *If only you knew how much I love you.*

She'd been so in love with her one-and-only child since the day she was born. It almost seemed unfair that Caitlyn was darn near perfect. Molly had been waiting for years for the other shoe to drop. Life was never this good. *People* weren't this good.

But there she sat, delicate face open and cheerful. She had big blue eyes and a cloud of wavy, strawberry-blond hair. Thanks to her father's genes, she was both shorter than her mother and finer boned. She gave an impression of fragility that her years in dance belied. Cait could be tough.

Bracing herself, Molly stirred the homemade chili simmering on the stove. "Cait, there's something I need to tell you."

Her daughter tilted her head. "Wow. You sound serious."

"It's about Trevor."

Cait stiffened.

Get it out quick. "There was another incident involving Trevor. Aaron Latter bumped Trevor in the hall between classes, and Trevor attacked him. He hurt Aaron badly. Mr. Whitlock had to pull Trevor off Aaron. I know how you feel about Trevor—"

"No, you don't." Cait was already scrambling off the stool. "What did you do? You didn't kick him out, did you?"

"I suspended him. You know I had no choice."

"Oh, right," Caitlyn said in an ugly voice. The hostility that filled her eyes was shocking. "Did you even ask him *his* side?"

"He has no interest in talking to me."

"Gee, I wonder why that is? God, Mom. How could you?"

Molly continued with her dinner preparations. She'd tell any parent not to overreact to teenage drama. Be matter-of-fact, she would say. Explain, but do not justify yourself. Be a reasonable adult. A role model.

She reached for the olive oil. "You know school policy on fighting. This is his second infraction within a week. And from what I'm told, this wasn't a fight. It was an assault."

"Oh, that's bull!" her darling daughter snarled. She grabbed her book bag and in a violent movement flung it toward a chair in the dining nook. It skidded across the seat and thudded to the floor. "Aaron Latter is a sneak and a liar."

"Cait, there were witnesses. Lots of witnesses." Explain but do not justify, echoed in her brain. *Yes, but where do I draw the line?*

"You know he didn't 'bump' Trev by accident, don't you? Aaron has been coming on to me. He's practically stalking me. Trevor told him to back off, all right? So the little passive-aggressive creep thought he could get away with smashing into him in the hall, like *oh, oops*."

It sounded reasonable. It might even be true. It also might not be.

"You've never mentioned having a problem with Aaron," she said mildly. She sliced a tomato carefully, aware she was clenching the knife handle too tightly.

Cait wasn't nearly as pretty when she was sneering. "I don't tell you everything, you know."

"I thought we had a good relationship."

Cait's pointed chin shot up. "*I* thought we did, too.

Until you decided you hated the only guy I've ever really liked. The only one who's ever really liked *me*."

The reasonable adult broke. "Okay, now that's ridiculous. Boys have been trailing around behind you since you were five years old. Remember Ben whatever his name was, who asked you to marry him?"

"That was *kindergarten!*"

Molly talked right over her. "You were the only girl in Mrs. Carlson's fifth-grade class to have a boyfriend. Who wrote you *poetry*."

"We were children! Like it's the same."

"Middle school dances," Molly continued inexorably. "I chaperoned them. Don't imply you weren't popular. You were the only freshman in high school invited to the senior prom—"

"Which you didn't let me go to."

"You were fourteen years old! He was eighteen." The knife was still clutched in her hand, but she'd given up slicing.

"I didn't care about him, okay?" Cait's pale, redhead's skin was a furious red. "I love Trevor, and you're…you're *persecuting* him because he likes me, too!" She shoved one of the stools and it crashed to its side on the hardwood floor.

"Caitlyn Callahan!"

"I'm through listening to you," Cait yelled, and raced from the room. The front door opened and banged shut.

Molly let the knife fall to the cutting board, braced her hands on the tiled countertop and closed her eyes.

Dear God, she asked, *why didn't we get this over with when she was thirteen? Why did raging hormones have to hit* now?

Easy answer: Trevor Ward.

"I do not hate Trevor," Molly said aloud. "I *am* more adult than that." She thought.

"Talk to me," his father said. "Tell me what's going on."

The anger that filled Trevor 24/7 rose like a storm-driven wave ready to crash on the beach. Trevor didn't know how to handle these violent impulses, this deep hunger to make everyone else hurt as much as he did. He couldn't have formed all this hostility and sense of betrayal into words even if he'd wanted to, and he didn't.

"Nothing's going on."

His father sighed. "Have you ever been in a fight before last week?"

He shrugged.

Dad had just slapped dinner on the table—a frozen lasagna nuked in the microwave, salad from a bag and presliced garlic bread, also nuked. He hadn't said a word during the drive home. When they'd walked in the door, he'd said, "Go to your room and don't come out until dinner," and continued toward his home office without looking back. Trevor had hesitated, but Dad hadn't looked or sounded like himself. There wasn't anyplace he wanted to be, anyway, he'd told himself, and gone upstairs where he threw himself on the bed and discovered he had enough adrenaline still heating up his bloodstream that he wished Aaron Latter was on his feet again and coming at him.

Now Trevor only wanted his father to get the lecture over so he could sneak out and meet Cait. So far, she was the only good thing to come out of moving to this crappy little town. When he was with her, his anger settled. He felt more *normal.* Horny, but normal. He grinned. Yeah, okay, that *was* normal.

"You find this funny?" his father asked coldly.

He kept his head down. "I was thinking about something else."

"I guess the first thing I need to figure out is how to keep your attention, then, isn't it?"

His first thought was *Oh, shit,* and his second—*Yeah, big scare, what can he do to me anyway?*

Dad held out his hand. "Car keys."

The legs of Trevor's chair scraped on the floor as he recoiled. "What?"

"You heard me. Your driving privileges are suspended."

Rage rose in him. Tide coming in. "That car's a piece of crap, anyway." He took pleasure in the slight flinch he detected beside his father's grimly set mouth. Dad had bought the heap of junk before Trevor had even shown up. He'd been *proud* that he already had a car for his son.

Trevor dug in his jeans pocket, pulled out the keys and tossed them toward his father. He wasn't real sorry when they landed on Dad's lasagna.

Without a word, his father picked them up, took the car key off the ring and handed it back to Trevor. "You might want to wash that," he commented, in the hard voice that didn't sound like the dad Trevor knew and had thought he loved. Then he calmly wiped his fingers on his napkin and started to eat.

Trevor stared at his meal.

"The cell phone is next," Dad remarked, as if he was commenting on something that happened at work that morning. "One more call from the school. You understand?"

"I'm not hungry." Trevor pushed back from the table.

"Understand?"

"Yes! I understand! Are you happy?" He hated the tremor in his voice. The little boy in awe of his daddy. The wriggling, squirming need to piss on the floor because daddy was mad at him.

"Happy?" For a moment their eyes met, the same espresso color. "No, I wouldn't say that."

"May I be excused?" Trevor asked with mocking courtesy.

"Certainly," his father said. "Check the refrigerator in the morning. Since you'll be home, anyway, I'll post a list of chores for you to do."

Trevor didn't say a word. He left the dining room and went upstairs. He'd already perfected the art of leaving the house via his bedroom window and swinging down from the arbor that covered the back patio. He and Cait were meeting at ten. Fortunately, he could walk anyplace in this nowhere town.

Tonight he'd get in her pants. She was dragging her feet. She hadn't done it before, she said. She wasn't sure she was ready. Furious, he turned on his music loud enough to shake the walls.

Well, screw that. Screw her. *He* was ready. Past ready. Desperate. He needed something, and she was it.

CHAPTER TWO

MOLLY DIDN'T DARE go so far as forbidding Cait to see Trevor. That was about the dumbest thing any parent could do, she had always believed. But oh, how she wanted to.

He did not appear chastened when he reappeared in school the following Monday. The black eye had already faded to mustard and lavender. All it succeeded in doing was making him look tougher. He seemed not to have shaved that morning, as if making a statement with the dark stubble. Molly noticed, as she noticed most things in her school. That was one of the mornings she greeted students arriving from the parking lot. His eyes met hers briefly, and she had to work to keep herself from taking a step back. The disquieting thing, she realized, was that there was no spark of rage. Instead, if she hadn't imagined it, he'd smirked. As if he knew something she didn't.

A mother's panic struck her. *Cait.* That son of a bitch. If he was planning to get to her through her daughter, she'd... Her stomach clenched. Do what? She couldn't even prevent whatever it was he had in mind, not without locking Caitlyn in her room for the foreseeable future. Sending her off to boarding school. And that was assuming she wasn't already too late.

I'll keep the channels of communication open, she

told herself, tamping down the fear. Cait and she had always talked, often and easily. Her daughter's recent behavior was an anomaly. She'd get over it.

But that same panic had Molly wondering, *When?*

She had spoken at length to Aaron and his mother— his father was apparently too busy to take time to discuss his son's behavior with school officials. The mother talked about pressing charges. Aaron's eyes got shifty and he insisted that was ridiculous, he could take care of himself. Molly pushed; he got shiftier. It would appear Cait was right; something *had* been going on that he didn't want his mother or anyone else to know about. He was not the complete innocent he had initially seemed.

"My daughter has mentioned you," Molly made a point of saying, and Aaron looked alarmed.

"Cait?"

"Yes." Molly had studied him unblinkingly. "Did you know she and Trevor are friends?"

The mother's head had been swiveling as she tried to figure out what this digression had to do with anything. Neither Aaron nor Molly enlightened her, but Molly was satisfied she'd made her point.

She still didn't like Trevor Ward—*although I do not hate him*—but she'd decided she didn't like Aaron Latter, either. Practically stalking, huh? Let him try that again.

Over the course of the next few weeks, Trevor managed to avoid getting into a fight. He still walked the halls of West Fork High School looking like an escapee gunfighter from the O.K. Corral, minus the black duster and—so far—the gun. Oh, God, horrendous thought— he wasn't *that* angry, was he?

Molly still caught glimpses of her daughter's shining strawberry-blond head at his side, barely topping his broad shoulder. Caitlin was going to the library to study a lot these days, after school and evenings. Or hanging out with friends, often unnamed.

"Does it matter?" she asked with apparent indignation. "Like there's anywhere in town to *go*."

There was Trevor's house afternoons when his father was at work. That was one place Molly would hugely prefer Cait not go. Or Terrace Park, the peculiar one-acre piece of old-growth forest somehow saved as a city park. The vast, tall, dark trees offered too many hiding places, especially at night. A teenage girl had been raped in the park only last year.

In her professional role, Molly had no reason to speak to Richard Ward, although she knew several of the teachers had called him. Trevor was not performing to ability in his classes. In other words, he was obliterating his chances of getting into Harvard or Stanford or possibly even the local community college. Coach Bowman had also called Trevor's father to ask why Trevor was refusing to go out for the basketball team. Coach Loomis had been sulking since school began because Trevor had refused to play football. West Fork had come within one win last year of taking the league championships. This kid who'd led his team to all-state in California could have taken West Fork to the Promised Land. It was killing Chuck Loomis that Trevor had refused. Gene Bowman was refusing to lose hope.

Molly wished him all the luck in the world. She'd love to see Trevor tied up every afternoon in basketball practice. Friday or Saturday nights at games. Whole weekends at tournaments! He could take some of his aggression out on the court in a healthy, culturally approved manner. He could be frequently unavailable to spend time with her daughter. Despite the many pluses, however, she was staying out of the campaign to win Trevor over. She had had to assure Gene several times that her intervention would hurt more than it helped.

One day the first week of October Molly overheard Caitlyn whining on the phone to someone—probably Trevor—that Mom hadn't let her take driver's ed this semester, so now she couldn't get her license until next summer even though she would turn sixteen in April.

To the best of Molly's recollection, they'd both agreed it didn't make sense for her to take the class until spring since it would be almost summer before she'd be able to drive, anyway.

Of course there was no mystery about Cait's new passion for getting her driver's license. When he couldn't hitch a ride to school with one of his new friends, Trevor had become a walker. Knowing Richard Ward had taken the kid's car away from him after the last fight did soften Molly's feelings toward Ward senior, if only slightly. Smart to hit a teenager the hardest where the privileges he or she took for granted were concerned. For a boy, the car had to be number one.

She would swear she'd never set eyes on Trevor's father before, but by some evil chance she kept seeing him now.

One Saturday she was pushing her cart filled with groceries out of the store and came nearly face-to-face with both father and son, striding across the parking lot toward her. Trevor looked sulky—gee, nothing new in that. His father looked sexy, in well-worn jeans and a faded T-shirt that clung to a powerful body. Oh, Lord, she thought, reacting to his loose-hipped, purely male walk.... One, she was disturbed to see, that his son shared.

The boy's stride checked briefly.

"Trevor," she said pleasantly, nodding. "Mr. Ward."

"*Ms.* Callahan."

Was she imagining the mocking emphasis on the *Ms.*? Molly's eyes narrowed. She'd expect it from the son, but not the father. No wonder his kid was such a butt.

The heavily laden cart had taken on a life of its own and she couldn't have paused even if she'd wanted to. "You need a hand?" said a reluctant voice behind her.

Father. Son hovered by the double doors, confusing them so that they slid open and closed, open and closed.

"Thank you, but no. I generally manage groceries on my own."

A flash in his so-dark eyes told her he'd heard her antagonism. He nodded and turned away.

"Mr. Ward," Molly called, ashamed of herself.

He paused and looked back, eyebrows up.

"Thank you. I mean it. It was kind of you to offer."

She had absolutely no idea what he was thinking. He only bent his head again and joined his son. The two disappeared into the store. Molly realized she hadn't seen them so much as glance at each other, never mind exchange a word.

She spotted him less than a week later behind the wheel of a moss-green cargo van that said Ward Electrical on the side. Molly had seen the vans before. In fact, hadn't they done the electrical work on the new elementary school? He must own the company.

She had pulled into a parking spot on the main street of West Fork's old-fashioned downtown. The Ward Electrical van had had to wait while she maneuvered. She turned her head as the van passed, and their eyes met. Inimical, she thought was the word. High school English teacher though she'd been, she had never until now put that particular word into real-world use. Mr. Ward did not care for her.

What ate at her was the knowledge that she deserved his dislike. He'd been a jerk, but she hadn't behaved any better. In fact, *she'd* been a jerk first. She'd had a headache, Trevor had quite honestly scared her and because of Trevor she was losing all closeness with her daughter, her only family. She prided herself on being a professional, but she hadn't been where either Ward was concerned.

Richard was in the bleachers on the evening in early October when the school held its first open house, mainly geared at freshman parents but open to all. Marta welcomed them, induced a few chuckles then introduced some of the staff, including Molly.

"Our vice principal, Molly Callahan," she said, "spent her summer ensuring that students were placed in appropriate classes and that when they got there, each and every one would find a chair to sit in and a desk to write on. This busy lady is part of our curriculum committee, deals with behavioral issues, oversees building maintenance and support staff. You are much likelier to meet with Ms. Callahan this year than me, although—" she smiled broadly "—I sincerely hope it isn't when your child gets in trouble."

A laugh rippled through the assembled parents, all looking awkward crowded on the bleachers. Probably feeling a hint of déjà vu. Unfortunately, that was the moment when Richard Ward, seated halfway up on the end of the senior class bleacher, caught her eye. He was not laughing.

After the speeches, teachers settled at tables hurriedly placed around the gymnasium and out in the main corridor. Parents circulated to chat with their particular child's teachers. Molly wandered around, greeting people she knew, pausing to talk longer with a few who had concerns. She kept seeing Richard, who was apparently determined to speak to every single one of Trevor's teachers. Probably he wanted to put faces with the voices he'd already heard on the phone when they called to discuss his son's shortcomings. Lucky man.

She slipped into the administrative offices to call Cait, who answered neither the home phone nor her mobile. Wonderful. Molly had a sudden image of all the unsupervised teenagers in town assembling at Terrace Park for some kind of bacchanalian party while their parents were all earnestly engaged in planning their futures. God.

A new headache nudged at her temple. She'd been getting a lot of them lately. Better drunken revelry, she decided, than Trevor and Caitlyn alone. She shook with sudden frustration and anger. What if they were in Cait's bedroom right now? Listening to the phone ring? Laughing? She could hear Cait, in that new snotty voice, saying, "Ooh, Mommy's checking up on me."

Putting on her game face, Molly let herself out of the offices only to see Richard Ward walking toward her.

Voices spilled into the broad corridor from the gymnasium and open area outside it. In the other direction, headlights were coming on in the dark parking lot outside. But momentarily, the two of them were alone and she felt the oddest pang of...fear?

Surely not.

Molly stiffened. "Thank you for coming tonight, Mr. Ward. I hope you were able to meet with everyone you wanted to."

"Yes, thank you." He looked gorgeous in a charcoal suit, white shirt and even a tie rather than his green work uniform.

She hated the knowledge that she could totally understand how Caitlyn had fallen so hard for this man's son. With hair long enough to be slightly unruly, mocking dark eyes and that lazy, long-legged stride, he was the sexiest man she'd ever seen.

He's a *parent,* she told herself. An electrician, for Pete's sake. A regular, garden-variety man. Maybe even married.

She didn't remember noticing the name of a stepmother in Trevor's records, but that didn't mean there wasn't one.

That splashed cold water on her involuntary leap of attraction. It hadn't occurred to her, for some reason, but of course he was. How many men his age who looked like that and made a good living hadn't been snatched up long ago? None. Molly made a mental note to check Trevor's records again. Only to satisfy her curiosity, of course. Yes, he'd come to school conferences alone, but his current wife wasn't Trevor's mother, obviously. A defiant seventeen-year-old son would be his responsibility, not hers.

"Good night, then." She offered him another vague, pleasant smile and passed by him close enough to touch as she returned to the gym and he continued to the outer doors and parking lot. If he wished her a good-night, she didn't hear it.

She had another hour to get through before she could go home and find out whether her daughter was Jekyll or Hyde tonight. With an odd ramble into frivolity, she thought, *Maybe I should I make it Jacqueline or...hmm, Heidi?*

"DAMN IT, ALEXA, *ANSWER*," Richard growled, listening to the phone ring. He'd left half a dozen messages. He'd have flown to California to confront her if he'd been positive where she and Brianna were living. The house had belonged to Alexa's husband, Davis, so of course she'd been the one to have to move out along with her children. A month ago, the two had been staying with friends. Brianna had texted that she and Mom had an apartment now, but Richard had yet to get an address.

"Richard."

She'd picked up. About goddamn time.

"You've been dodging me," he said.

"You know my life is a mess." She had an irritatingly little girl voice that always caught him by surprise. Hard to imagine why he'd thought it was cute when they were in high school together. Now it only grated. "I don't need more to deal with. Trev flipped out. It was too much for me. The two of you have always been tight. I thought he'd be happy to be living with you."

"He's damn near flunking out of school, he's been in two ugly fights and is a hair away from getting expelled, and every word he deigns to speak to me drips with sarcasm and hostility. I can safely say that he isn't happy."

"Oh, no," she whispered.

"Lexa, what happened? This had to be almost an overnight thing. He's not talking. You need to tell me."

"I don't know!" she cried. "Okay? Davis and I were

having problems, and maybe I just didn't notice something. All I know is that he suddenly hated me, Davis and everyone else."

"Brianna?"

She let out a breath that might have been a sob. "Maybe not her. I don't know. I think he calls her sometimes."

"She told me he does."

"Did you ask *her?*"

"Not yet." It seemed underhanded, using one kid to get a handle on the other. And he'd always found it harder to talk to Brianna.

"Well, try," his ex snapped. "Trevor sure doesn't talk to *me*. He doesn't answer when I call and hasn't called me once. He's all yours, Richard. Isn't that what you always wanted?"

It was all he could do not to say, *Yeah, but I'd have liked to get him before you screwed with his head.*

That wasn't fair, anyway. As little as he liked Alexa, she'd done fine with the kids. Brianna seemed like a normal teenage girl—i.e., incomprehensible to him—but what was new about that? Trevor had thrived until whatever happened happened.

They talked for a couple more minutes. Alexa got sulkier and sulkier. He found himself responding in monosyllables. He finally asked if Brianna was there and his daughter came on.

"Hi, Daddy."

Daddy. Call him a sucker, but that warmed him. Not so much when she was trying to persuade him to buy something for her, but when it popped out for no reason, yeah.

"Hey, honey. How are you? You settled into school?"

She'd had to change schools, too, which wasn't fair, but her mother couldn't afford an apartment in Beverly Hills where Davis lived. The guy was rich enough to have made it possible if he'd wanted, but why would he? The kids weren't his. At least the break hadn't happened mid-school year.

Brianna was fourteen, and a freshman in high school now. Only a year behind Trevor's apparent girlfriend, Caitlyn Callahan. Had that occurred to Trev?

"It's okay," Bree said, tone telling him it really wasn't. "At least I still talk to Lark."

His daughter might be a near stranger to him, but Richard did know that Lark was her most recent BFF. Lark's daddy was with one of the big Hollywood talent agencies. Brianna had been moving in slightly scary circles. He'd wondered without ever asking her if she told anyone that her father was an electrician.

"That's good," he said cautiously. "Gotten to know some new kids?"

"Oh, kinda. The classes are way behind the ones I was in last year."

"I'm sorry to hear that." He felt helpless, as he often did when talking to her. *He* couldn't have offered her what Davis Noonan had. He'd had painfully mixed feelings about the advantages this man he'd never even met had given his children. His feelings about them losing those advantages were even murkier. "I'm betting you'll rise to the top wherever you are," he said in the hearty tone any self-respecting kid would see through.

"Oh, Dad." Rolled eyes. He knew it. He'd been demoted to "Dad," too.

"Trev is having a tough time," he said abruptly.

"Yeah, he doesn't say much."

Unhelpful. "I was hoping he did to you."

"Nuh-uh. I think he's mad at Mom and you, too, but I don't know why." She paused. "Is that why you wanted to talk to me?"

"Partly," he admitted, shamed. He tugged at his hair hard enough to hurt. "I always want to talk to you. You know that."

"I kind of wish I'd come for the summer."

He squeezed his eyes shut. "I wish you had, too, honey. I miss you. It's been too long."

Bree hadn't spent this past summer with Richard, either. She'd seemed reluctant with her brother not coming, and Richard hadn't pushed it. He was sorry now.

"Maybe I can come for Christmas," she added. "Except then Mom would be alone, so maybe not. Plus I wouldn't know anyone there."

"You know me and your brother."

She made a noncommittal noise. He tried to coax some more information from her about new friends, teachers, anything, but got nuggets like "not really" and "they're fine." Finally he gave up and they signed off.

In frustration he thought, *This is as good as it's going to get. I'll watch her graduate from high school and probably college, help pay for a wedding, walk her down the aisle if stepfather number four or five doesn't get the nod, and I'll never really know her. My own daughter.*

He'd actually had doubts about whether she really was, although he rarely let them surface. He hadn't guessed when Bree was born that Alexa was sleeping around, but later... He'd wondered, that's all. Unlike Trevor, she had her mother's coloring and enough of her mother's looks there was no being sure. It didn't make any difference, though. He'd loved his little girl from the first time he held her, and never stopped. It didn't really matter if biologically she was his or not. It was only that she was more like her mother. Girlie.

He sighed and scrubbed a hand over his face. Brooding was getting him nowhere.

What he had to ask himself was whether Alexa had lied to him just now. He had a hard time imagining that she really had no idea what had turned their all-star son into a wannabe juvenile delinquent.

And—hell—what about Brianna? Was she lying, too? Was there something none of them wanted him to know? He grunted with near humor. *If I were trying to keep a secret, would I confide it to my powder keg of a son? My mall-mad daughter?*

No, for God's sake, that was idiocy. Sooner or later, Trevor would blow up and all would be revealed. Had to happen.

Whether Richard could fix what was wrong, though, that was another story.

Sitting there alone in the quiet house, he admitted to himself that he could use help. None of his friends who were married had teenagers, though; they hadn't started families as young as he had. Counseling would be useless without Trevor's cooperation. And Richard would be damned if he'd ask for help from Molly Callahan, who *cared* so much she had only suspended Trev instead of expelling him. Big of her.

As much as he disliked her, Richard wished he could keep himself from noticing her luscious body, glorious hair and exquisite skin. Or the fact that she didn't wear a wedding ring.

That didn't mean she wasn't married, he reminded himself, and then thought, *Poor schmuck.* She probably

gave him that chilly, commanding stare over the dinner
table until he ate every last bite of his broccoli.

Richard shook his head hard. *Quit thinking about her.
Get your head where it needs to be: on your own kid.*

Yeah, that might be more productive—if he had the
slightest idea what Trev's problem was.

TREVOR DIDN'T GET WHAT was going on with Cait. She was
shy when he saw her at school the day after they got it
on the first time. He almost kind of liked that. He liked
knowing he was the only guy she'd ever had. She'd been
major tight, and he'd gotten a real charge out of breaking in. Hah! Like he'd fiddled and fiddled with the dial
on a safe, and there'd been that magic moment when the
numbers tumbled into place and the lock clicked open.
Man, it felt *good.* But he knew it hurt her. So he'd resolved the next time to make up for it.

But her shyness hung on. And even though he'd
screwed her, like, five or six more times since then, he
could tell she wasn't enjoying it. She lay there under him
stiff, and seemed relieved when it was over. She didn't
talk to him the same way anymore, either. He thought
she was avoiding him.

It was almost mid-October now. Determined to make
her tell him what was wrong, he lay in wait outside
school at the end of the day. She came out the usual door
with a cluster of her friends. Something happened on her
face the minute she spotted him. She said something to
the other girls, who all turned and looked at him, then
Cait separated herself from them and came over to him.

"Were you waiting for me?"

"Yeah, I want to talk to you."

"I have dance."

"I know you do." It had kind of pissed him off that she would never ditch one of her dance lessons for him. She had lessons three days a week, and often went to the studio in the evening or even on the weekends for more informal sessions. She'd told him that, if she was going to stay limber and be really good, she had to work out and dance every single day. He'd gone to watch a couple of times, and she was good, he had to admit. She looked amazing in her leotard, too. And there was the way she moved. It was so different from how other girls moved. Even the other girls at the dance school. Cait looked like the real thing. Maybe she was, or would be. He knew she'd been in the Pacific Northwest Ballet *Nutcracker* for a couple of years when she was younger.

"Can I walk you over there?" he asked.

"Um." She shrugged. "Sure." They crossed the parking lot and reached the sidewalk. She sneaked a look at him. "What do you want to talk about?"

"You're being weird lately. Like you don't like me anymore."

She kept her head down and her mass of hair hid her face. "It's not you."

"Then what is it?"

"Me," she said softly. "It's me, okay?" Her voice rose there at the end.

He caught her arm and turned her to face him. Her eyes were darker than usual, almost purple like storm clouds could be. She was so beautiful, he wanted to kiss her, but when he started to bend toward her she took a step back.

"I need time. I'm a little freaked, okay?"

Shock slammed him, like a fist in his gut. "Freaked about what? Me?"

"I've never had a boyfriend before."

He waited, but she'd clammed up.

"And now you don't want one?"

She squeezed her eyes shut for a minute. Her hands gripped the cloth handle of her dance bag so tightly her knuckles shone white. "I do, but…"

"You don't."

"I do! I just wish…"

He knew what she wished, and it made him mad. "That we could hold hands? Maybe kiss each other but keep our tongues in our mouths? And our clothes on?"

"Maybe." She swallowed, and now her eyes held appeal. "Sometimes."

Angry and hurt and he didn't know what else, Trevor backed up yet another step. "I thought you were grown-up. My mistake to hook up with a little girl."

Her chin came up. "I'm not a little girl."

"You know what?" he said. "Let's forget about all of this, okay? There are plenty of girls who want me. Ones who are ready for something real, not make-believe like playing with Barbie dolls or having a tea party for your stuffed animals." The cruelty came easily. Slice and dice. He told himself he didn't care about the way her eyes dilated or she panted with shock. "Run along to your dance lesson, little girl." He was walking backward now, opening distance between them. "See you around," he told her with deliberate carelessness.

She gasped, whirled and ran, leaving him feeling bloody even if he was the one doing the slicing. *Bitch,* he thought. *She played me. I hope she's crying. She deserves to get hers.*

He wanted to go smash windows. Faces. Something.
No more Cait to make him feel normal. Warm.

Who cares? he told himself. *Who needs her?*

CHAPTER THREE

MOLLY PAUSED IN THE HALL outside her daughter's bedroom door, cocking her head to hear music or a voice. Nothing. Probably Cait was listening to her iPod while she worked on a school assignment or talked with friends online or texted. After a moment she knocked. "Cait?"

The "Yeah?" didn't sound very encouraging, but Molly opened the door, anyway. How things change. Six weeks ago she'd have been welcome anytime in Caitlyn's bedroom. Now she had no idea what was happening in Cait's life. Maybe today Molly could get her to open up.

Sure enough, Cait sat cross-legged on her bed, an earbud in and her smartphone in her hands. She looked up with an expression that said, *Why are you bothering me?*

Molly sat at the foot of the bed, anyway. "Is something going on with you and Trevor?" she asked bluntly. "I haven't seen you with him lately."

"Bet you're really sorry, aren't you?" Resentment gave a razor edge to every word.

"I'm sorry for anything that hurts you. Please believe that, if nothing else."

Dark smudges surrounded Cait's eyes. Heavier than usual makeup, or had she rubbed her eyes, forgetting that she wore mascara? Wanting to reach out to her, Molly restrained herself.

Cait shrugged. "We broke up, so I guess you can go out and celebrate."

"Honey…"

"I don't want to talk about it, okay?" Cait stared wildly at her. "Especially not with *you*."

Molly flinched at the sheer venom and knew her daughter saw it. She wanted to say something parentlike, wise, understanding, but her mind was a giant blank. After a moment, she nodded, stood up and left the room without saying another word. She heard the sob behind her as she closed the door, but she didn't stop, felt no temptation to go back.

She went to her own room and sat in the easy chair where she often read. It had to be ten minutes before she was calm enough to feel rational. Mostly rational. Right at this moment, she couldn't figure out how parents went on after scenes like this and looked at their children with love. She couldn't even figure out why this particular scene had hurt so much. All she knew was that it had.

On instinct she changed to running clothes, including the iron maiden bra she had to wear when active. She'd use the middle school track. She was less likely to be recognized there than at the high school. She ought to be putting on dinner, but if Cait got hungry tonight she could feed herself. Molly didn't even knock on her daughter's door on the way out to tell her where she was going.

She found the track deserted and, after stretching, began to run. Slowly at first, then pushing herself harder and harder. She was on the third mile before she recognized the stew of emotions inside her as a sense of betrayal. The person she loved the most had turned on her, and all the child psychology she could summon, all the reason, didn't seem to help.

She doesn't really hate me, no matter how it sounded. How it looked. I know better. I know if I'm patient, when she's eighteen or twenty she'll return to me, my loving daughter. I know that. I do.

Hormones. Pulling away. Cait's behavior was typical. Probably more typical than the way she'd breezed through the usually difficult middle school years.

I'm an adult. I'm the parent.

Yes, she was. But did that excuse Cait?

She was running all out now. Too fast, her lungs heaving. The slap of her feet on the track was all she heard.

I love her.

I don't deserve this.

Finally she had to make herself slow, then walk. Her eyes stung from sweat and her thigh muscles felt like jelly.

The childish hurt had faded, replaced by a crushing sense of failure. What was she doing in a profession for which she was obviously so ill qualified? She cringed at the superiority she'd felt as she counseled parents from her own lofty height as the mother of the perfect child. To think she'd dared when she knew so little about being a parent or even a teenager. She certainly hadn't been a usual one herself. She had never been able to rebel.

Who was I to talk? she marveled. And then, *No wonder Richard Ward looked at me like that.*

She felt stiff and slow and older than her thirty-five years when she got back in her car and started for home.

CUTE LITTLE CAITLYN Callahan seemed to be a thing of the past. So far as Richard could tell, there wasn't another girlfriend, per se, although there were certainly girls. Trevor was coming home smelling of cigarettes first, then booze and finally pot. They had one ugly confrontation after another. Richard wondered if there were still military-style boarding schools.

It was nearly the end of October, which meant midsemester grades would be coming out. Richard warned Trev that if he was failing, he'd lose his cell phone.

He had always believed you taught your kids your values, then trusted them. When treated with respect, people were more likely to push themselves to meet expectations, he'd been sure. Worked for employees, should work for kids, right?

The day he searched his son's bedroom was a low. The very necessity made him admit that Trevor was in real trouble. That, as a parent, *he* was in real trouble.

He worked quickly, efficiently, trying not to let himself think too much about the way he was violating Trev's privacy. Drawers first—underwear and socks, shirts, jeans. Nothing untoward. Closet—mostly unused sports equipment and shoes in a jumble on the carpeted floor, a few jackets carelessly hung, unpacked boxes on the shelf. Richard lifted those down, one by one, but found them still taped shut and identified in bold black marker—*Trev's Summer Clothes. Trev's Ski Parka, Quilted Pants Etc. Trev's Books.* And so on. He put them all back where they'd been. Moved on to the desk.

There he found precious few signs that school assignments were being completed, but a few returned quizzes and tests that gave him hope. Apparently Trevor had been advanced enough in school that the routine work was a gimme for him. Maybe enough to save him with passing grades?

It was a sad day when that was all he could hope for.

Actually, that wasn't the only positive. He also failed to find any drugs. So the pot he'd smelled probably hadn't been Trevor's. He didn't find any cigarettes, either. Or even matches or lighter. Maybe Trev hadn't gotten as stupid as he'd feared.

He did find a couple of magazines featuring naked women in lewd poses, but those weren't any surprise. What teenage boy didn't have some under his mattress?

Once he was sure Trevor's room looked the same as when he'd entered it, Richard went downstairs to his home office and refuge. He sat behind his desk to brood. His mouth curved wryly as he remembered those long-ago days when he, too, was a teenager and unable to think about much besides girls and sex. His curiosity had raged from the time he was maybe eleven or twelve. Mom wouldn't have touched the topic with a ten-foot pole, but Dad had sat him down for a few awkward conversations that were less than informative. Mostly he'd tried to drive home a singular point—be very careful not to get a girl pregnant. Richard grunted. Dad must have felt as much of a failure when Lexa turned up pregnant and Richard had to give up college to marry her as he did now, unable to understand or reach his own kid.

His smile died as he wondered whether Trevor was actually sleeping with those ever-present girls. Another thing Richard hadn't found, come to think of it, was condoms. Huh. How would Trevor react if his father presented him with the gift of a box of them? Or would that seem too much like a green light to go crazy sexually, so long as he wore the condoms?

Another question to which he had no answer. He could imagine Trevor's reaction if his father tried to sit him down for a conversation about safe sex.

Did Molly Callahan know her daughter was no longer seeing Trev? If so, she no doubt felt profound relief. Or had she ever known Caitlyn *was* seeing Trev? It wasn't as if kids dated the way they once had.

He grunted again. Yeah, of course she'd known. Maybe she wasn't a cast-iron bitch; maybe she'd seen his son as a threat to her daughter. Richard knew how he'd feel if Bree were seeing a guy with Trevor's behavioral issues. Maybe Ms. Callahan had some excuse for her hostility.

A part of him wished he knew for sure. He was uncomfortable to realize she'd surfaced in his thoughts not because she was Caitlyn's mother, but because he had been thinking about sex. Something he hadn't had in way too long. Hadn't even especially wanted, except in an easy-to-dismiss way when a woman momentarily caught his eye. Casual sex had gotten to be less satisfying at his age, and after the disaster that was his marriage he'd never been sure he was willing to go that route again. Trust once decimated was difficult to resurrect. Most women would want to start a family, too. Been there, done that, and less than satisfactorily. He couldn't see himself starting all over. So he'd found himself dating less and less often, with the result that opportunities to take a woman to bed came rarely.

I'm thirty-seven years old, and I've consigned myself to middle age. I didn't even notice it happening.

Being a full-time father to Trevor seemed to be hastening the process.

But a picture rose in Richard's mind's eye again of Molly Callahan, pushing that cart out of the grocery store. She'd looked ten years younger in jeans and a snug sweater, hair in a ponytail. He could close his eyes and see her. The way the jeans had fit over her long legs and firm, full ass, the sweater over breasts that would be more than handfuls even for a man with big hands. The pink painted on her cheeks by chagrin, the shame and vulnerability in her eyes when she'd called after him to apologize, if obliquely, for her rudeness.

Of course, *he'd* been so miffed at her instant rejection, he'd then been rude. He could imagine what she'd think and say if he called and asked her out to dinner.

Since that was a clear impossibility, it might be best if he kept assuming she really was a bitch, instead of suspecting she might have some excuses for coming across that way.

THE HIGH SCHOOL HELD an annual harvest dance, Halloween with its pagan connotations being verboten. It was the first dance of the year, which meant freshman girls in particular giggled and talked about little else when clustered at lockers. This year's was to be held on Friday night, two days before Halloween.

Molly dreaded dances. Even when they'd had an open, loving relationship, Cait had hated knowing her mother was there, however much Molly swore, cross my heart and hope to die, that she didn't look for her daughter, tried not to see her even when she did, did not memorize what boys she danced with. Of course, Molly perjured herself when she swore, because she couldn't help keeping a watchful eye out for her own kid. It was behavior out of her conscious control. Someday, when Cait had children of her own, she'd understand, Molly told herself.

Caitlyn announced at the last minute that she wasn't going to this dance.

"You can dance with your friends," Molly suggested helplessly.

Expression mutinous, Cait shrugged. "I don't feel like going."

"Trevor probably won't be there. Seniors usually don't bother."

"I don't want to. That's all." She gave a nasty smile. "You have fun, Mom."

As usual, Molly planted herself out in front of the gymnasium as reassurance to parents and warning to kids. Most of the students arrived in clusters, many from the parking lot. Others, especially the freshmen and sophomores, were dropped off by parents. Molly paid no particular attention to a black pickup pulling to the curb until Trevor leaped out. He hurried away, undoubtedly anxious to disassociate himself from his dad.

Molly made a point of smiling at him. "Trevor. Glad you came."

Instead of staring his usual challenge, his gaze touched hers with alarm and skipped away. He ducked his head and hurried past her into the gym.

Hmm, she wondered. What was that about?

She glanced back to see that the pickup was still there. In fact, Richard Ward had gotten out and was walking toward her. The night was cold and he wore jeans, work boots, a flannel shirt and down vest. His eyes were shadowed by the artificial outdoor lighting, but she thought they were wary.

"Ms. Callahan."

"Mr. Ward." She turned her head to smile at some students. "Sarah, Danielle, Micayla. Have fun."

"Chilly night to have to stand out here," Richard remarked.

"Yes, it is." She'd pulled out her wool peacoat for the first time and had the collar turned up over a scarf wrapped around her neck. She even wore gloves. She could see her breath. His, too, come to think of it.

He remained silent as she spoke to more kids and waved greetings at a couple of parents. She saw out of the corner of her eyes that he'd shoved his hands in his jeans pockets. When there was a momentary lull, he spoke. "I keep expecting to hear from you."

She faced him. "Trevor hasn't been in any more fights, thank goodness. We had some vandalism, but as far as I can tell he wasn't tied to it. Which is not to say he doesn't still worry me."

"Me, too."

Well, that was honest. It didn't so much surprise her as make her aware anew of how badly she'd misjudged him. After seeing him earnestly making the rounds talking to Trevor's teachers, she'd been forced to realize that he did care about his son and was, in fact, taking full parental responsibility. He still made her uncomfortable, but that wasn't his fault. Seeing him only reminded her of how poorly she'd handled that meeting—and probably the phone call preceding it.

Okay, and then there was the fact that he reminded her for the first time in a long while that she was a woman, with a woman's needs. Right now, for example, she was painfully aware of his size, broad shoulders, dark, tousled hair and the angles and planes of his face that made it look…austere. Although that might not be the bone structure. Molly had a feeling this man was suppressing a whole lot.

"I gather he and your daughter aren't an item anymore," he said after a minute.

"Yes, so she tells me."

"Did she say why?"

"No." Molly frowned and really looked at him. "They're young. Pairings don't usually last long."

"Maybe not." He rocked back on his heels. "I met Trevor's mother in high school. Dated her the last two years, and married her."

She opened her mouth and then closed it. She didn't know why she was shocked that he'd told her so much. It hadn't been a throwaway, making conversation kind of comment. Had he really gotten married at eighteen? She was horrified whenever she heard about students graduating and getting married right away.

Not that she could say much, married at twenty and a mother at twenty-one. Yes, but see how that had turned out. Maybe it's why she *was* horrified by the idea of it happening to anyone else.

"But you're divorced," she heard herself say, and winced.

"I didn't say it was a good idea. Only that some high school romances get serious."

She nodded.

"I have the impression Caitlyn hurt him."

Oh, so that was why he was loitering at her side? Wanting to blame *her* daughter? Molly's anger fired right up. Maybe her first impression was right after all;

maybe he was the kind of parent who always wanted to blame someone else.

"Funny," she said sharply. "I have the impression *he* hurt Cait. She didn't even come tonight."

"Really." He continued to stand there, rocking subtly on the balls of his feet, watching her. Cars pulling up to the curb were having to maneuver to get around his pickup.

She greeted more people. There he stood. Exasperation and something that felt a little bit like panic finally made her turn back to him.

"Mr. Ward, I'm afraid I need to be available to other parents. And I'll have to go inside soon. If you'll excuse me…?"

She would have said his face was expressionless, but now it became *really* expressionless.

"Of course," he said. "Sorry. I wanted… It doesn't matter. Poor timing. Hope the evening goes smoothly." He nodded and walked away, climbing a moment later into his pickup and accelerating away from the curb without once looking back at her.

I wanted… What?

An ache in her chest told her she should have guessed he needed to talk to her about something specific. Of course he hadn't hung around only to make disjointed, meaningless conversation. Probably he had hoped to discuss Trevor. What else could it be?

Why in heck hadn't she asked him, as she would have any other parent, whether he needed to talk? Suggested they arrange an appointment instead of icily dismissing him?

Oh, but she knew why. He intimidated her. He made her feel things she didn't know how to handle. She could talk alone with the father of any other student in this school district without once thinking of him as a man. But with Trevor Ward's father... She couldn't forget he was a man. Attractive, enigmatic and probably unavailable, assuming she could even imagine herself *wanting* him to be available, which she didn't.

Ugh. She didn't lie even to herself very well.

WAY TO STRIKE OUT, Richard congratulated himself. But, God, had he behaved like an idiot, or what? Standing there shuffling his feet, sneaking peeks at the object of his adoration—who was trying to do her *job* and had absolutely no time to chat with him, never mind flirt.

It appeared he'd lost any touch he'd ever had. Richard couldn't believe he'd done that. He hadn't intended to. He had never consciously decided, *When I see her again, I'll ask her out.* No, when he saw her out front of the gym greeting arrivals, impulse had overcome him and next thing he knew he'd been standing beside her trying to think of something to say.

So, of course, his conversational foray had been to accuse her kid of breaking his kid's heart. He flinched at the memory. Really slick.

He'd been surprised Trevor wanted to go to the dance at all, far less was willing to accept a ride from him. Not that he'd done so gracefully; when Richard offered, Trev had given a typically sullen, one-shouldered shrug that said, louder than words, *whatever.* One of his favorite words in the English language. So favored, he'd learned to convey it wordlessly. Still, he had accepted. Of course, he hadn't talked during the short drive, but he had actually muttered a "thanks" before he jumped out. A word Richard would have sworn Trevor had deleted from his vocabulary.

Home again, Richard found the house felt empty and too quiet, a ridiculous thing to think when he'd lived here alone since his divorce but for the kids' visits and his own two, year-long tours in Iraq. Then, living in barracks with other National Guardsmen, he'd have given anything to be home in his quiet, empty house. He had nothing to complain about.

He turned on the TV but found nothing interested him and turned it off. He'd never been one for noise for its own sake. The sound of canned voices did not make him feel any less lonely.

Richard set down the remote and looked around his living room. Funny that he hadn't realized he was lonely. The kids were on his mind a lot, sure, but that wasn't the same thing. By logical extension, he thought, *I could call Bree,* but reminded himself it was Friday evening and she was sure to be out. Hell, Lexa probably would be, too. He'd be stunned if she didn't already have another guy on her string. Maybe two or three. He knew from pictures of her with the kids that she'd stayed beautiful. Maybe Davis hadn't been paying enough attention to her. Could be he'd gotten too wrapped up in work. Alexa needed to have a man completely besotted with her or she'd look for another one who would be. Eventually Richard had come to feel sorry for her, so insufficient unto herself. She had to see a dazzling reflection of herself in someone's eyes to feel as if she was worth anything.

Took him long enough to figure that out. But then, good God, he'd been only months older than Trev was now when he made his seventeen-year-old girlfriend pregnant. Mind-boggling thought.

Grimacing, he reached to turn on his computer. At least if he worked, he could accomplish something concrete. Bree's dad might be an electrician, but he was a pretty damn well-to-do one. He planned to have his bid for the electrical work on a small strip mall in Monday morning. No time like the present to finish it up.

IT WASN'T FULL DARK WHEN the doorbell rang Sunday night, but Molly knew who she'd find on her doorstep. The little ghosts and robots and princesses came out early.

She usually enjoyed Halloween and had been determined to try to enjoy this one, too. West Fork was the kind of town where it was still safe for children to knock on doors begging for candy. Too bad Cait had already ruined Molly's favorite part of the holiday—carving the jack-o'-lanterns. They'd done it together since Cait was big enough to draw a face on the pumpkins with her marker and help spoon out seeds and slime. This year, when Molly announced that she'd bought two pumpkins, Cait had said flatly, "Wow."

"You don't have dance tonight. I thought this would be a good evening to carve them."

Her daughter only shrugged. "I don't feel like it."

Without another word, Molly had marched downstairs, spread newspaper on the table to contain the mess and done it herself. She didn't have a grain of Cait's artistic ability, though, so hers were simple—triangular eyes, noses, wide mouths with missing teeth. But, by God, they had jack-o'-lanterns, one on the porch steps and the other on the railing.

Not half an hour ago, she'd lit candles inside them. Wrapped candy was heaped in a huge ceramic bowl on a side table by the front door, ready to hand out. She'd gotten dinner on the table early—although not as early as she'd planned—so they'd be ready. Cait had even come down when she called.

She then sat pretending to eat, head bent so her hair shielded her face, responding in monosyllables if at all to Molly's one-sided chatter. The few glimpses Molly had gotten of Cait's face had scared her. She'd been starkly pale and utterly withdrawn. Something was wrong. Even *more* wrong.

In irritation, Molly thought, *Sure, there is. Something earth-shattering like Trevor acquiring a new girlfriend.* She was getting exasperated enough at Cait's histrionics to keep her from panicking. The sound of the doorbell was a relief.

She opened the door to a cry of "Trick or treat!" and found two small faces grinning up at her. The little girl wore a remarkably clever horse costume—she was a palomino with a shining golden mane and tail—while the boy was a pirate.

"Happy Halloween," she told them, dropping candy into their proffered orange buckets and waving at the dad who hovered on the front walk. Another group was already turning up toward her porch.

She hadn't quite finished dinner, but that was okay. Maybe Cait would condescend to take a turn. At least that didn't involve interaction with her mother, the enemy. And she hadn't said anything about going out.

To Molly's surprise she appeared from the kitchen and grinned at the latest group. "Wow, you're so cute. And you're scary!" she said, handing out the candy. She

mimicked fear at a Frankenstein. Giggling, the two carefully climbed down the porch steps to rejoin a shadowy
adult figure—Mom this time?

Studying Cait carefully, Molly thought there was
still something odd going on. Did she seem…frenetic?

Wow, I'm getting paranoid.

"You should have seen the horse," Molly said, closing the door and smiling at her daughter. "The costume
was pretty amazing. Almost better than yours."

Cait rolled her eyes. "Which you designed and sewed
by the sweat of your brow. And yeah, I remember you
had bandages on every finger by the time you were
done creating the tail. How could I forget? You've only
bragged about my purple horse costume nine million
times."

"I hadn't even thought of it in years," Molly said, as
evenly as she could manage. "I apologize for mentioning it. Will you get the next trick-or-treaters?"

Cait yanked open the closet and grabbed a parka. "I
have to go somewhere."

Molly had started toward the kitchen, but now she
turned back. "*Have* to?" When there was no answer,
she asked, "Where and with whom?"

"'With whom.' God, Mom."

She crossed her arms. "You didn't mention a party."

"I'm not going to a party, okay?" Cait exclaimed with
that new ugliness. "It's like six o'clock. It's not even
dark! What's your problem?"

"I asked where you're going. Is that so unreasonable?"

"Yes! You don't trust me at all." She flung open the
door, startling a solitary Mutant Ninja Turtle who had

been reaching for the doorbell. He scuttled back a few steps.

"Trick or treat?" he whispered.

"Here!" Cait grabbed a whole handful of candy bars and dumped them in his bag so hard it rattled. "I'm going," she told her mother, and took off down the steps, yelling over her shoulder, "Deal with it." The parent waiting on the sidewalk took a step onto the grass to let her tear by. The flashlight the woman held wobbled.

"Thank you," the little one mumbled, and Molly pulled herself together enough to say, "Happy Halloween."

Then she shut the door, all her pleasure in the evening gone. Boy, did Cait have a real talent for puncturing every happy moment these days, as if she sensed and resented her mother's mood. Depressed? Has a headache? Good enough, I'll give her a break. Cheerful, optimistic? Hell, no. I'll flatten her.

She's being a teenager, that's all. You're taking it ridiculously hard, Molly told herself. Cait had spoiled her up until now, that's all. Good heavens, she wasn't using drugs—at least that Molly could tell—she hadn't reeled home drunk yet, she wasn't being dropped off at all hours by boys who screeched up to the curb outside the house. Also, as far as Molly knew, Cait was even keeping her grades up. So she'd become snotty, sulky, secretive and all too frequently angry. Not that unusual.

Deal with it, Molly thought with near humor.

The doorbell rang again, and she found a smile for the next round of children.

By eight-thirty, she was tempted to blow out the candles and turn off the porch light. Any trick-or-treaters now would be teenagers, and she didn't feel all that obligated to offer them candy. On the other hand—her gaze strayed to the bowl—she was bound to be tempted by the leftovers, and she struggled with her weight enough without ripping open Butterfinger or Snickers bars uncontrollably only because they were there.

She cleared the table in the long lull and began loading the dishwasher. Most of their dinner had to be scraped in the garbage. Molly had scraped quite a lot of food in the garbage lately. Cait seemed to enjoy throwing her scenes at mealtimes. Hey, Molly thought, maybe she should weigh herself. Could there be a silver lining to all this? It had seemed as if the waistband of her navy blue skirt was rather loose this morning.

Unlike her heels, which she still wore in her hurry to get dinner on the table. On the thought, she kicked them off. One flew halfway across the kitchen, the other only a few feet. She wiggled her toes, decided she'd ditch the panty hose as soon as she'd finished cleaning up the kitchen and reached for a dirty pan.

The doorbell rang. She jumped, remembered *why* it was ringing and turned, stepping automatically around the open dishwasher door. At which point, she planted a foot on the pump lying on its side and stumbled back into the kitchen trash container, which she'd pulled out from the cupboard to make cleanup easier. Even as she swore, it toppled over, spewing the uneaten food, crumpled wrappings, cans that should have gone in recycling, and…what was that?

She stared, disbelieving, at a little white stick with a bright blue dot at one end. Buried at the bottom of the garbage amidst carrot peels.

Suddenly frantic, she crouched and dumped out the rest on the kitchen floor. The doorbell rang again, more insistent. She ignored it, scrabbling through the trash. A brown paper bag held something, half-squashed. With shaking hands, she pulled it out. A home pregnancy test kit. Open. A second stick slid out and plopped onto a glob of leftover casserole. Molly turned it over and saw that it, too, had a blue dot. It only took her a minute to find the instructions. *If no color appears, you are not pregnant,* she was informed. *If color appears, you are.* Simple.

Dizzy, she dropped to her knees. All she could think was, *My fifteen-year-old daughter is pregnant. Oh, dear God.*

CHAPTER FOUR

MOLLY KNEW THAT she would never, so long as she lived, forget the expression on Caitlyn's face when she finally arrived home at nine-thirty, dashed straight to her bedroom and found her mother sitting in her chair, the two sticks from the pregnancy test kit lying on the desktop in front of her. Her gaze flew to her mother, then the damning evidence and back to Molly.

"You searched the *garbage?*" she whispered.

"I knocked it over by accident." Molly had become very nearly numb by now. "You should have disposed of them in the can."

"I was going to, but there wasn't anything in it. I thought you'd notice…" Cait swallowed. She still stood a foot or two inside the room, frozen in place.

"You didn't think I'd notice your belly swelling?" *How polite I sound.*

"I…I…" Tears spurted and Cait's face contorted. With a sob she threw herself across the room and face-down onto her bed. Her whole body shook with the force of her tears.

Molly's eyes stung. On a rush of pity, she moved to sit on the bed and gently rub her daughter's back. "Oh, sweetie. I know you were scared. I do know."

She kept murmuring; Cait kept crying. It was a storm of misery and grief and fear. Molly would have given a lot to have joined her. But maybe strangely, she felt steadier now than she had at any time in the past six weeks.

"I love you," she said, bending down to kiss Cait's head. "I love you so much. We'll figure out what we have to do. We will."

"How can you love me?" her child wailed.

Through her own tears, Molly laughed. "I will always love you. Haven't I told you that a million times? That no matter what happens, no matter what you do, I will love you because I'm your mother?"

Cait managed to roll over and look up through swollen eyes. Her skin was blotchy; tears dripped from her chin and snot from her upper lip. Molly reached for a dirty T-shirt on the top of the hamper and handed it over. "Wipe and blow."

She did, and almost looked worse afterward. Molly sat back down and embraced Cait, who laid her head on Molly's shoulder and clutched her, too. They sat like that for a long time—a couple of minutes, at least. Silent, breathing in and out. Molly soaked in the closeness and tried to shut her mind for this brief, peaceful interval to all the decisions to be made. To the fact that everything had changed for Cait, irrevocably.

At last a long breath shuddered out of her and she straightened. "Would you like a cup of tea? Or cocoa?"

"Cocoa, please."

They went downstairs. Molly put water on to boil and Cait sat in the dining nook waiting. They had instant, thank goodness; Molly hadn't been sure, since they didn't drink it often. She set a spoon in each mug, poured in the boiling water and carried them to the table, where she sat across from Cait.

"Have you told Trevor yet?"

Head bowed, concentrating on stirring, Cait shook her head. "That's where I went tonight. I tried."

Molly had guessed as much. "Did you find him?"

"Finally. At a party. But he was with some girl." She clenched her jaw. "He wouldn't go off where I could talk to him. And I didn't want to yell out to the whole room, 'Hey, guess what, I'm pregnant.'"

"No, I don't blame you."

"What can he do anyway?" she asked fiercely.

It was hard, so hard, to hide how angry Molly was. "Depending on what you decide to do, there are ways he can take responsibility, too. He *is* responsible. At least as much as you are. He's two years older, Cait."

"We didn't use a condom the first time," Cait said dully. "He did after that, but I could tell he didn't like how it felt."

That son of a bitch, was all Molly could think. "At seventeen, he surely understood the consequences," she said after a moment, trying to hide her rage.

"I've been so scared." The swollen eyes were pathetic. Her nose was starting to run again and Molly handed her a napkin. "I kept thinking my period would start any day, that this couldn't be happening."

"How pregnant are you?"

That made Cait drop her eyes. A new tide of red rose from her neck to swallow the blotches on her face. "The first time was, um, six weeks ago," she mumbled. "So I guess…"

That meant if they were going to seriously consider abortion—and how could they not, given Cait's age?— it had to be soon. "Oh, sweetie," Molly murmured. She waited, but Cait didn't say anything. "Didn't you know you could talk to me?"

The wet eyes met hers again. "I was so scared," she repeated. She buried her face in the napkin, finally wiped and blew again. "And I've been such a butt."

"Yes, you have. But remember—"

"No matter what I do, you will always love me because you're my mother," she recited, sounding watery.

"Right."

"Mommy. What do I *do?*"

"That's something we'll have to talk about and think about carefully. But I suspect you know the options. Really, there are only three."

"I could get an abortion," Cait said tentatively.

Molly nodded. "That's one. Two, you can have this baby and give it up for adoption." It was hard to go on, seeing the stricken look on her daughter's face. "Or three, you have it and keep it."

"But…how can I?"

"With great difficulty. There was a time both Trevor's parents and I would have said the two of you had to get married. He could finish the school year and then get a job."

"But…he broke up with me."

"There were consequences to his choosing not to use a condom," Molly reminded her. "Seniors in high school are planning for the future. They're thinking about grades, how to pay for college, how to get training for a trade that interests them. A few are even planning to get married once they graduate. Trevor made a choice about the future when he was either in too big a hurry to bother with a condom, or decided he didn't like how sex feels without one." She paused, feeling cruel, but knowing this had to be said. "So did you, agreeing to have sex without setting limits."

A sob hitched in Cait's throat, but she didn't leap up and race from the room as Molly had half expected.

"So you think we should get *married?*" she asked after a minute.

"No. I said there was a time that would have been expected. Nowadays... Well, I suspect most girls in your situation have an abortion. No matter what, you're too young to marry anyone, and whether you want to admit it or not, Trevor is not a good candidate. He's an angry young man who has been lashing out at everyone around him. I don't believe he's capable right now of being any kind of husband or father."

"He was...he was really sweet to me."

"Until he ditched you?"

"It wasn't like that." Cait looked wretched. "I think... I think it was my fault." Molly snorted, and Cait shook her head. "He said I was acting like a little girl, and he'd made a mistake hooking up with someone my age. And...I guess I was, I don't know, kind of not sure how to act and..." She stumbled to a stop, seeming to run out of words.

"Over your head."

Another sniffle. "I guess. He's older and he knew what he was doing and I didn't and... But I liked him so much, and when he liked me, too..." The last came out as a wail.

Molly felt a burn beneath her breastbone. She understood. How could she not? She'd been a teenager, hopelessly aware of a boy who would never in a million years notice her. And then a freshman in college when a boy like that *did* notice her—and she, too, had ended up pregnant long before she'd planned for any such eventuality. Yes, she'd been older than Cait, but any wiser? Not so much.

"Right now," she said, "I think we both need to go to bed."

"I can't go to school tomorrow!"

"Yes, you can, and you have to." She held up a hand when Cait would have interrupted. "You're not going to be any less scared or upset on Tuesday or Wednesday. Or even next Monday. And if you should decide to carry this baby to term..." Her throat wanted to close up as she envisioned her increasingly pregnant daughter walking the halls of the high school. Or transferring to the alternative school? "Chances are good you won't make it all the way through the school year. So you'll miss days then. You can't afford to miss any now."

Cait gulped.

"Do you want me to confront Trevor with you? I could call you both to my office...."

"No!" Her daughter leaped to her feet, her face a study in alarm. "You wouldn't!"

"You have to tell him."

"I know I do." She swiped at her eyes. "I will. But I need to do it my own way, okay?"

"Fair enough," Molly said, although she didn't agree. "Just...pick your time carefully, okay? Maybe after school?"

Cait nodded. She was crying again. Molly's heart was wrung by pity, but also some anger, and it wasn't all aimed at Trevor. She would have sworn Cait was so mature for her age. Molly had nearly treated her as an adult. They'd talked openly about everything, including sex and birth control. And then brooding Trevor

Ward had walked into West Fork High School and Cait's brains had scrambled.

Hormones do that.

I thought I'd Kevlar-vest-armored her against making the same mistakes I did. So what happened?

Trevor happened.

And the truth was—she felt hollow, thinking this for the ten thousandth time and finally understanding it was true—you can't protect your children. Not 24/7, without fail. Not the way you want to.

I didn't believe it, Molly admitted, and now *she* felt grief.

"Caitlyn Callahan called," Richard told his son. They didn't get that many calls on the home phone. The ring had startled him.

Trevor grunted, one foot on the bottom step.

"The third time this week."

"Yeah, like she can't talk to me at school." After that momentary pause, Trevor took the stairs two at a time.

Richard stared after him. What was going on? He'd only caught a glimpse or two of her, but enough to see that Caitlyn was an exceptionally pretty girl. *Really* pretty. There was a reason Trev had cut her from the herd within days of starting school here. Richard still didn't know who'd dumped whom, but unless this girl was completely lacking in pride, he had trouble seeing why she'd make a nuisance of herself pursuing his son once he'd lost interest. There had to be plenty of other boys who'd be glad to fill the vacuum.

Frowning after Trevor, Richard gave some serious thought to calling Molly and asking what she knew. But hell, he knew that was overstepping. He had no real grounds for this uneasy feeling. Maybe girls had gotten pushier than they were in his day. Even then, there'd been a few who didn't hesitate to call a boy, and call again. Let Caitlyn back Trevor into a corner at school if she was determined enough.

He tried to shrug it off, tried not to regret the lack of any good excuse to call Molly, maybe even see her. In the week since the high school dance, he'd come to his senses about asking her out. It was a bad idea all around. She would have said no and he'd have been humiliated. As long as Trevor stood between them, that wasn't happening, even assuming she'd have been otherwise interested. Maybe next year, once Trev had graduated—if he did. Maybe then, if Richard could determine whether she was really single.

He went to the kitchen to find something to throw together for dinner. He wasn't much of a cook, which embarrassed him some. But why would he be? Lexa had done the cooking when they were married, and later there wasn't much motivation, not when the only person he was feeding was himself. Summers when he had the kids, he'd tried harder; made sure he served a vegetable with dinner, grilled steaks, made salads. Even followed a few recipes. The last summer they were here, Trev and Bree had taken turns putting dinner on the table most days, and both of them were pretty decent cooks. Lexa's influence, Richard guessed. Went without saying that Trev hadn't so much as turned on the coffeemaker for his father this year.

Trev slouched downstairs for the hamburgers, baked beans and corn Richard served for dinner. For the first weeks, Richard had tried talking during dinner about his day, maybe mentioning some things he'd read in the morning paper, offered an anecdote from when Trev was little. Talking, he'd discovered, was worse than the silence, so sometime in the ten weeks Trevor had now been with him, Richard had given up. They ate in complete silence tonight, although he wanted to ask, *Why are you dodging that girl? Why can't you make it clear you're not interested? Or is she intent on saying something you don't want to hear?*

He felt a little chill at that last thought. What could she possibly want to say that would have his big bad son ducking and weaving? Was there any chance Trevor actually still had a conscience, and was avoiding the admission that he'd treated her poorly?

But—*how* had he treated her poorly?

"Please clean the kitchen," he said, and pushed away from the table. "The Steelers are on, playing Kansas City."

"Yeah, I don't care about either team."

Neither did Richard, but he still enjoyed watching an occasional game. He wasn't a fanatic; he didn't give up every Sunday to stay glued to the television. But tonight he thought it would be a good way to unwind.

His phone rang, and he had to go looking. He'd set it down on the kitchen counter when he started work on dinner. He didn't recognize the caller's number, which surprised him, but it was a local one.

"Hello?"

"May I speak to Mr. Ward?"

He knew who this was. "Ms. Callahan?" he said in surprise. Out of the corner of his eye, he saw Trevor turn slowly from the dishwasher, a dirty plate in his hand.

"That's right." She sounded all buttoned-down, not

pissed but not friendly, either. "Are you aware that Caitlyn has been trying to reach Trevor?"

"Yes, actually I am. I passed on a message this afternoon."

"Since he's refusing to speak to her, I have to ask if we can meet." There was a pause. "At my home. And I'd appreciate it if you could bring Trevor."

Oh, shit. This couldn't be good. His eyes were locked with his son's. Trevor couldn't possibly hear what she was saying, but he was braced for something, and it wasn't good.

"Yes, Ms. Callahan. When?"

"Is Trevor home now?"

"Yes."

"This evening would work for us." So Caitlyn was to be included in this showdown. Oh, shit, he thought again. "If tonight's not good…"

"Tonight's good," Richard said. "Where do you live?"

She gave him her address and he told her he didn't need directions. He'd lived here his entire life, and had worked on what seemed like half the houses in town. Given the address, he knew exactly where she lived— a neighborhood of upscale town houses built…oh, five or six years ago. Ward Electrical had done the wiring, so he even knew the layout options. Each had a pocket front yard and a not much bigger backyard. They were nice places, though—two story, with clean styling he liked, the garages off alleys that were as wide as some city streets.

"We'll be there in fifteen minutes," he said, still not looking away from Trevor, who was shaking his head frantically. Richard pocketed the phone. "You got the gist of that."

"Us?" He let loose some obscenities, followed by, "What's this about? Is Mommy the vice principal going to chew me out because I broke her little girl's heart?"

"I really doubt that's what Mommy the vice principal has to say," Richard said grimly. "Trevor, did you have sex with this girl?"

He had his answer in the panic on his son's face.

"How old is she?"

"She's... She wanted it, too!"

"How old?" he ground out.

Trevor swallowed. "Uh...fifteen. I think."

Richard closed his eyes. "Goddamn it, Trevor." As if all this would be any better if the girl had passed her sixteenth birthday. Was this a nightmare? Had Trevor just ruined his life, the same way his dad had ruined his?

"Forget the dishes," he said. "We're going over there right now to find out what this is about."

Trevor tried to say no. Vehemently, profanely, even physically. Richard all but dragged him out to the pickup, thrust him in the passenger side. "You *will* come with me. For the first time since you got off that airplane, you will behave like a decent human being. Do you hear me?"

Breathing hard, eyes black with fear, Trevor finally nodded. Richard went around and got in. Neither said another word, not while the garage door rose, not during the short drive. Not even when he parked at the curb in front of one of the town houses, painted a warm gold with darker gold-and-brown trim.

Molly opened the door, and studied Trevor with slightly narrowed eyes. "Thank you for coming," she said, and stood back to let them in.

For a moment, despite his tension, she was all Richard saw. Her hair was loose, a cloud of wavy, wayward fire. It was the first time he'd seen it that way. Brown cords emphasized those long legs and hips he fantasized getting his hands on—when he'd had enough of touching her hair. A cowl-necked sweater in something soft bared enough throat and collarbone to jolt him. No freckles. Why didn't she have freckles?

He gave his libido a good yank and deliberately looked around. Away from Molly.

She led them into a living room that surprised him. Cream walls were hung with textile art, everything from an antique crib-size quilt to a weaving that he guessed was South American. The rugs scattered on the hardwood floor were all interesting, too, some likely vintage if not antique. Bookcases were mostly full of books, but held some art that he thought might be African or South or Central American, too. Different. The coffee table looked Shaker, the sofa was a dark red plush fabric and the two easy chairs were covered in a dark blue and sage green, respectively. Somehow the colors of furniture, rugs and wall hangings all worked together. He saw it all quickly; it was only an impression, but he was impressed.

Intimidated, too, which got his back up. Had she decorated the room to please herself, or to show off her education and cultured tastes? It bothered him suddenly that he hadn't changed out of his usual work uniform of dark green trousers and a matching shirt with his name stitched on the pocket. *Yes, I am blue collar.* He wasn't usually that sensitive about his profession, but in this case the reminder struck him as healthy. It would be good to keep some distance.

"Please. Have a seat," Molly said, without a trace of warmth. "Caitlyn?" she called.

Her daughter ventured into the room. Her averted face meant she didn't look at either Trevor or Richard. Some instinct made Richard grip his son's shoulder and give a single, reassuring squeeze. If what was coming was what Richard expected, Trevor needed to know he had support—so long as he did act with any sort of decency and honor.

Richard sat at one end of the sofa, Trev at the other. Mother and daughter took the chairs facing them.

"What's this about?" he asked bluntly. Trevor, he saw, was staring balefully at Caitlyn.

"Caitlyn is pregnant," Molly said, equally blunt.

He jerked with shock. He'd expected it, yes. But he knew now that he hadn't really. Maybe this was what it felt like to drive to the hospital when you got a call telling you your kid had been in a car accident. You might bargain with God the whole drive, but you didn't really believe this person you loved more than any other in the world could actually die.

Before he could say anything, Trevor leaped to his feet. "You're just saying this because you're mad," he accused.

Face bleached pale, Caitlyn gaped at Trevor. "I wouldn't!"

"Sit *down*," Molly ordered, and maybe long practice gave her voice enough snap his son obeyed. Dropped, as if his knees had given out.

"But we used…" His face went stark.

"We didn't the first time," the girl mumbled.

"I pulled out." Color slashed over his cheeks as he darted a look from his father to his former girlfriend's mother. His mouth opened, closed then worked a few times.

All the breath left Richard and he bent forward, elbows on his knees, and let his head sag. Oh, damn. Oh, damn. Was his gifted son really that stupid?

There was a good long silence after Trevor's so brilliant remark. "And you actually believed that was good enough?" Molly's incredulity was almost disguised. Almost.

"The guys say there's hardly any chance..."

"The guys are idiots," she told him crisply.

Back to the wall, he glowered at Caitlyn. "How do I know it's mine?"

She gasped and jumped up in turn. "You...you... you *jerk*."

"I'm just asking. I've seen you with Jed Sawyer."

"He's a *friend!*" Her voice vibrated with outrage.

"How am I supposed to know?" Trevor snarled.

Molly looked at Richard. "Is this how you encourage him to take responsibility for his actions?"

His head went back. "You're blaming *me?*"

"He's your son."

"I didn't even want to have sex!" Caitlyn was yelling. Tears ran down her cheeks. "But I liked you. You *knew* I wasn't ready."

Oh, hell. Trevor was back on his feet, too, his shoulders hunched like an angry bull. Or maybe it was one that felt threatened. "You could have said no."

Richard found himself rising to his feet, as well. This felt like a bar brawl in the making. He was stunned, angry, scared, all at the same time. And deeply ashamed of his kid.

"And then you ditched me." The girl's eyes were wild,

her hair seeming to have gained volume and fire from her emotions. It wasn't really that red, was it? Not compared to her mom's.

"You're the one who got weird!" Trevor bellowed. "I had a thing for you. If you'd told me no, I would have been okay with it."

"Oh, right. Oh, sure." Caitlyn's hands were curled into fists at her side. "When I tried to talk to you, you made fun of me. You told me I wasn't grown-up. That it was your mistake to hook up with a little girl."

Richard groaned, which brought Molly's furious gaze back to him.

"Well?" she demanded.

Voice reaching near hysteria, Caitlyn kept on as if the two parents weren't in the room. "You wanted a girl who was ready for something 'real.' Remember that? One who didn't still play with Barbie dolls. You got what you wanted, and then you told me to run along!"

"Well, you're getting yours back, aren't you?" Trevor spat. "Bet you're really satisfied. It's all my fault. Like you weren't there." Except he added a few more words, ones that had Molly's eyes going slitty.

Richard raised his voice. "Sit down! Both of you."

"Finally, some sense," Molly snapped.

He turned a dirty look on her. "You should have known better than to have set us up like this."

"Set you up?" Now, finally, *she* shot to her feet. "This is how *you* take responsibility?"

"What kind of responsibility are we talking?" he asked her. "What are you trying to do, push my son into marrying her?"

"And I suppose you assume she'll get an abortion," she

said, equally nastily, "and oh, thank goodness, Trevor's off the hook."

A sob broke from Caitlyn, who spun and raced from the room. The thunder of footsteps on stairs silenced them all until the slam of a door. Richard felt a nerve in his cheek twitch.

Trevor stared after her for a long time. "This can't be happening." He sounded like he was talking to himself.

"It's happening," Richard said.

Trev turned a look of hate on his father. "Yeah, thanks, Dad. I really needed that." He spat another expletive and walked out. The slam of the front door was louder than the one upstairs, and it resonated through Richard.

He'd automatically turned to try to stop Trevor. Now he stood with his back to Molly, head hanging again, and pinched the bridge of his nose so hard it hurt. What a mess. *And I'm not making things better.* It took him a minute, but finally he was able to square his shoulders, lift his head and face her again.

"I'm sorry," he said simply. "Can we start again?"

CHAPTER FIVE

DEEPLY ASHAMED OF HERSELF, Molly sank back into the chair. "Yes," she said. "Of course we can. You're not the one who should be apologizing. I am." He frowned and she shook her head. "You're right. I did blindside you." She hadn't known she was doing it because she was angry, but she understood now that she'd wanted to see their faces, Trevor's and Richard's both, when she told them.

With a sigh, he came back to the sofa and sat, too. "I guess I knew from the minute you called. I could tell Trevor was antsy, avoiding Caitlyn. I worried without quite putting it into words."

"It would have been better if I'd told you on the phone so the two of you could have some time to absorb the news before we talked. I really am sorry I didn't do that."

He nodded. "This might have gone smoother, but maybe not. I can't say I'm proud of Trevor right now." His mouth twisted. "Not that I've been proud much these past couple months."

She looked down at her hands, disturbed by how the dark emotions in his eyes affected her. "I don't think Trevor's recent behavior has much of anything to do with Caitlyn being pregnant. Nice boys get their girlfriends pregnant, too."

He made a sound she couldn't identify. She lifted her head to see a bleak expression on his face. "This is one of the last things in the world I wanted for him." Then his eyes met hers. "Dumb thing to say. You feel the same. Probably worse."

"No matter what, Caitlyn will be more profoundly impacted."

"I guess so." He hesitated. "How long have you known?"

"Almost a week. Since Halloween." She huffed a laugh. "Trick or treat. She wanted to tell Trevor her own way. It was only today that she gave up."

"It's good she came to you."

Her laugh was sharp. "She didn't. I'd like to think she would have eventually, but I don't know. It was a total mischance that tripped her up." That made her laugh again, but no more happily. "Believe it or not, I tripped over the kitchen trash and knocked it over. Guess what spilled out?"

"Confirmation from a clinic? No." He rubbed a hand over his chin. "It'd have to be a home pregnancy kit."

"Yep. Friday morning was garbage pickup. Neither of us had put anything in the can by Sunday and she was afraid I'd be curious if I saw a teeny tiny bag at the bottom when I took something out. So she stuck the two test sticks and the packaging in the bottom of the kitchen garbage bag, figuring I'd never have reason to dig through it."

"I searched Trevor's room the other day." Richard's voice was hoarse.

She stared at him.

"Sorry. That's not exactly relevant, is it? But... It's the kind of thing I'd have sworn I'd never do. And then there I was, trying to find out whether he's gotten into drugs."

"Has he?" Molly sighed. "You don't have to tell me. I'm sorry."

"We've got to quit apologizing to each other." A lop-sided smile gave her butterflies. "And the answer is no. I didn't find a thing. Not even cigarettes or a lighter. It was…a relief."

"You really don't know why he's…"

"Not a clue. His mother claims she doesn't, either."

Molly nodded, not sure why she was. She wasn't agreeing with him; he hadn't said anything that begged for agreement. She couldn't think of anything to say. They sat together for a rather long, silent period that he finally broke.

"You got mad when I mentioned abortion."

"I think I was mad in general," she said ruefully.

"So you're not discounting the possibility?"

She studied him narrowly. *Was* that his preference? She wanted anger to rise, but couldn't make it. Of course that's what he'd be hoping Caitlyn chose to do. He was Trevor's father; his first interest had to be his son, and there was no question abortion provided an out for Trevor. No fuss, no muss, problem gone. He was un-likely to have any later qualms, the way Cait might.

And that, naturally, was part of why Molly tight-ened every time she thought about Cait going that route. Trevor didn't deserve a Pass-Go-Collect-Two-Hundred-Dollars card.

But Molly knew that the possibility of down-the-line regret wasn't the whole reason she hated desperately to think of Cait undergoing an abortion.

"This is your grandchild, too, that we're talking about," she pointed out.

He closed those so dark eyes. "Grandfather. God."

She couldn't tell him the other reason the whole concept bothered her. It was personal, and had nothing to do with what was right for Cait.

"Ultimately it has to be her decision," Molly said.

He looked at her again. "You don't think Trevor should have a voice?"

"Was he even admitting to any responsibility?"

He heard the barb in her question, but didn't rise to it. "Be fair. You and Caitlyn had some time to process. What happened tonight was pretty much a knockout punch for him. Give him a chance to stagger to his feet."

He was right, which made Molly feel ashamed again. "We'll...keep you informed," she said stiffly.

"You'll do more than that." His voice was hard. "This *is* Trevor's baby, too. If it's given up for adoption, he'd need to sign to relinquish his parental rights, just like your daughter will. If there are financial consequences, he'll bear them. He has to have a part in this decision. He and Caitlyn are in it together."

"When he won't even return her phone calls?"

"That was then. This is now."

"What if he's not interested?"

"Let me be more accurate. *We're* all in this together."

"So one of the Wards is taking responsibility?" Oh, that was low. Even before she saw his expression, she wished she could pull the words back.

"Responsibility—" he rose to his feet "—is my middle name. I was barely nineteen when Trevor was born. As big an idiot as he is, except I thought my girlfriend was on the pill. But you know what? I married her without one accusation. Was it the right thing to do? I still don't know. But, by God, I took responsibility." He sounded unutterably weary. "Even as big a jackass as he's been lately, I don't wish Alexa had had an abortion. So don't tell me I'm pushing your daughter that way. I was asking you to talk to me, that's all."

Throat thick, she stood, too. Oh, heavens, how many times tonight had they popped up and down? "Can I say I'm sorry again?"

"I meant it when I said let's ditch the apologies. Maybe neither of us is at our best. We need to talk again, but obviously this isn't the time. I'll give you a call, or you can call me."

"Yes."

"Good." He nodded and left before she could pull herself together.

She couldn't seem to do anything but stand where she was, staring after him even though she'd heard the front door open and close. Quietly, unlike when his son tore out of her house.

Had tonight's meeting—confrontation—helped in any way? Or had she only ramped up the hostility? Molly hated this overwhelming feeling of inadequacy. It made her realize how arrogant she'd been, even though now it was easy to see that life hadn't been as perfect as she'd wanted to believe it was.

She only wished that if she had to be brought crashing down, Cait hadn't had to go with her.

TREVOR RAN UNTIL HIS breath was whistling in and out and his lungs were on fire. He ran harder than he had even when he'd been determined to win every sprint, to be the best. He ended up in Terrace Park. With dusk having descended, it was dark under the trees. He walked up to one, wrapped his arms around it and laid his cheek against the bark. Ground his cheek against it. With shock he heard the sob and realized it had come from him.

He swore. Softly, louder, finally screaming out rage that he knew was really fear. He swiped his forearm across his wet face and sank to the ground with his back to that same huge, ancient Douglas fir.

Oh God oh God oh God things like this aren't supposed to happen to me. Maybe this was his payback for being so shitty to Dad when really it was Mom— Trevor stopped that thought dead. No. Dad had lied, too. More with what he didn't say than what he did, but he'd lied all the same. If he really loved Trev and Bree, how could he let them live with Mom, when he *knew...?* His claiming he loved them, that was a lie, too.

Trev knew only a couple of other guys who'd gotten a girl pregnant, and they were idiots. Plus, the girls had gotten abortions—one of them without her parents even finding out—so everything was all right.

The tormented look on Cait's face when her mom said that, about her getting an abortion, made Trevor afraid that's not what she'd do.

He'd talk to her, he thought desperately. Talk her into it. *Not* getting one was stupid. If she had that baby, nothing would ever be the same for either of them again. She was fifteen. He remembered the things he'd said, about her still playing with Barbie dolls and holding tea parties for her toys, and winced. But he bet she'd been doing both those things not that long ago. He knew Bree secretly played by herself in her bedroom long after she was pretending to her friends to be cool and into boys.

And Bree…he cringed again. Bree was fourteen. Oh, man. He'd kill the guy who got his sister pregnant.

The guy? You mean, the one like me?

He used the hem of his shirt to wipe his nose and then to furiously blow it. Did anyone else at school know about this? If Cait had told all her friends, *everyone* would know in no time. Maybe a bunch of them already did. He didn't like thinking there'd be some jerks who'd be bowing to him because he'd cashed in her v-card and was so virile, he couldn't help getting her pregnant. Those same guys would be looking at her like she was some kind of slut, and trailer trash because, man, she'd have a squalling brat by the time she was sixteen. Would the admin even *let* her stay at the high school, or did they exile pregnant teenagers to the alternative school? Wow, did West Fork *have* an alternative school? Yeah, they must. Every place had losers.

Oh, damn. He dropped his head back against the tree and stared at the lights he could see outside the boundary of the park.

If either of them was the loser, it was him. He felt familiar fury rise in him as he imagined some jerk making filthy comments about Cait as she passed in the hall. Someone like Aaron Latter, a *real* loser. Filled with so much anger and turmoil he didn't know where to put it—high tide, oh, yeah—Trevor would want to smash any guy's face who said something about Cait. He didn't know if he could stop himself. If he *should.* Wasn't that the right thing to do? Defend his girl?

Get kicked out of school?

If they made her go to the alternative school, he'd go, too, he resolved. All for one and one for all. It was only fair.

He had known she didn't want to have sex, and he hadn't cared because it would make *him* feel good. And now he felt like such an asshole, and he didn't only hate Mom and Dad, he hated himself, too. And the thing was, he still really liked Cait but he knew she must hate him. And why wouldn't she, when he'd jumped up and said *How do I know it's mine?* when he didn't even mean it.

This time, when he felt hot tears on his face, he didn't try to stop them from falling.

NO POINT IN EVEN PRETENDING to go to bed until Trevor came home. If he came home. *Where else would he go?* Richard asked himself, and didn't know. He'd have gone out looking for his son, but had no idea where to start, either, which was a sad thing as a parent to realize.

He kept thinking about Molly and wondering whether she felt as useless as he did tonight. Did she have anyone she could talk to? Would he and she get to a point where they could? How much more awkward would it be if she knew he was lusting for her?

At 11:36, he heard the front door open. He stepped out of the kitchen, catching Trev heading for the stairs. A vise closed over his chest. Trevor looked like hell. Gaunt, as if he'd somehow managed to lose a whole lot of weight in less than four hours. His eyes were swollen, his mouth compressed, his hair spiked.

"I was worried about you," Richard said quietly.

His son shrugged. "Yeah, sure." He hadn't managed to inject the usual vitriol in his voice, though.

"Take it how you want. I'm here to talk when you're ready."

Another shrug. Trev gazed at his feet.

Richard nodded and went back into the kitchen,

where he poured the coffee he hadn't wanted anyway down the sink. If Trevor went upstairs, it was soundlessly. The picture of him still standing there, not moving, was disturbing. *I have to let him come to me.* Yeah, what are the odds of that? his more cynical side asked.

Richard went about setting up the coffeemaker for morning. When he turned off the lights, he found the downstairs deserted. Trevor's bedroom door was shut, as it always was, but a light showed in the crack beneath it. Richard stopped, wanting to knock, wanting to say only, "Are you okay?" but knowing there was no point.

He has to come to me.

True but unlikely.

HE WENT OUT ON SOME SMALL jobs the next day, the kind he wouldn't usually do but that didn't require his full attention. He wired a new garage, replaced some outlets in a house dating from the early sixties and finally went out and checked up on a bigger job, one he had two of the guys working on. They were both standing outside smoking when he arrived and ground out their cigarettes the minute they saw him, expressions wary. He didn't say anything about it, though. If the work was moving slower than he thought it should be, then he'd say something. Otherwise, they were entitled to breaks. Unless he watched them all day through binoculars, he couldn't know if they were taking too many. He could only judge on the quality of the work.

"Hey, boss," one of them said, and it struck Richard that the guy couldn't be more than twenty. Yeah, he'd come to work for him right out of high school. Was this what he wanted to be doing? The pay was pretty damn good, but maybe he'd had other dreams. *Probably not.*

I'm tarring him with my brush. Jeez, he's probably making twice as much an hour as his high school buddies.

Richard had actually thought of asking whether Trevor wanted to work for him this past summer, but the Boys & Girls Club job had kept his own offer unspoken. He didn't know what he'd been thinking, anyway. The last thing he wanted was for his son to come to work for him. Ward & Son Electrical? He hadn't seen any choice in his day. He'd known he was lucky to have such a good paying fallback. Thanks to his dad, he and Alexa had done okay. After the divorce, he'd been able to pay decent child support.

He wanted better for Trevor. Then, irritated at himself, he thought, no, not better. Damn it, Richard was proud of what he'd done with Ward Electrical, which had been his old man alone until Richard joined him. Now, with Dad retired in Arizona, Richard employed nine men and one woman as electricians as well as a receptionist and a half-time bookkeeper. The most respected and one of the largest in the tricounty area, his electrical contracting business did grocery stores, malls, schools as well as housing developments. He still did some hands-on work himself, but not much. Mostly he was in the office now.

What he'd wanted was to be an engineer. He'd dreamed of giant dams and bridges, not light switches. To satisfy himself, in the empty years after Lexa left with the children, he had gone back to school and worked his butt off on top of the job to get a degree in civil engineering with a specialty in structural engineering, but he knew he'd never use it. What sense did it make to walk away from a successful business to start all over working for someone else? None, of course. Mostly, he was satisfied because he had the degree and now he knew that what he did for a living was *his* choice.

To his surprise, Trevor was home before him. Richard had gone wearily to the kitchen to think about what they'd have for dinner when Trevor spoke up behind him.

"We could order a pizza or something."

Wonder of wonders. Richard schooled his expression before he turned. "Why don't we go out?"

Trevor shuffled from foot to foot. "Uh, yeah, okay."

Richard had a favorite pizza parlor that on a Tuesday night was likely to be quiet. During the short drive, he glanced at Trev. "You get a chance to talk to Caitlyn today?"

"Yeah, well, I tried, but when I appeared, she disappeared."

Richard only nodded.

"I guess that's justice, huh?"

What? Is the real Trevor Ward alive and well after all?

"That's probably how she sees it," Richard said neutrally.

Trevor scowled out the window.

In the restaurant, they ordered, then carried their pitcher of cola back to the table. "How come you never drink?" Trevor asked, surprising him.

Richard slid in on one side of the booth. "I have a beer once in a while, a glass of wine if friends serve it at dinner."

"Yeah, but you don't usually."

Funny the subject had never come up before. "Your grandfather was a heavy drinker. Probably still is.

Walked in the door and went straight to the fridge for his beer. He had at least a six-pack every night. Yelled at your grandmother if she'd forgotten to buy some and then he'd go right out to the store. I didn't like it."

"I never noticed," Trevor admitted.

"That's because he doesn't get falling-down drunk. Doesn't look that drunk at all, which is actually a bad sign. He's a functioning alcoholic, but an alcoholic all the same. Wouldn't admit it. Your grandmother scoffs at the idea, too."

"So…you think you might've been an alcoholic, too?"

"You mean, I inherited the tendency?" He frowned. "I didn't think about it that way. All I knew was, I might have to—" *I might have to give up going to college and work side by side with my father, but I didn't want to be any more like him than I could help.* That wasn't even fair, he knew. His father had been faithful to his wife, he hadn't abused her or their kids, he'd been a good provider. He wasn't that bad. "I wanted different for you and Bree," was the best Richard could sum it up.

"Like, me not getting a girl pregnant my senior year of high school?" Bitterness dark in his eyes, Trevor looked at his father.

"That, too," Richard admitted honestly.

He let Trevor go for the pizza. Waiting, he felt sad and exhilarated both, a crazy mismatch of emotions. This was the first time they'd really talked since… Hell, he thought it was a phone conversation they'd had back in July. Somehow they hadn't connected in August before Alexa contacted him. He'd figured that Trevor was busy with his job and friends, but in retrospect he realized that was the beginning.

Do I dare ask him outright?

No, he decided. One problem at a time.

Trevor set the pizza in the middle of the table and they each dished up a slice.

"What would you have said to Caitlyn today?"

"She goes by Cait."

"Okay."

Trevor set his slice down. "I guess I'd have said I was sorry for being such a…" He swallowed whatever word he'd been about to use and said "jerk" instead.

"You mean last night?"

"And before, too," Trev mumbled, head bent.

There was a lot Richard wanted to say or ask, but he only waited.

"When Mom got pregnant…um…" His cheeks had reddened. "Didn't you use a condom?"

"She was on birth control pills."

His head jerked up. "Then how…?"

Truthful answer: *I don't know.* Or, worse, *I think I do know.* What he said was, "They can fail, too. No method is a hundred percent. She might've forgotten to take a pill or two, or if a woman is on some medications they can interfere with how a hormonal contraceptive works."

Trevor sat staring at him and Richard absolutely could not tell what he was thinking. "So you didn't do something stupid like I did," he said at last.

He'd trusted Alexa. That was stupid. Maybe. He never *knew,* not really, only suspected. He hadn't asked or accused, because that might have made building a life together impossible, and by then they had an unborn child to think about.

"I guess not. Things happen."

"I don't want it to have happened," Trevor said, barely whispering. "I want her to get an abortion."

"I don't blame you." Richard was hurting, too.

"So why does *she* get to decide?" Trev's eyes were suddenly hot with rage and his voice trembled.

"You should be involved in the decision. But reality is, this is her body. What if you were trying to insist she have the baby and keep it? Would that be right for you to force that choice on her?"

"I wouldn't!"

"Are she and her mother churchgoers? Abortion might be a choice that would be morally repugnant to them."

"Wow." Elbows planted on the table, Trev buried his head in his hands. He was rocking, Richard saw, and yanking at his hair so hard it had to be painful. "I keep thinking I'll wake up."

Richard felt compassion, sure, but this was one of those moments he realized how mad he was, too. No condom. God help them all.

"I don't know if they go to church," his smart/stupid kid mumbled. "How should I know?"

How should I know? He'd gotten the girl pregnant, and he didn't know whether she believed in God. Oh, face it; what boy his age *would* care? All that mattered was would she or wouldn't she.

That probably wasn't any fairer to Trevor, Richard realized, than his earlier thoughts had been to his father. So what. *I don't have to be fair.* Serenity wasn't a by-product of parenthood. More like an antonym.

"Let's take the rest of the pizza home," Richard decided, and went to get a box.

CHAPTER SIX

AT THE SOUND OF THE BELL over the door ringing, Molly
swiveled in her seat. She was ridiculously nervous. The
new arrival was Richard Ward himself, tall, imposingly
handsome, glancing around the sandwich shop until he
spotted her at the table in the back corner. And, damn
it, there was that loose-hipped walk that always stirred
something in her.

She'd been the one to suggest they meet for lunch,
completely separate from their kids. He hadn't argued,
hadn't asked why.

She half rose when he reached the table, then sank
back down. She wasn't in the office. "The waitress left
you a menu," she said inanely.

He nodded and pulled out a chair next to her, not the
one across the table. Their knees might bump. They
would bump. He took up way more than his fair share
of space, and that, too, unsettled Molly. She was a big
enough woman; she was taller than most men with
whom she dealt.

Oh, get a grip! You're not an adolescent. But she was
feeling a lot like one right now.

"Mr. Ward, thank you for coming," she said with
more composure. *This is Trevor's father. Trevor's father, Trevor's father.* She'd chant it as many times as
she had to. This was not a date.

A faint smile touched his mouth. "Don't you think we're past Mister and Missus?"

"Richard," she amended.

He chose quickly from the menu and they both gave their orders. Then he regarded her gravely. "Has Caitlyn—no, Trevor says she prefers Cait—has she made a decision? Or are you wanting to tell me to butt out?"

"I'd have suggested coffee instead of lunch if I were going to do that."

Now he outright grinned, and her heart damn near stopped. "Not option B, then."

"Or A." Molly looked down at her place setting. "Partly I'm back to apologizing—"

"No. Let's not get mired there."

He was being more generous than she deserved. She swallowed and met those dark eyes again. "Okay. Thanks. Really I only wanted to talk. Listen to you, since I didn't the other night."

"Have you told anyone else?"

Molly shook her head. "Cait and I agreed not to for now. She swears she won't tell even her best friend. If she decides to get an abortion, she could move on more easily if no one knows but you, me and Trevor." She paused. "Assuming Trevor will keep it quiet?"

"I think I can vouch for him." He studied her for a moment. "He says now Cait won't talk to him."

She made a helpless gesture. "She's hurt, scared, confused.... Do you blame her?"

"No. Neither does he. He said he guessed it was justice, after the way he dodged her."

"Really?" she said, surprised. "That sounds…"

"Almost mature?"

Molly laughed. "I was trying to think of a really tactful way to say it."

He smiled, too, mouth and eyes both. "Surely as a high school administrator, you must have a thesaurus worth of euphemisms at the tip of your tongue."

"You'd think so, wouldn't you."

Their drinks came. Richard waited until the waitress was out of earshot. "Will you tell me about you and Cait? I asked Trevor if you were churchgoers, for example, and he had no idea. Is Cait's father in the picture? Trevor thought you were divorced."

Her first uneasy thought was, *why does he want to know about me?* Was there any chance some of this chemistry she felt went both ways?

Get a grip, she told herself again. *Remember the way he stared at you that day when he had to wait for you to park. Inimical. Remember?* If they'd been adversaries then, they were more so now.

"I am divorced, and have been since Cait was a little girl. She was four when her dad and I separated and five when the divorce went through. She gets birthday and Christmas checks from him, and that's about it. He started out with more enthusiasm. You know, the usual every other weekend thing, but that became once a month, then once every few months, and then..." She shrugged. "Church? We go, but not as faithfully as we should. I didn't grow up in a church. I started when she was little, thinking Sunday school was one of the things parents did."

"Even though yours didn't?"

He was sharp, she had to give him that. "I didn't have a father. Don't remember my mother well. She was killed in a car accident when I was seven. I grew up in foster homes after that. I guess you'd have to say I learned parenting from the book. Literally." She was trying hard to make it light, almost if not quite a joke. "I have quite a library of *Now Your Child is Eight, Now She's Eleven* books. Either I skipped a few chapters in the *Now She's Fifteen* one or the author left out some essentials."

The kindness in his eyes was almost unbearable. She had to look away from it. He waited a minute before responding. "When something like this happens, it makes you go back and rethink everything you've ever done, doesn't it? Trevor surprised me by asking some things about my parents, so I guess he's doing the same thing. You can't help thinking the 'why' of this isn't an accident. It can't be as simple as a horny teenage boy and a girl with a crush on him. There has to be something bigger. Something we didn't teach them. Some cosmic reason we didn't."

"Someone didn't teach Trevor to use a condom," she said sharply, then closed her eyes tight in shame. "Oh, God. I'm sorry. I swore I wouldn't do this."

"Hey." His big hand covered hers on the table and squeezed before releasing her. "I set myself up for that one."

She opened her eyes to see that he was laughing, and for some reason she did, too. "The real lesson is, teenagers do stupid things. With the best will in the world, we can't stupid-proof them," she said at last, feeling a thousand times better.

"No, we can't," he said, wryly enough to remind her that he'd gotten his own girlfriend pregnant when he was a senior in high school.

She opened her mouth to say, yet again, *I'm sorry,* but closed it.

"I keep thinking, what if I hadn't knocked over the garbage. What would Cait have done? Would she have told me?"

"What were her options?"

Their lunches arrived, and they both pretended enthusiasm. He reached for the ketchup, making her aware of the flex of muscles beneath the crisply ironed shirt. And, oh, damn, his knee did slide against hers.

Molly angled her legs away. "I don't know. Go to a clinic, I guess. Find a way to get an abortion without telling me? Run away from home?" she said when they were alone again.

"How likely is that?"

"Not likely," she said. "We were good friends until she fell head over heels for your son and decided I was the enemy because I wasn't really happy about her boyfriend."

"Understandably unhappy."

He steered her skillfully back to telling him about her life. No, she admitted, there was no man around, no pseudo-dad Cait might have turned to. She didn't say, *I can't remember the last time I went on a date.* Never mind the last time she'd slept with a man. How did single mothers do that on any kind of regular basis? Especially without any loving extended family to serve as babysitters and backup? And, heck, it was harder now than when Cait was little. How did she justify having a sex life when she was steering her daughter to *not have one?* She did admit she'd been only twenty-one when Cait was born.

"Yes, she was an accident. I was a junior in college,

and almost as blown away when I realized I was pregnant as Cait is now." For the first time she thought about
the fact that she and Richard had both experienced much
of what their kids were now. It seemed like an especially
cruel slap from fate.

"How did you handle it?" Richard asked. He'd been
eating and listening, somehow keeping her talking with
a question here and there. "I gather you did marry her
father."

"Yes. And although it was really hard, I managed to
stay in school. I went straight on to grad school, too.
That was when…" *Whoa.* She waved a hand. "Irrele-
vant. The one thing I can say is, once Cait was born I
never once regretted her."

"No, I felt that way about Trevor, too." His mouth
quirked. "Until the past couple of months. I can't deny
there've been a few moments of 'What the hell did I
do?'"

Molly laughed, as he'd no doubt intended. "What
about you?" she said. "I take it your marriage didn't
last."

"Not forever. We stuck it out for six years." He was
quiet for a moment, a frown gathering his dark brows
together. He wasn't looking at her, and she suspected he
was seeing another time and place. "I have a daughter,
too. Brianna. We call her Bree most of the time. She's
still with her mother."

"How old?"

"Fourteen. I was appalled when I first realized Trev
had hooked up with your daughter because I'm thinking, *Wait. Don't you realize she's barely older than your
sister?*"

"You sound like you miss her."

"Yeah." He grimaced. "Truth is, sometimes I feel like I hardly know her. I've had her for occasional summers, a few weeks over the holidays...." He shrugged. "You know how it is. The older she's gotten, the more of a mystery to me she is."

Molly found herself wanting to touch him. It was probably just as well that his hand wasn't lying there conveniently close. "I suspect most fathers feel that way when their daughters became teenagers," she said gently.

His eyes met hers finally. The skin was crinkled at the corners. A smile that hadn't reached his mouth. "You're probably right. The sad part is, I thought I did know my son. Turns out I was wrong."

"Maybe you did. Maybe he's not the same person he was a year ago, or whenever you last spent time together. Or maybe the person he was is only submerged."

"Submerged." He shook his head. "How do you change that fast?" He seemed to be appealing to her, but didn't wait for an answer, even assuming she'd had one. "No, it's been even quicker than that. I was thinking back the other night. I must have talked to him for an hour toward the end of July. I heard all about his job—he worked at a Boys & Girls Club, supervising kids, coaching. Yeah." He grinned ruefully. "Marvel at the idea, I don't blame you. But that's the kind of kid he was. Until..."

"Until what?"

"I have no idea. He won't talk about it."

They talked about that, too. He was easy to talk to, she couldn't help thinking, and he seemed to be relaxing with her, too.

He told her that his ex-wife had remarried twice now,

and that she'd separated from husband number three in August. That might or might not be related to Trevor's current problems. "He never seemed that attached to the guy. Davis." He said the name carefully, as if it left a taste in his mouth, but Molly couldn't tell what kind. He wasn't jealous, was he?

"Did Trevor have a girlfriend?" she asked. Oh, she hated to mention this, but… "Is there any chance he got her in trouble, too? That he was…I don't know, running from it?"

Richard stared at her. "God. That's an ugly thought." But almost immediately, he was shaking his head. "That doesn't make sense. No, he didn't have a girlfriend, or, at least, not anyone serious. There was someone, but her dad got transferred to Houston and they moved the previous summer. And if he'd gotten another girl pregnant, surely he wouldn't have been stupid enough to leave off the condom the next time he got in a girl's…" He stopped, cleared his throat. "Sorry."

She, who had winced at the words that almost came out of his mouth, gave what was probably a sickly smile. "Teenagers are stupid, remember?"

"Yeah, and he was clearly bewildered by the idea that pulling out wasn't an adequate and recommended form of birth control."

Silly to become self-conscious, but she did. She could talk about pregnancy with this man, but change the topic to sex—yes, the act itself—and she was instantly flustered. So aware of *him,* all man.

"Yes, he was. I haven't asked Cait yet if she was fine with it at the time, too."

The way he watched her was almost enough to have her squirming in her seat. She'd never seen eyes of such a dark brown—except his son's. His hair was as dark, thick, wavy enough to keep it looking disheveled most of the time. With that lean face and stark cheekbones, he had the fallen angel look. Except she associated that with men who exuded sin, and somehow he didn't. If she had to guess, it would be that Richard Ward had spent a lifetime disciplining himself.

"What about you?" she asked on impulse. "You haven't mentioned a wife. Lucky woman, to have to put up with Trevor's cheerful attitude."

"No wife. I've never been sure..." He stopped himself, expression closing down. Yes, definitely disciplined. "If nothing else, I didn't want the kids to see both parents with revolving spousal doors. They've adjusted with their mother. I figured, enough is enough."

Did that mean he never intended to remarry? She didn't know why that shocked her, as she wasn't exactly in the market for a second husband, but...she wouldn't rule it out, if she met someone. The right someone.

Tempted to roll her eyes like a teenager, she thought, *Uh-huh. Sure. What you mean is, a completely trustworthy someone.* Her standards this time around would be so exacting, she couldn't imagine finding him.

And, oh, yeah, he couldn't be someone wanting to start a family.

Richard Ward wouldn't be, it occurred to her. He *had* two kids.

"You're going to live alone, all so your kids don't have to get to know a new stepmother?" Molly congratulated herself on her tone, casual, possibly a little amused.

"Let's just say I've never gotten to the point of seriously considering it," he said slowly, those dark espresso eyes on her face.

What was he thinking?

"So, do we have a timeline?"

"A what?"

"For a decision. You didn't say how far along your daughter is."

"Oh." That kind. "She's seven weeks now. So yes. Obviously, an abortion has to happen in the next few weeks."

"Surely the sooner the better."

"Yes." She bent forward, her stomach cramping. How strange. Painful cramps had once been a way of life for her. Menstrual cramps, but stress-related stomach ones, too. Divorce had miraculously cured the second.

"Trevor wanted to know why the decision was Cait's. Why isn't it his." Temper flooded her, but he shook his head. "I told him because it's her body. That said…I ask that you think about him, too. He's not ready to be a father."

She was still sizzling. "I doubt you were, either. You need to stop pushing. I said I'd talk to you, not give you a vote."

His eyes narrowed. "I seem to remember a promise that you'd listen to me."

Oh, hell. "I've listened."

"Have you?" He pulled out his wallet and tossed some bills on the table. "Seems to me that mostly you talked and I listened." Their gazes met. "I've left enough to take care of the bill."

And he walked out on her again.

Which she completely deserved, Molly admitted. *What is* wrong *with me?*

Excellent question.

TREVOR STALKED CAIT the next day. Only way to put it. He told himself she was asking for it.

Even so, she stayed surrounded by friends all day and almost got away after the last bell because she didn't stop at her locker the way she usually did. She zipped out of class and shot across the commons for the front door like an Indy 500 driver with her foot to the floor. Fortunately, Trev had been careful to take the desk closest to the door himself in *his* last class, he clock-watched and, since he'd never even pulled out his binder to take notes, was able to launch himself through the door while the bell was still ringing. The two of them reached the double exit doors at almost exactly the same minute. They were the first there although the commons was now flooded with jostling bodies.

"After you," he said, bowing and opening a door.

"Um…I was going to wait for Jenna."

"You don't have dance today." He had her schedule down.

Her cheeks flushed. "I was going over to the school, anyway."

Sure she was. "Then I'll walk you."

She gave another desperate glance behind him in hopes of spotting a whole crowd of her friends, no doubt, that would provide her with camouflage. Not happening. He had her in the crosshairs now.

"Is talking to me so bad?"

"I know what you want to say."

"What's that?"

"You want me to…" Her eyes got super wide at the same time as she shut up.

Wow, good thing. He shouldn't have pressed her when there were other people around. Trevor took her arm and steered her toward the sidewalk. "Were you really going to dance?"

Her gaze slid his way. "I guess I don't have to."

"We can just walk, then. Cut through Terrace Park."

"Okay," she agreed.

She looked really hot today. Not that she ever didn't. Her hair was the prettiest he'd ever seen, especially in the sun. And there was some sun today, the first in close to two weeks. Cait wore jeans, flip-flops that showed off toenails painted bright pink and a formfitting long-sleeved T-shirt. Also hot pink, which gave, like, a pink tint to her reddish-gold hair.

God, he'd had such a thing for her. He was still confused about how it could have gone so cataclysmically bad. Well, the pregnancy part he got; that was his fault. But the rest.

They were all by themselves when she spoke. "Abortion. That's what you want me to do."

His heart began to pound hard, as if he was about to go out on the court for a big game. "You can't really want a baby."

Her blue-violet eyes flashed at him. "Of course I don't!"

"Then what's the deal?" he asked reasonably. He thought.

"The deal is that we made a baby, okay? This isn't like…like I shoplifted something I can get rid of in a Dumpster so no one ever knows I did it."

"It's hardly even some cells yet." Trevor didn't actually know. Didn't *want* to know. And why would she?

"I think it might be a couple of inches long now," she said in a small voice.

He looked down at her, scared by that voice. Even more scared by the expression on her face. She was sort of inward looking, her eyes soft.

"See, my mom got pregnant with me by accident. She was only twenty, a junior in college. She could have had an abortion, but she didn't." She stole a look at him. "Your dad doesn't look like he's very old, either. How old was he when you were born?"

"Nineteen. He was nineteen," Trevor answered, feeling hollow.

"See?" Like that said it all.

"But you're fifteen. You're not nineteen or twenty. That's really different. You're not even close to graduating from high school."

"I'm not talking about keeping the baby." She wasn't looking at him anymore. They'd almost reached the park. "Only...only *having* it, and giving it a chance. You know?"

"You'd keep going to school? Do you know how everyone would look at you?"

"I could maybe take second semester off. Or go to the alternative school."

"Everyone would still know."

She stopped dead and faced him. "So I should kill this baby just to keep people from talking?"

Kill this baby. Oh, man. He was so screwed.

"It's not a baby yet."

Cait ducked her head. "I don't know."

"We made a mistake. Mostly, *I* did," he admitted.

"This can ruin our lives. Yours more than mine. No one will ever look at you the same way again." He paused. This was really crummy of him, but oh, well. "You'll have to quit dance."

She jerked, and he saw that it hadn't occurred to her.

"Going back after a year would be really hard."

"Not a whole year."

"Close."

"Why are you doing this?" Eyes drenched but angry, too, she looked at him. "No, forget it. I know why. It doesn't *feel* good." Her contempt ripped through him. "You didn't care about me, and now I don't care about you. So stay away from me."

She turned back the way they'd come and started walking, faster and faster, finally breaking into an awkward run. Her flip-flops slapped against the sidewalk, her book bag bounced on her back. Feeling like he had a big, jagged rock in his chest, Trevor watched her go.

MOLLY STOOD IN THE MIDDLE of the restroom, crossed her arms and stared at the two boys. Aaron Latter had a bloody nose, Trevor an eye already swelling and discolored. The opposite one from last time, she noted clinically. Chuck Loomis, football coach, six foot three and beefy, stood between them, a meaty hand locked on each boy's arm. Trevor at least stood straight. Aaron seemed to hang like a wet noodle. He held wadded toilet paper to his nose and was sniveling. A third student hovered by the urinals. He was a scrawny kid with a huge Adam's apple, eyes wide and scared. Molly sorted through her mind for his name. She knew he was a freshman. Something Russian, or maybe Ukrainian... Something like Russ...Ruslan. Ruslan Balanchuk. Did he go by Russ?

She had never actually spoken to the boy before. Had Chuck bullied him into staying?

"Ruslan…" She hoped she'd gotten the pronunciation right. "I gather you saw this fight."

The boy bobbed his head, his nervous gaze flicking to the two taller boys. Trevor wasn't looking at him, but Aaron had turned his head. Molly could imagine what he was trying to convey with his stare.

"Let's step out in the hall," she said. "Then you can go back to class. Chuck, if you don't mind waiting with Trevor and Aaron."

She escorted Ruslan through the swinging door. The hall, five minutes after the bell had rung, was deserted.

"What did you see?" she asked gently.

"Aaron was bad-mouthing Cait." A lurid red tide rose from his skinny neck to his face as he likely remembered who Cait's mother was. His accent was subtle; his family must have been here since he was a little boy. "He called Trevor names and said, um, that he'd done bad things to Cait. And then he punched him."

"He punched first. You're sure."

He nodded hard. "Trevor kept saying, 'Shut up. Don't talk about her that way. You don't know anything.' He said it over and over. But Aaron was totally in his face." His voice was gaining enthusiasm and speed. "He never did punch back. He just, kind of, grabbed Aaron and threw him away. He fell against one of the bathroom stalls, you know, face-first. That's when his nose started gushing. And I opened the bathroom door and yelled, and Coach Loomis was going by."

"Okay." Molly smiled at him. "You did right. You might have been hurt if you'd tried to break it up yourself. There's some hard feelings between those two."

"The stuff he said about Cait…I mean, I don't know why he would."

She half laughed when she didn't feel at all like it. "I can only imagine what it was. I'm sure he was only trying to get a rise from Trevor. I suspect it was all nonsense. Cait was his excuse."

"Oh." His face cleared. "Okay."

She scribbled a hall pass and sent him on his way, then returned to the bathroom.

"Trevor, please go to the nurse's office and get some ice on that eye. I'll talk to you after that. Aaron, you come to my office with me."

He launched into a scurrilous attack on Trevor's motives and parentage. She raised her eyebrows. "Coach Loomis, perhaps you won't mind escorting him."

"With pleasure."

Aaron had clamped his mouth shut by the time he got to her office. He sat sullenly refusing to talk to her or make eye contact until his mother retrieved him. Molly spoke to her alone, telling her the same thing she had Richard—if her son got in one more fight, he would be expelled. No recourse. "In the meantime, he's suspended until Monday."

Mommy argued and repeated things she'd no doubt heard from her son about Trevor, but Molly stood her ground.

"This time, Aaron is entirely at fault. He knows the rules. His behavior was unacceptable."

Then she sighed and went to the nurse's office, where she was startled to find Richard already sitting next to his son. Trevor's head was down and he still held the ice pack to his eye, which must hurt like the dickens. Richard had an arm around him.

His eyes, dark and hot, met hers. He looked considerably less friendly than he had yesterday when she'd had lunch with him. He squeezed Trevor's shoulder and then stood.

"Mr. Ward," she said formally. "I didn't expect to see you here."

"Trev called me."

"Really." She glanced at his son, who was peering at her through the one good eye. More déjà vu. "Trevor, how's that eye?"

"It hurts like a mother..." Intercepting his father's warning look, he didn't finish.

"I'm sorry," she said, taking the seat on the other side of him. "Please tell me what happened."

"It wasn't me."

His father loomed, but to his credit didn't say anything. Molly didn't let herself look up at him.

"I know." She smiled at his surprise. "Ruslan said Aaron was bad-mouthing Cait, you told him to stop and Aaron punched you. He said all you did was push Aaron away. That he fell against the bathroom stalls."

"He said that?"

"Yes. Isn't it true?"

"Did he tell you what Aaron said?" He sounded desperate. She saw him scan the office as if to be sure they were alone. "He said everyone's talking about her. That she keeps having to go to the bathroom to puke. People think she's knocked up."

Molly was glad she was sitting. "Oh, no."

"You didn't know she was sick?"

"I know she's nauseated every morning. But she seems okay in the evening. She didn't tell me she was sick at school."

"He said everyone knows she's pregnant and I'm a…" Again he hesitated. "A you-know-what for fu… uh, screwing her and then dumping her."

Molly didn't say anything. She was still combating the dizziness. *You did screw her. You did dump her.* Not helpful. Not even the entire truth. Cait had her share of responsibility. She could have said no. Or, at least, you have to wear a condom. Or, better yet, you have to wait a month until I can get on birth control. *And* you have to wear a condom.

Water under the bridge. She was overwhelmed by the knowledge that disaster had struck. They shouldn't have dawdled. If Cait was getting an abortion, she should have done it. Before the whispers started.

"Did you know people were talking?"

He shook his head. "But maybe they wouldn't in front of me."

"Or around her."

She pulled herself together and stood. "Okay. She and I will talk tonight."

There was hope on his face. "Do you think she'll agree, you know…?"

"I don't know," she told him honestly. She didn't. She didn't know how *she* felt about it. No, not true—she did know. She felt as if she was being pulled apart. What was easiest for Cait, what would be right for her in the long run, what really *was* right…if there was any such thing. And then her own ache, the one she couldn't seem to squelch that kept her from being clearheaded. Finally she looked at Richard, and saw lines of puzzlement on his forehead as he studied her. So he hadn't figured her out yet. Imagine that.

How could he, when she was so confused herself?

"Mr. Ward…Richard. Perhaps I can call you tomorrow?"

He gave a clipped nod. "Trevor's free to go?"

"Yes." She looked at the boy. "Trev, it would have been better if you'd walked away, but I understand why you felt you had to defend Cait." She hesitated. "I even appreciate that."

He gave her a lopsided grin that must have hurt, because he winced. "But you'll deny it if anyone asks?"

Despite the now ever-present ache, Molly laughed. "Something like that."

The bemused lines on Richard's face were still there, but now his eyes were warm. He nodded. "Molly." And steered his son out.

She sank back into the chair with a groan. Dear God, now what?

CHAPTER SEVEN

WHAT NOW? THE ANSWER wasn't really that tough. Take action, of course, which they should have done long since. It was nearly the middle of November, for Pete's sake. To make the right decision, they needed information. Molly would make sure they got it.

The next evening she spoke to Richard on the phone. "We saw our family doctor today. He gave Cait something that should help reduce the nausea. I wish she'd told me sooner."

"Why didn't she?"

"She didn't realize anything could be done, and she was sure nobody had noticed."

He grunted in a male commentary that said it all. Of course someone had noticed. Several someones. And *they'd* told someone else, who'd told someone…. It was likely that the entire school was now talking about why Caitlyn Callahan was having to excuse herself from class to hang over the toilet several times a day.

"You were never that naive?" Molly said defensively.

"Nope." Then, as if curious, he asked, "Were you?"

Her irritation subsided. "No. But I didn't grow up…"

"Protected."

She had to clear her throat. That gentle voice he sometimes used had an unsettling effect on her. Colton, Cait's father, had been demanding, exciting, charismatic, but never tender.

Which should have been her first clue, she thought wryly.

"Yes," she admitted. *Forge on. Don't let him know he got to you.* "I made appointments for us to visit a couple of adoption agencies tomorrow," she said briskly. "I've let Cait drift, which wasn't smart. She needs a clear picture of all her options."

"Are you always smart?" he asked mildly.

"Doesn't everyone try to be?"

"I don't know. I doubt most people think it through like that. What's the smart thing to do? What's the dumb thing? Which am I going to do?"

She chuckled at that. Hard not to.

But he went on. "Kidding aside, most of us react, don't you think? Emotions get in the way of clear thinking. Sometimes that's even good."

"Is it?" Had any decision she'd ever made for emotional reasons turned out to be right?

Refusing to consider terminating her pregnancy. That was right. And an irony, since Colt was the one who'd wanted her to abort pregnancy and inconvenient problem all in one go, while barely three years later he was pushing her to get pregnant again. Having to get married while he was still a student didn't suit him. The minute he was finished with law school and ensconced in the family firm, having a son and heir had become all-important. He'd wanted a Colton the Fourth—and seriously talked about naming his son that, despite his jokes when she first met him about how ludicrous it was for his parents to have made him the Third. She'd tried to imagine a family barbecue if someone called out, "Colton!" and *four* generations of men and boys came running.

Water under the bridge.

"How can Cait's decision not be made with emotions?" Richard asked simply.

"Because that doesn't help. There'll be grief no matter what she decides. Abortion or adoption, one kind of grief. If she were to keep the baby and raise it, she'd be giving up everything a teenage girl and young woman expects. Still loss."

"I do see that," he said after a pause.

"Does Trevor?"

"He's already grieving in his own way, you know. He's discovered he isn't who he thought he was."

"Invincible?"

"That, of course. He also knows he wronged Cait in several ways. That's damaged his sense of self. The responsibility you've talked about…it's pretty damn scary for a kid his age."

Unsaid was how well Richard knew what his son was feeling. "What about you? Did you and—Alexa?—is that her name? Did you discuss abortion?" Molly asked.

"Not to speak of. I raised the idea once—she got hysterical. It was our baby. How could I possibly suggest any such thing."

Curled on one end of the sofa, conscious of the quiet house around her since Cait had disappeared upstairs to her bedroom shortly after dinner, Molly continued tentatively. "Have you thought about that? I mean, this is our grandchild."

He made a noise she couldn't quite interpret. "I'm thirty-seven years old. You're, what, thirty-four, thirty-five? Doesn't the idea of becoming a grandparent at your age secretly horrify you?"

"Um…yes?"

Richard laughed, a quiet, rich sound. "Honesty," he teased.

"I'm so confused," she heard herself admit. She clutched the phone, as if it was a lifeline.

"I don't totally see why. Caitlyn still has the chance to walk away from this. To say, 'I'm too young.'"

"You could have done that, too. So could I."

"But we were both…"

"A few years older. I know." All these feelings crowded in her chest like an overfull room. She needed air to breathe. "I've got to go," she said, knowing she sounded abrupt and suddenly not caring. "Good night, Richard."

She cut him off, still speaking. Why had she thought he of all people *would* understand? Dropping the phone on the coffee table, Molly stood and walked to the French doors that led out to a patio and her tiny backyard. She stared out at the darkness, not sure she was seeing more than a few feet past the glass. It felt symbolic. Maybe if she stepped outside, there would be enough moonlight to ease her panic. But she made no move to open the door.

If only Cait would talk to her.

When Molly had told her about the fight between Trevor and Aaron and the possibility that there was speculation Cait was pregnant, her expression had been almost as stricken as when she realized her mother had uncovered her secret. But this time, she hadn't said, "Mommy, what should I do?" She'd only said, "No one can prove anything."

"No."

Cait had nodded when Molly suggested a doctor's appointment, although her face had been white and oh, so young when she followed the nurse into the exam room for her first ever pelvic. The doctor had wanted to talk to her privately first. Molly had been allowed in only at the end, when they sat down to talk.

The trouble was, after that first night when Molly confronted her, Cait had retreated inside herself. Instead of defiant and angry, she was withdrawn. Molly couldn't tell if she was practicing denial, agonizing over what she saw as a very private decision or wanting to talk to someone—anyone—other than her mother. Denial was Molly's best guess, and it was dangerous.

I'm right to push, she told herself. If Cait were to carry the baby to term, it should be because she'd made the choice, not because too much time passed and she no longer had a choice. *I can do that much for her.* Really, was this any different than insisting your kid get unwanted vaccines, confess to the neighbor that she'd thrown the ball that broke his front picture window, finish that assignment tonight even if every single one of her friends was going to Wild Waves water park instead because *their* parents weren't mean and said it was okay?

No. It wasn't. Helping her daughter make a truly informed decision was her duty as a parent. So there.

RICHARD TOOK A CHANCE and went over to Molly's the next evening. Trevor was out, God knows where, and he'd found himself unbearably restless. He didn't like how last night's conversation had ended. He'd blown it, saying that. *I don't totally see why you're confused.*

She'd given him a chance to listen, and he'd shut it down. Scared, he supposed, for Trevor's sake.

She might be less than thrilled to find him on her doorstep, but he had to try to talk to her. To make up for his insensitivity, to give her a chance to talk in case she didn't have anyone else she dared confide in.

Yeah, he admitted honestly, *and because I want to see her, too.* Last night, listening for nuances in her voice, he'd wished he could see her face.

He was relieved when she came to the door, not Cait. "Richard?" she said, obviously startled.

"Hi." He shoved his hands in the pockets of his parka. "I was hoping you'd give me a few minutes."

"Well, of course." She backed inside. "Wow, it's cold."

A puff of icy breath accompanied Richard into the entryway. "Yeah, they're talking about a scattering of snow Monday."

"Oh, ugh," she muttered, as she took his parka and hung it in the closet.

Richard raised his eyebrows. "Where's that youthful wonder? The first snowfall of the year…"

"The disaster transporting students becomes."

"Tell me you're not one of the people who decides whether school is going to be canceled."

Over her shoulder, Molly wrinkled her nose at him. "You mean, one of those people who is on a conference call at 5:00 a.m.? Why, yes, I am."

His gaze traveled over that luscious body. He wondered if she had any idea how lovingly that pair of faded jeans fit her ass. He even appreciated the big, sacky T-shirt she wore, because it made her more approachable. Her hair was bundled loosely in an elastic, but curly tendrils escaped to lie against her cheek and the nape of her neck. And—oh, damn—she was barefoot. Richard was taken aback to discover how erotic feet could be. As he took a seat and watched her settle into what was obviously a favorite spot at one end of the sofa, he remained fixated on those feet.

They weren't dainty. She must wear a size nine or ten, but then she was a tall woman. She had particularly narrow feet with high arches and exceptionally long toes. He switched his gaze briefly to her hands and realized her fingers were long, too. As were her legs. He wondered how deft she was with those toes....

He was already aroused. Richard moved in an effort to make himself comfortable and hide his reaction from her.

"I should have offered you coffee before I sat down," she said suddenly.

He shook his head. "I'm fine. I drink too much of the stuff as it is."

"Me, too. And waste entirely too much money on lovely, frothy, calorie-laden drinks that may or may not actually be coffee."

He laughed. "I love that espresso stand on the corner of Wall and Fifth."

"Oh, yeah. Me, too." For a moment they smiled at each other, no complications, but finally her expression faltered. "What did you need to talk to me about, Richard?"

He leaned forward, elbows braced on his knees. "I do understand why you're confused," he said abruptly. "Or, at least, that you are. Maybe not entirely why, because I'm not a woman and it's not my daughter who is pregnant."

She stared at him for a long time, her eyes astonishingly vulnerable, the gray so much softer than it seemed to him at first meeting.

"I'm sorry," he said. "That's what I came to say. And to tell you I really will listen if you need to talk any of this out." Or anything else, but he didn't say that. "I, uh, didn't know if you've told any friends. If you have anyone else you can vent to."

"No." She tried to smile, but it wouldn't take shape. "No, I haven't told a soul. I have friends, but…"

When she didn't finish, Richard broke the silence. "Mine all have kids that are way younger. When I first realized what was going on with Trev, it hit me that I didn't have anyone to talk about it with."

Molly nodded. "I've gotten close to the mothers of some of Cait's friends, but right now they're the last people I want to tell that she's pregnant."

"Is she home?" he asked, and she shook her head.

"She's at the dance school. She assists with a class of younger students."

It turned out he didn't have to say much. She started to spill. She hurt at the knowledge that Cait would lose dance, if only temporarily, should she continue the pregnancy. No, she was unlikely to go on professionally with it anyway; she was likely too tall, and she didn't have the single-mindedness required.

"But she loves it."

She told him that her daughter wasn't talking to her. Her face pinched with unhappiness. "It's not that she's sulking or anything like that. Not like when she was mad at me over Trevor. She's just…retreated. Gone deep inside. And…it's always been the two of us." She stole a look at him that was both shy and filled with pain. "Now she's shut me out."

Richard moved without thinking about it. One minute he was on his side of the living room, the next he'd taken the middle cushion of the sofa and her hand in his. Ms. Molly Callahan wasn't as tough as she'd appeared. Not even close.

"I've been feeling some of that with Trevor," he said. "It's not the same because I didn't have the chance to raise him, but I thought we were tight. Finding out how wrong I was hurt."

She gave a laugh that wasn't quite a sob. "And in the middle of all this, I have to ask myself why I'm getting my feelings hurt when my daughter is facing something so life-altering. And mostly it is her I think about, but sometimes…"

"You're human," he said softly.

She looked down at their hands, her paler fingers entwined with his. "Yes." Her voice was even quieter than his. "I guess that's it."

"Hey." He squeezed slightly. "We're entitled to have feelings, too. God knows our kids have been sharing plenty of them."

Her small giggle pleased him. *No, not tough at all.*

A minute later she regained enough composure to become self-conscious, and retrieved her hand from his. He was sorry. He relaxed where he was, stretched his legs out as far as the coffee table allowed and asked her if she and Cait had had an appointment at either adoption agency today.

Turned out they'd gone to both places. That was one of the reasons, he realized, that she was distressed. Cait, apparently, had listened but barely mumbled one- or two-word answers to any questions asked of her.

"Then on the way home, she said, 'I can talk for myself you know, Mom.' Not mad, but warning me off."

Molly might not be tough, but she did have a take-charge personality or she wouldn't have gotten as far as she had in school administration by her age. He didn't feel much sympathy for her daughter.

"Did she not want to go?"

Molly made a face. "Who knows? If not, she didn't say so. Heck, I may find out she's decided to get an abortion and done it without even telling me. At this point, I wouldn't be shocked."

"Can she?" he asked.

"Without parental consent, you mean?" When he nodded, she said, "I don't know. I'm assuming there are ways."

"Would you be angry?"

She shook her head. More of her hair slipped from the elastic. "Hurt that she was so determined to shut me out. See, there I go again. But I'm not sure I could help it. I've made it clear that I'll support her decision. So if she decides not to let me support her…" She blinked a couple of times, and he took hold of her hand again.

"When they lay that squalling baby in your arms at the hospital, they should warn you what they're going to turn into. You worry you'll fail this small creature without realizing the creature metamorphoses into a hideous monster for one stage of its development. Maybe if we knew from the get-go, instead of misty eyes and melting heart, we'd start out wary."

He loved what a smile did to her face, and to a mouth that was a whole lot softer than it had appeared at first meeting, too. She kept it firmly compressed entirely too often.

"You're right," she declared. "Baby books should carry warning labels. 'Forget childbirth, having a kid *really* hurts when they hit their teens.'"

"You've got it."

This time they grinned at each other like idiots.

Finally she appeared to notice they were holding hands and wiggled her fingers until he released her. He wasn't letting her get shy. Shy? The formidable Vice Principal Callahan? "Tell me what you learned today."

That got her going again. She admitted that she'd expected a sales job. Any adoption agency must have dozens to hundreds of desperate couples waiting for that perfect baby, and subconsciously Molly had assumed that would color how they dealt with teenage mothers on the fence.

"But it wasn't like that at all. Both the women we talked to today were cautious, to say the least, kind and really good to Cait." She rolled her eyes. "At least, they tried to be. They were pretty matter-of-fact about how it works. We heard about traditional and open adoptions."

He tensed a little at that idea. "Open?"

"Caitlyn, at least, could stay in touch. They vary all the way from adoptive parents sending photos and maybe notes once a year to ones where the birth mother practically becomes part of the family."

"What about the birth father?"

"I'm guessing that's a possibility, too."

He nodded. "How did Cait react to that idea?"

"Who knows?" Molly said with exasperation. "But at least she was listening."

"They must get birth mothers who back out at the last minute."

She looked at him in surprise.

"I'm thinking back to your expectation that you'd get a sales pitch. It wouldn't do them any good to channel used car salesmen. Even if the kid signs on the dotted line, there's still a period she can back out, even after the baby goes home with the adoptive parents, right?"

"Right. The law is weighted on the birth parents' side." She was nodding. "Of course you're right. It must be awful to let a couple think they're getting a baby, then have it yanked away at the last minute."

She told him she thought she'd make herself a cup of tea, and Richard followed her to the kitchen. He kept listening for the front door, wondering what her daughter would think to find him here, but Molly didn't seem to be worried.

Conversation strayed while they waited for water to boil and then tea to steep. He told her he'd been the electrical contractor for this development and done the work personally on some of the town houses. "Not this one," he said, looking around a kitchen with pale cherrywood cabinets and countertops of a granite warmed by gold and pink tones. "I keep my hand in, though. Sitting in an office all day doesn't suit me."

"I never thought it would suit me, either," she said, handing him one mug. They moved toward the dining nook and chose seats across the table from each other. "I loved teaching," she said, her hands cradling the mug. "Honestly, I'm still of two minds about whether I want to stay on the administrative track or go back to the classroom. The pay is better now, though, and that counts when you're a single parent."

"Cait's father doesn't pay child support?"

"Sure he does, but so much and no more. Braces? My problem. Do you know what braces cost these days?"

"To the penny," Richard assured her. "Trevor didn't need them, thank God, but Bree did. After that hit, I added some orthodontic insurance for my employees. Some of them have kids."

"Those braces came close to taking Colt's entire year of child support checks." She shrugged. "I've been trying to build a decent college fund for her."

He saw her flinch as it occurred to her that fund might not be needed now—or, at least, not for its original purpose.

"Oh, Lord," she whispered.

He felt compelled to offer reassurance. "Things will work out," was the best he could come up with.

Her eyes flashed indignation. "What does that mean?"

He had to laugh. "That things will work out somehow or another? It doesn't promise that they'll work out well."

"Thanks a lot!" But she was smiling, too.

She stiffened at the same moment he heard the sound of the front door opening. "I'm in the kitchen," she called.

Richard found himself hoping the kid would go straight up to her bedroom, the way Trevor usually did. No such luck. She appeared in the kitchen, pretty and ridiculously young, wearing jeans and a shiny pink leotard.

"Mom, Sabrina told me..." Her eyes widened. "What's *he* doing here?"

"Cait!"

Her face got mulish. "Well, what is he doing here?"

"Talking to your mother." He drained the last of his tea and stood. "We have some feelings about what's happened, too, you know. Sometimes talking them out with someone who understands can help."

She'd been raised to be polite, he suspected, because now she flushed. "I'm sorry," she muttered.

He smiled at her. "It's okay. Looks bad, I know. Two adults, alone in the house..." He shook his head solemnly, pleased when she laughed. If she only knew, he couldn't help thinking. She sure as hell wouldn't like the way he'd contemplated her mother's toes and what they'd be capable of doing. He didn't suppose that she saw her thirty-five-year-old mother as a sexual being. Which made him reflect on what Trevor would say about his father lusting after the mother of his former girlfriend. Probably nothing very nice.

"Thanks for the tea, Molly. And for letting me drop in."

She stood, too. "No problem." She glanced at her daughter. "Let me walk Richard to the door, hon."

"Richard?" The kid sounded outraged.

Even laughing, he felt every year and then some as he headed for the front of the town house.

"Your daughter is a puritan," he suggested to Molly, while she got out his parka.

She laughed—okay, giggled—and then pressed her fingers to her mouth to hush herself. "Possibly. I'd never noticed."

"There's a certain irony."

"No kidding." There was the grown-up, sardonic. And then she gave him an uncertain smile. "Thank you for coming, Richard. And for listening."

"No problem." Not letting himself hesitate, he took a chance, stepped forward and kissed her lightly on the cheek. "Call anytime," he said, and went out, not looking back. He felt a little uneasy to discover he took with him a whole lot of sensory impressions: the velvet texture of her skin, the gentle, pillowy feel of her cheek beneath his mouth, the tickle of her hair and an illusive, sweet scent. And his last glimpse—those long toes curling, because he'd kissed her.

CHAPTER EIGHT

TREVOR COULD NOT BELIEVE that Cait was still dodging him. He had some rights here, didn't he? Shit, yeah, he did.

He tried to catch her between classes; she was as quick as a minnow in a lake, darting away. After school—she never again made the mistake of leaving without having surrounded herself with girlfriends first. Postdance—more friends, or else her mother or another girl's mother was waiting in the car out front. Her phone never seemed to be on anymore, but he sent texts.

Cant we talk?

The only response he got was:

When Im ready so quit stalking me.

Sure. He sent back:

Ill quit stalking when you talk.

She ignored that one.

The weird thing was, he didn't know what it was he needed to say, or to hear from her. Only that he felt like his skin had shrunk and now it itched and prickled and he felt trapped inside it. It was a little like when he'd thought sex with her would make him feel all better, but…different, too.

Because he knew what an asshole he'd been and he needed her to say it was all right even if it wasn't.

No.

Lying on his bed, he groaned and pushed the heel of his hand against his forehead. He needed her to say it because she meant it. But he also knew that wasn't happening. Because she was majorly, totally screwed over. And it *was* his fault.

His phone rang and he rolled over to snatch it up. Not that it would be Cait, but… He was disappointed anyway when he saw the number. Bree's. She'd left a couple messages, and he hadn't called her back.

This time, after a brief hesitation, he answered.

"Hey," she said. "You've disappeared."

"Yeah, well, things have been…" He tried to think how to explain without explaining. "Happening," he finally concluded.

"Like what? Did you decide to go out for basketball?"

"No." Man, he knew the coach would still take him, and there were moments when he really missed playing, but… How fair was it if he got to play a sport he loved while Cait had to quit dance?

"Do you tell Mom everything?" he said abruptly.

His sister huffed. "You know I don't. Did I ever tattle?"

A grin tugged at his mouth. "Yeah, when I shaved the head on every one of your Barbie dolls."

"I was five! And that was mean."

"They'd gone to boot camp." Another huff. He was

still grinning. It was wiped from his mouth, though, when he took a deep breath. "This is *not* for Mom. Swear?"

"Swear."

"My girlfriend is pregnant. Um…she used to be my girlfriend."

There was a long, shocked silence. "Used to be? You've only been there for, like, three months?"

"Yeah, uh, we didn't last long." He sat up on the edge of the bed.

"Long enough."

Trevor blinked at his sister's tart tone. Suddenly she didn't sound so much like a kid. He grimaced. A kid? She was…not even a year younger than Cait. He knew when both their birthdays were. Eight months and… six days.

In sudden alarm, he asked, "Have you, um…?"

"Had sex? No way!"

"I'll bet some of your friends have," he said.

"Well, sure. But I haven't met anybody I liked that much. And even if I did…I'm going to try to wait until I'm in college," she finished in a rush.

He was surprised by his tangle of emotions. He hated the idea of some guy screwing his little sister. Scoring. Even worse—wow—of her pregnant.

"That's a good idea," he said.

"One you've lived by." Before he could counter that, she went on. "Is the girl a senior, too?"

"Uh, no." He realized how much he'd been saying that: *uh.* To give himself time to think, maybe. "She's a sophomore."

"And you got her *pregnant?*"

"She was there, too."

Bree made a sound he took as disgust, and Trevor let his head fall forward. *I am such an asshole. And there's no way I can make it better.*

"What are you going to do?" his sister asked.

"I don't know." It was a really hard thing to admit. To accept.

Almost as hard as accepting that there probably wasn't anything he *could* do.

"How were things at school today?" Molly asked brightly. She drained the spaghetti.

"I didn't puke, if that's what you mean," her daughter said disagreeably.

"That's not what I meant, but I'm glad. The medicine's helping, then."

"I guess."

Cait did help carry food to the table and filled her plate although then she looked down at it in dismay. "I'm so hungry! When I'm not sick, all I want to do is eat. I'd be a whale if I…" She put on the brakes.

Molly opened her mouth to say, *You're eating for two,* but, thank God, thought better of it in time. "You're active," was all she said. "Didn't you dance today?"

"Yeah. It does make me hungry." Apparently she gave herself permission to eat, because she started in on the spaghetti with enthusiasm.

Molly finished a bite of broccoli. "So, did you have any thoughts about yesterday?" she asked, ultracasual.

Pasta dangling from her fork, Cait stared at her. "Yesterday?"

"You know. The two agencies."

She shrugged and put the bite in her mouth.

"I think I liked the first one better. I don't know how

you'd feel about an open adoption, but they sound as if they embrace the concept instead of offering it grudgingly. It might be easier, if you choose adoption, not to close the door on your child."

This stare smoldered. "Can't you let it alone, Mom?"

"Sometimes talking things out is the best way to clarify your thinking," she said very carefully.

"Is that what you're doing? Clarifying *your* thinking, so *you* can make up your mind what I should do?"

Molly put down her fork. She was beginning to be fed up with Cait's sullen, "me against you" attitude. "No," she said. "You know that's not what I'm doing."

"Do I?"

"Have you told any of your friends?"

"Of course not!"

"Then who do you have to talk to?"

Silence.

"Trevor?"

"I don't want to talk to him!" Cait was flat-out glaring now. "*He's* the one stalking me now."

"Because you won't talk to him."

"Why should I?"

"Because you have to talk to somebody," Molly said, trying for patience when the well was dry. "Seems to me, your choices are him or me."

"Both of you want to decide for me. You don't listen. You tell me what to do. You always have," she claimed, in that sweeping way teenagers had of making a parent feel guilty for every single decision ever made. She dropped her fork with a clatter. "I'm not hungry anymore," she announced, pushing back her chair.

Molly might have felt really crummy if Cait's hand

hadn't snaked out and nabbed a piece of garlic bread, which then disappeared behind her.

"All right," Molly said, voice steely. "Here's the deal. You're now over seven weeks pregnant. You and I both know you shouldn't take more than three more weeks to make up your mind about an abortion. After that, it's off the table. Do you fully understand that?"

"Yes!" Cait yelled, face red and tears starting. She ran from the room.

Taking the garlic bread with her.

MOLLY WOULD HAVE GONE out to the garage to make her phone call, if only it wasn't so cold. As it was, phone in her hand, she strolled to the foot of the stairs to be sure Cait really was safely closeted in her room before dialing.

"Molly," Richard said, in that quiet, deep voice that for no good reason seemed to settle some of her turmoil. She'd been counting on it. "I was hoping you'd call tonight."

"Hah!" She kept her voice low and walked to the living room, where she could hear any footsteps on the stairs—and wasn't right beneath Cait's room. "You were probably hoping for a few days of peace."

"No. Cross my heart and hope to die."

She could hear his smile, which made her grow one, too, however wry and painful it was. "Thank you for saying that. I hope you meant it. About listening. Talking."

"I meant it."

Sincere? Not? Given that she'd already made the phone call, what could she do but take him at his word?

"So what's up?" he asked.

"Oh, the usual drama with my daughter. How dare I try to open a discussion about the adoption agencies, open versus closed adoptions, never mind the fact that she's seven plus weeks along. Seven weeks!" She was breathing hard again. She wished suddenly that he was here. That—maybe—he was holding her hand. The first time he'd done that, she'd hardly noticed on a conscious level, but the feel of his big, warm hand wrapping hers was nonetheless imprinted on her sensory memory. When was the last time anyone had offered physical comfort to her? Anyone but Caitlyn, who used to be generous with hugs but now seemed to bitterly resent her mother?

"Yeah, that's been on my mind, too," Richard said.

Molly had to think what he was talking about. *Seven weeks.* That was it. "What is she thinking? No, don't even try to answer that."

"I wasn't going to." There was an undertone of amusement, but sympathy, too.

"Has Trevor opened up to you any?"

"Initially he did. More recently, he's been close-mouthed. Less angry, though. It's as if once he realized how badly he'd screwed up, he became a little less focused on the flaws of his bumbling parents."

"One of his teachers commented in passing that Trevor blew him away with a paper."

"A paper? He actually turned one in?"

"Apparently."

"Huh."

On a spurt of resentment, she thought, *Crisis hits, his kid turns a corner for the good and mine for the bad. How fair is that?*

Fair enough. Trevor was older. He *should* be more mature.

"So, did you get her talking at all?" Richard asked.

"Only long enough for her to yell that all I ever do is tell her what to do. I don't listen."

There was a moment of silence, long enough for her to remember Richard, too, had told her she didn't listen.

"I was pissed," he said. "I didn't mean it."

"You read my mind?"

"Hard not to."

She sighed. "Maybe I don't."

"From all I can gather, your daughter was popular, amazing at dance—according to Trevor—and smart. Not a cheerleader only because it would have gotten in the way of dance. Homecoming princess."

"Straight-A student. That's more important than popular."

"Agreed. She's gotten mixed-up lately. Doesn't mean you didn't raise a great kid. Give yourself some credit."

Molly drew her legs up, dug her toes into the sofa cushions and rested her forehead on her knees. "Thank you. I needed somebody to say that."

"You're very welcome." The undercurrent of amusement was in his voice again.

She cleared her throat. "So. I was thinking."

When she didn't continue immediately, he made an interested sound.

"What if you and Trevor were to come over for dinner?" Molly said in a hurry. "If we ruled no talk about… you know."

This silence had her antsy. She lifted her head. *Did I just say that? What was I thinking? That we could all be* friends?

"There's nothing I'd like better," he said. "Well, that's not true. Dinner without our kids, that might be better."

She laughed, her unease settling. She loved how he could do that.

"I can run it by Trevor," he said. "But from what he says, Cait won't willingly be on board."

"Maybe it should be a surprise party…. No, forget I said that. There's a disaster in the making. I tried that already, didn't I, and you and Trevor didn't like it very well. Okay, it's a lousy idea."

"No, it's not," Richard said, to her surprise. "Chances are Cait feels isolated, but is scared of being pushed into a decision before she's ready. Maybe something like this could make her feel…supported."

"And maybe," Molly said slowly as the realization hit, "I'm involving you and Trevor when I shouldn't be. You wanted to be kept in the loop. That's, um, a courteous, long-distance relationship, not an up-close and personal one."

"I like up-close and personal."

Her pulse tripped. "You're being nice," she said lightly.

"No." His voice deepened some. "I almost asked you out once."

"Once?" she repeated stupidly. "During one of our congenial little chats?"

Richard chuckled. "High school dance."

Oh, God. That's why he'd loitered beside her, hands in his pockets, making pointless conversation? He was waiting to get her alone?

Her heartbeat had rocketed now. "I didn't have a clue."

"I noticed. And realized I'd picked a really stupid

time and place to ask. Pretty poor month and year, too, when we were bound to be dealing with each other over Trevor. I decided to wait until he'd graduated."

"Oh." Brilliant. *I am so out of practice.* Then, *Do I want this?* "Instead, we may be cograndparents."

"Not quite what I pictured," he admitted. "Anyway, I thought it was fair to tell you."

A panicky fear that the subject might be closed for good had her speaking up. "I...don't know what I would have said. You'd gotten tangled up in my mind with Trevor. By the time of the dance, I guess I knew you weren't the irresponsible parent I'd imagined you, but..."

"You were still mad."

"Yes."

"If you hadn't been?"

No question there. "I'd have said yes."

"Ah." His quiet satisfaction was apparent. "Well, why don't we hold the thought? Or bring our kids on our first date."

He made her laugh so easily. "Let's do that. I'll sound out Cait. You do the same with Trevor."

"Got it." The smile was there again, which warmed her. "Did we talk out your mood?"

"Yes, I think we did. Thank you. You've been a life-saver."

"When I wasn't threatening you with my buddy the superintendent."

"Do you know him?" she asked, curious.

"Yes, he put an addition on his house a couple of years ago. I'm not so sure he'd agree that the fact that I wired it made us best buds, though."

The call ended on another laugh. Molly was left wondering what she would have said that night, if Richard had taken her by surprise the night of the dance and asked her out.

TREVOR STOOD IN THE DARK, looking up at Cait's bedroom window. Her blinds were closed, but not tightly. He could see that her light was on.

He'd expected to have to climb over their back fence, but found he had been able to reach over and unlatch the gate. Light poured through the kitchen window and the French doors, so he'd had to move carefully to reach the back of the house without getting spotlighted like a deer by night hunters. Now he cautiously eyed the possibilities.

They had an arbor, too. Not as sturdy as Dad's, but doable. It didn't reach quite underneath Cait's window, either, but he thought he could knock on the glass. If she'd open up, he could grip the sill and swing himself up.

Assuming she didn't freak, of course. Scream. He'd left the back gate open for a quick getaway, in case.

Was this a totally dumb-ass idea?

No. He *had* to talk to her. As far as he was concerned, she'd chosen the time and place. Dad said she'd checked out adoption agencies last weekend—without telling him a word about it. He especially wanted to talk before they both got to participate in the nice, civilized dinner party put on by her mother. Because that would relax him and Cait, sitting down to eat under their parents' eagle eyes.

Do it, he decided, crouched and jumped. Easy as a slam dunk, his fingers locked over the rough wood of the crosspiece. He dangled for a moment, swung and, when the momentum was right, levered himself up. He sat atop the beam for a moment, then rose to a crouch, toed over to the house and braced an open hand on the siding. Okay, now, if he leaned…stretched… Yeah. He rapped lightly on the glass.

For a moment, nothing happened. Then the blinds were parted and he saw her face. He waggled his fingers. Blinds snapped shut. He waited, until finally they rose and then she opened the window.

"Trevor?" she whispered.

"Yeah, can I come in?"

"Are you *nuts?*" Her hair was tousled, her face scrubbed clean, making her look even younger than usual and she wore… Wow. Some kind of saggy-baggy T-shirt thing.

He kept his voice low. "No. I want to talk to you."

"Now?"

"When?"

"What if my mom comes in?"

"Does she?"

"She's watching a TV show. She probably won't come up until it's over." The answer was grudging. Cait stuck her head out and looked down and then sidelong to where he stood atop the arbor. "What if you fall?"

"I won't."

She rolled her eyes but relented. "Oh, fine."

He got a grip okay, but there was one distinct thud as his feet hit the side of the house. Cait and he both went still. The strain on his shoulders was huge. Even so, he let a good minute pass before pulling himself up and half falling through the window.

Cait immediately let down the blinds and pointed

to bare floor behind her bed. "Sit down there. If Mom comes, drop flat, okay?"

"Sure." He sat, back to her bedside stand, and stretched out his legs. He couldn't see all of her room from here, but enough. It was almost as girlie as Bree's at Davis's house. A couple of posters of ballerinas were the eye-catchers. One was doing some kind of leap and seemed suspended in air. Impossible and dazzling, he had to admit. Another was being lifted by a guy, who looked gay in tight dance clothes but obviously had some serious muscle.

Otherwise, her bedspread was fluffy and powder pink, there was a barre like at the dance school screwed into one wall intersecting with the one that had floor-length mirrors on the closet doors and the whole room was completely neat. Unreal.

She plopped on the bed cross-legged and looked down at him. She was not happy. "Say whatever it is you want to say."

"Why are you avoiding me?"

"Because I know what you want."

They'd had this conversation before. And, no lie, Trevor did want to say again, *Get an abortion. Please, for both our sakes, get an abortion so we can both forget this ever happened.* But he'd seen the way she reacted last time, and whether he liked it or not, he heard what she'd said.

He felt queasy when he thought, *What if Mom had aborted me? Well, duh, I wouldn't be here. Cait wouldn't be pregnant. Or, at least, I wouldn't be the father. There might've been some other guy.*

"No," he said. "That's not it. I wanted to say...I was

an asshole. I know I was. And I want to make up for it, if I can. I wish you'd talk to me. That's all."

"Right. Sure. You want to hold my hand and dry my tears and be super nice guy."

"Yeah. If that's what you need from me," Trevor said, feeling guilty because no, that's not what he *wanted*.

"What if I said what I *need* is for you to leave me alone?"

He was here because he hated being helpless. He needed some control. But…he looked at her face, and saw his sister. It shook him up. What if this was Bree? What if she needed space? To decide for herself, not for anyone else?

Trevor made a getting-up motion. "Then I will."

She burst into tears.

"Oh, shit." He got to his knees and reached clumsily for her. She fell against him and clutched him hard. "Shh," he kept saying. God. All they needed was for her mother to burst in here now, find him here. "Shh," he said against her hair, more desperately. "It's okay."

"It's not!" Cait whispered fiercely.

No. He guessed it wasn't.

She finally unwound her arms and sat back. She grabbed some tissues from a box in her drawer and swabbed at her face, not looking at him. Trevor stayed where he was, kneeling in front of her.

"I'm sorry," he said. "I wish there was something I could do."

She blew her nose and gazed at him from puffy eyes. "It was nice of you to come over. And…well, to keep bugging me the way you have been. You could have, um, just figured it was my problem and ignored me."

"I'm not that big an asshole," he muttered. "It took two. It's *our* problem."

"And your dad's and my mom's, too, apparently."

He tried out a grin. Crooked, one that he hoped said, *We* are *in this together.* "I noticed."

"Can you believe they want us all to have dinner together? Like, what?"

"I don't know what," he admitted. "I guess it makes them feel good. Like they're involved or something."

"It's my baby." Her eyes slid to his. "Ours."

"Yeah." Oh, shit, oh, damn, oh… "You don't want to get an abortion, do you?"

Her face froze.

"It's okay. You can tell me."

"It feels wrong."

"You really think it's a baby and not…"

"Some cells?"

"Yeah."

"I don't know," she said. "I don't. I don't think abortion is necessarily wrong. Maybe I'd do it without even thinking if it weren't for Mom having me when she wasn't ready for a baby."

Feeling like he had a baseball lodged in his throat, Trevor nodded. He couldn't say anything. *I'm the one who is going to freak,* he realized. The lump was stuck. It was never going away. *If she has her way, I will have a child. The rest of my friggin' life, I'll know. Somewhere out there, I have a kid. One who'll believe neither of us wanted him.*

Who'll be right that neither of us wanted him.

Without knowing he planned it, he was on his feet. "I should go." He could talk after all.

Eyes as wide as swollen lids would let them be, Cait stared at him. "Okay."

"It's hard to think about it." He nodded toward her belly without actually looking at it.

She nodded.

"Whatever you decide…" He sucked in a deep breath. Oh, man, this was hard. "That's okay," he finished. "Whatever *you* decide. Not your mom."

She kept staring.

"I'll marry you if that's what you want. Okay?" The idea scared the shit out of him, but he had to offer. "If you decide on an abortion, I'll take you and pay for it. No matter what your mom thinks."

Cait took a shuddery breath and nodded.

"All right." He tried out another smile, which pretty well fell flat, but oh, well. "See you for dinner."

A whispery sound that might have been an almost giggle came from her. He turned away and squeezed his eyes shut. Sick and scared, he lifted a leg over the windowsill.

"Be careful," she said, sounding alarmed.

"Yeah." He grinned at her. Better this time. "Piece of cake."

Hang by your hands. Toe away from the wall. Drop and roll. He rose to his feet as if it was nothing and took a bow. She was definitely smiling when he faded into the darkness.

He'd really liked her. He still really liked her. But… married? Trevor couldn't believe he'd said that. Oh, man. What if she took him up on it?

CHAPTER NINE

RICHARD COULDN'T DECIDE if this was the most idiotic idea on the face of the earth, or a good one. As he rang the doorbell, Trevor waited a step behind him, sulky but seemingly resigned.

"I hope she doesn't cook something weird," he muttered. "Like Mom—"

Richard started to turn. Trev hardly ever mentioned his mother, and when he did he shut down fast, like he was now. But why was he mad at his father, too, if it was his mother who had enraged him in the first place?

The door opened, but it was Caitlyn standing there. "Come in." She didn't roll her eyes but might as well have. She didn't even look at Trevor.

"Thank you," Richard said, nodding. Watching her hang his and Trevor's coats in the closet, he wondered how Molly had compelled her semiwilling compliance.

"Come on back to the kitchen," Molly called.

There was a formal dining area, but she'd set the table in the nook attached to the kitchen. He guessed that's where they ate all their meals, and he'd have done the same. It had the same warmth as the kitchen and was surrounded by glass.

Molly looked good. He'd discovered he really liked her when she got out of her take-me-seriously suits. Tonight was jeans and a snug sweater in a reddish-brown.

She was definitely a generously proportioned woman, and made no attempt to hide it. He hoped she wasn't one of those women who tried to starve her body into submission on a regular basis.

Richard sniffed cautiously, and relaxed when he recognized something Italian.

"Manicotti," Molly told them. "I hope you like it. It's a favorite of Cait's and mine."

"Sounds good to me," he said heartily.

Trevor grunted.

"Cait, why don't you help me dish up. Richard, I could open some wine if you'd like that…."

He shook his head. "I'm not much of a drinker. Water's fine."

Eventually they all settled around the table. He hadn't sat down to a meal with a woman and two kids since the days before he walked in on Lexa with her lover. Trev was six years old then, which made it…eleven years ago. This felt more than bizarre.

Molly smiled at his son. "Trevor, I don't think I even said hello. I hope this isn't too awkward for you, given that our interactions haven't always been positive."

Trevor stared at her with obvious incredulity.

She cleared her throat. "Cait and I were talking today about Thanksgiving. Are you staying here with your dad?"

Trev's gaze flicked to his father. "I guess."

"You must miss your sister."

"I talk to her," he said after a minute.

"Maybe if I bought her a ticket she'd come up for Thanksgiving," Richard heard himself say. "Hell, it's next week, isn't it? I should have thought of it sooner.

I suggested Christmas, but she wasn't sure she wanted to leave your mom alone."

"Maybe," Trevor mumbled.

Richard guessed it was his turn to plow some conversational ground, so to speak. Not his strength. "So, Caitlyn," he ventured, "I hear you're quite a dancer." He winced inwardly at the avuncular tone, which was pretty well guaranteed not to go over well. "Is it ballet?"

She stared at him. Her mother shifted in her seat, which seemed to snap her out of her state of disbelief. "Um, I do ballet, but I do jazz and modern dance, too."

"Even belly dance," her mother said brightly.

"Really?" That was Trev. "Hey, cool. I didn't know that. Do you ever perform?"

Richard gaped at his son, then closed his mouth. Had that been an involuntary exclamation of interest, or was Trevor actually making an effort?

"Um, yeah, sometimes," Cait said. "I belong to a troupe, and we do dinner shows once in a while. You know that club in Everett? We've got a show there in December." She shot her mother a spiteful look. "Mom doesn't like them."

"I never said that...."

"You didn't have to," her daughter shot back.

"I love the dancing. You know that." Her conflict was apparent on her face. "It's the part where you shimmy around with people giving you money that reminds me a little too much of strippers. When I saw that creep stick a dollar bill in your cleavage..."

"Some old guy?" asked Trevor.

"That was gross," Cait admitted. "He had, like, gray hair and kind of a wobbly chin. And I didn't like the way he looked at me."

"Belly dancing is sexy," Molly said. "The problem is, most of the troupe are older than Cait. In their twenties, at least."

"Bathsira, our leader, is, I don't know, thirty-five or something," Cait contributed.

Molly's age, Richard thought with amusement. He wondered if fifteen-year-old Cait had thought to equate a dance partner with her aging mother.

"Bathsira?" Trevor echoed. "Really? In West Fork?"

Cait's chin came up. "That's her stage name. Her real name is...it doesn't matter. We all have stage names."

"Yeah? What's yours?"

"Mariam."

"That's pretty." Trevor was eating with astonishing enthusiasm. He'd polished off his first serving of manicotti and even the green beans and was reaching for the serving dish.

"I thought so," Cait said. "Here, do you want some more garlic bread?"

"Yeah, cool."

Trevor coaxed Cait to tell them the stage names of some of the other dancers, then asked if she'd perform after dinner.

"No! You'd just make fun of me, or..." Her cheeks got pink.

"I wouldn't," Trevor claimed. He shoveled in a big mouthful of manicotti.

"The dancing really is beautiful," Molly said. "And Cait's won some local contests. Somehow her body flows."

There was a moment of silence, during which they all undoubtedly thought about Cait Callahan's body, and what it was up to right now. She ducked her head. "Geez, Mom."

"Well, you're good."

Cait looked at Trevor. "You should try dance. Some pro athletes do it, you know."

Trev snorted.

"Coach Bowman would give his right arm if Trevor would only play basketball," Molly said.

Caitlyn turned her blue eyes on him. "You should, you know," she said earnestly. "If you're that good. Why aren't you playing?"

Richard made a fist under the table and gave it a surreptitious punch. He avoided meeting Molly's eyes.

Trevor looked down at his plate. "I'm still thinking about it."

"Our team could use some help," Molly said matter-of-factly.

He hunched his shoulders. "Even if I wanted to... It's not fair," he finished in a burst, "if Cait can't keep dancing."

When nobody said anything for a minute, Richard did. "I'm proud of you for thinking about that." He cleared his throat then nodded toward the garlic bread. "Molly, would you mind handing that to me?"

She did, and he passed it on.

"I wouldn't mind," Cait said tentatively. She was looking at Trevor. "Really. It might be fun to watch you play." She flushed. "If it wouldn't embarrass you."

He swallowed hastily. "You mean having you there? No! I mean, I'd like it if you'd come to games." Now his cheeks had reddened, too, and he stole a look from his dad to her mom. "If I decide to play."

"I hope you do," Molly told him.

Richard had feared the forbidden topic would act as a clot in the conversation, but somehow it didn't. Next thing he knew the kids were comparing teachers, with Molly throwing in an occasional dry comment or raised eyebrow that kept Trevor and Cait one step inside the lines. Richard himself stayed mostly silent, but inwardly he rejoiced. He hadn't seen Trevor this animated since a year ago summer. Caitlyn really was a beauty when she smiled and teased. He could understand the fascination, because it was her mother he kept watching, although he hoped not too obviously.

Instead of her daughter's delicacy, she had a lush, earth-mother thing going. Dark wings of brows, hair of that rich auburn, determined to curl whatever she did to it. A mouth that was wide and generous when she was relaxed. And that skin—damn, that skin. Cream, was all he could think.

Cait's was different, more of a porcelain that went with her almost-blond hair and blue eyes. Molly's begged to be touched, as his itching fingers attested. He'd give one hell of a lot to see her naked, with those plump breasts and luscious hips and long, long legs....

He tuned in to realize he'd missed something. Dessert, it turned out. Molly was asking who wanted their apple pie à la mode.

"You have to ask?" he said, and she flashed a grin at him.

He pushed back his chair. "Hey, I'll give you a hand. Uh, do you have milk? Apple pie. How can I eat it without milk? Trev? Cait?"

They both voted yes.

In the kitchen, Richard murmured in Molly's ear. "You're a genius."

Her smile was so close he could have kissed it. Wanted to know what it would feel like to kiss her when she was smiling.

Thank God she wasn't looking at him. "Will you get the ice cream out of the freezer?" she asked, as she wielded the knife on a beautiful, obviously home-baked pie.

She let him dig out scoopfuls of ice cream to crown each slice of pie. Only when she handed him the first two plates to carry to the table did she murmur in turn, "I am, aren't I?"

He was grinning when he set plates in front of Trevor and Cait. His son studied him with suspicion, but was easily distracted by food.

"This is awesome," he exclaimed, after his first bite.

"I baked it," Cait said shyly, earning a look of pure admiration from him.

"Really? My sister won't bake at all because she's always on a diet."

Richard hadn't known that. One more thing he didn't know. "Why?" he asked. "Has she put on weight?"

Trevor shook his head. "She looks okay to me. *She* says she'd be fat if she wasn't careful."

Cait set down her fork.

"She's not athletic," he told her. "And she doesn't dance or anything like you do. You'd be too skinny if you ate nothing more than a few green leaves like she does."

Trevor could be accused of sensitivity. *Did I raise a good kid after all?* Reality check. *Yeah, maybe not me. Maybe Alexa.*

Richard backtracked. "Green leaves?"

"Don't freak, Dad."

"Is she starving herself?"

He shrugged. "Sometimes she pigs out."

"Tell me she's not bulimic."

His son stared at him. "How do you know about things like that?"

"I read the paper. I watch TV."

"No, she's not bulimic. She doesn't, like, stick her finger down her throat or anything." He frowned. "At least, I don't think so. She just worries every time she has something like pizza and eats nothing but salad the next day."

Richard sat back, less than reassured. "Are there many girls at the high school with eating disorders?" he asked Molly.

"I don't always know," she said. "I'm aware of a couple."

"There's more than that," Cait contributed. "Mostly they're not that bad."

"Will you tell me if they get that bad?"

Cait flicked a glance at Trevor. "Maybe. Probably. I mean, if I think they're killing themselves."

Her mother sighed. "Okay."

Cait had only finished half her dessert when she set down her fork. "You want the rest?" she said, seeing Trevor's avid gaze.

"Really? You're done?"

Assured that she was, he inhaled it.

"You want to go upstairs?" Cait asked.

Richard could imagine how Molly felt about that. By all means, let the two close themselves in the girl's bedroom. But she only looked at him. "Coffee?"

"Sure."

He helped her clear the table, then while she was filling two mugs nodded toward the ceiling. "You don't mind?"

"Barn door? Anyway, I think the last thing they're going to do with us in the house is have wild sex. So no. I don't mind."

"They were both on their best behavior. I wonder why."

They headed toward the living room by unspoken agreement. "I issued a few threats. How about you?"

"Maybe one or two."

She took one end of the sofa, him the other. He'd rather have sat in the middle, right next to her, but was as aware of his son and her daughter upstairs as Trev and Cait no doubt were of their parents down here.

"I don't know if this accomplished anything." She frowned toward the fireplace. "I don't know what I thought it would accomplish."

"An easing of tension," Richard suggested. "And I think it worked."

The lines on her forehead smoothed and her pretty, dove-gray eyes met his. "Maybe. I wonder what they're talking about."

"Better we don't know."

Molly wrinkled her nose. "Isn't it awful when you suspect your own child, who not that long ago worshipped and adored you, now makes fun of you behind your back?"

His mouth curved. "I doubt if Trev makes fun of me. I'm going to guess anything he has to say is more obscene than that."

She made another face. "In fairness, it's hard for Cait. Imagine when you were in high school if your mother had been the vice principal."

"That would have sucked," he said with a laugh. "But Cait, she seems to have been a good kid, so it can't have bothered her too much. And it hasn't hurt her popularity any, has it?"

"Maybe in certain circles." Molly sipped her coffee, which he'd been amused to see she seemed to like with plenty of cream and sugar both. Maybe it said something that he liked it bitter, her sweet.

"But not the circles you'd want her in, anyway."

"No," she allowed, then smiled at him. "Have I thanked you for being so nice, and after I wasn't at first?"

"We didn't hit it off that first meeting," Richard conceded. Except he'd felt the first twinges of lust, angry as he was.

"No. Or the first phone call, either."

He remembered back. Cast-iron bitch. He'd been so sure.

"I wanted you to tell me what to do," he said. "I didn't have the slightest idea. I still don't."

She listened willingly when he told his fear that it was too late for him to become a full-time parent.

"Did you ever think of, I don't know, contesting custody, or asking for alternate years, or…?" Molly asked, expression compassionate.

He grimaced. "Yeah. I was okay until Lexa got married and announced they were moving to California. I might have made a stink, except I was in the National Guard and half expecting to get sent to Iraq."

Her eyes widened. "Did you?"

"Yeah. Year-long tour." He looked away from her. "Twice."

He didn't know what she saw on his face, but her voice dropped to a whisper. "Oh, Richard."

"There wasn't any way I could have had the kids." He kept his gaze fixed on the framed photos and pair of unusual candlesticks atop the fireplace mantel. "I didn't come home in great shape, either. Especially after the second tour."

"You were injured?"

"Not on the outside. I was one of the lucky ones." He spared her a glance but didn't let himself drown in her sympathy. "It was a year or more before I could sleep through the night after coming home, though." He shuddered slightly, hoped she hadn't noticed. "I had flashbacks. I was angry. Jumpy."

"PTSD."

"I don't know. If so, I'd say most returning vets are coming home with it." He shrugged. "I got better. But God knows I wasn't in any shape to be a single parent."

Miraculously, she was the one who scooted a cushion closer to him and laid a hand on his arm. "I'm sorry."

His fingers curled into fists, the only way he could keep himself from touching her. From driving those same fingers into the dark fire of her hair.

"Are you still National Guard?"

He shook his head. "I got out. Barring something that pulls me back."

"I had no idea."

"Why would you?" That sounded unfriendly, and he didn't mean it that way. "We didn't know each other." He frowned. "Why didn't we? West Fork isn't that big a town."

"Cait and I have only been here three years. We lived on the east side before I got offered this job. Cait wasn't thrilled." A quick, wry grin pulled at her mouth. "She consented to the move once we determined the dance school here was acceptable."

He found himself looking at her, maybe having some trouble tracking her words. "Molly," he said, huskily.

Her lips parted. They stared at each other.

And then, goddamn it, came the sound of a door opening upstairs, voices, the clatter of footsteps, and the moment shattered. Cheeks pink, Molly whisked herself back to her end of the sofa and snatched up her coffee cup. Groaning inwardly, Richard drained his coffee and lifted his eyebrows at his son, who had taken the last three steps or so with one leap and thud. Cait had stopped three-quarters of the way down, her hand on the rail.

"You ready to go?"

"Sure," his son said.

Molly hustled to the closet and handed out their parkas. "Thank you for coming. I enjoyed having you."

"We enjoyed dinner," Richard said.

"It was good," Trevor agreed. He zipped up his parka. "Thank you, Ms. Callahan."

"You're very welcome, Trevor." She smiled impartially at them. Richard thought her eyes were a little shy when they met his. "And Richard."

He'd have given damn near anything to kiss her good-night. He would already have kissed her, if his son didn't have such terrible timing. Maybe it was just as well. Trevor needed to come first, and the Callahans, mother and daughter, could do him some serious damage.

Trevor and he were in the truck, Richard ready to

turn the key in the ignition, when Trev spoke. "I don't think she's going to get an abortion."

His head snapped around. "What?"

"I told her I'd marry her if that's what she wants."

Richard heard the defiance and the misery, but that didn't stop him from saying, "Are you crazy?"

"So the truth comes out," his son said disagreeably. "You didn't want to marry Mom."

Richard didn't swear much, but this would have been the moment if he hadn't gritted his teeth hard. How in hell was he supposed to handle this?

Trevor turned away to look out the side window. "It doesn't matter."

"It matters," Richard said grimly. "And the answer is, no. I didn't want to marry your mother. I wanted to go to college. I wanted to grow up. I wanted to do something else with my life, not go to work for my father. None of that means I didn't love your mother." He thought a white lie was justified under the circumstances. "Or that I didn't want you once I realized you were a possibility." He wrapped both hands around the steering wheel. "Can't you understand that?"

Trev's chin dropped to his chest. "Yeah." His voice came out thick. His breath rushed in and out. "I'm scared that's what she'll want."

"Son." Eyes burning, Richard pulled his boy into a rough embrace. "I doubt that'll happen. She's fifteen. That's not what her mother'll want. But…" His own breathing shuddered. "I'm behind you, okay? Whatever you need."

He'd have sworn he felt tears on his neck. They stayed that way a long time in the dark.

CHAPTER TEN

IN THE NEXT WEEK, Molly developed the unwelcome suspicion that Cait was enjoying the role thrust on her. She'd never in her life held such power over others. She was the martyr, suffering visibly; everyone else had to wait on *her* decision. And yes, she was probably genuinely scared and uncertain, but she was also petulant and, in a strange way, triumphant. Molly began to feel she didn't know her at all.

Clearly, Cait was taking that decision down to the wire. Maybe she'd shared it with Trevor—but Molly doubted so, from the wary way he watched her on the occasions she saw them together.

The teenagers were talking, Molly knew that much. Secretly, which was disconcerting. A couple of times, she saw Trevor waiting for Cait after school. Once Molly arrived home to see him hurrying away from the house down the sidewalk, hands in his pockets and face averted. Cait seemed to be spending a great deal of time closed in her bedroom on the phone talking to someone.

Which was probably good, because she sure wasn't talking to her mother.

Molly might have found those days unbearable if not for Richard. One of them called the other almost every night. She thought about the few times he'd touched her, however casually. Maybe it was just as well that phone conversations allowed no opportunity for good-night kisses. Assuming, of course, he wanted to kiss her, and she wasn't positive he did.

They'd plunged into such intimacy so fast, she was unnerved. The sound of his voice on the phone, warm, slow and deep, made her quiver. She was embarrassingly eager when he suggested getting together. He was certainly the sexiest man she'd ever seen, with his lean, dark face lit by a flicker of a smile. The sight of his very male saunter made her knees weak. She could hardly remember being so affected by a man, and gee, that had turned out so well.

Every time her self-esteem hit a low ebb, she reminded herself he had wanted to ask her out. Maybe he felt as cautious as she did, but he was definitely interested. That gave her something to hang on to.

The weird part was that in the meantime he had become her best friend. Her confidant, her prop, her reminder that it was possible to laugh.

He talked, too. Less willingly than her, she thought, but what man was happy baring his deepest feelings or most regretted failures?

So, okay, they hadn't gotten there yet. She hadn't told him about her marriage; he hadn't told her about his. Neither had talked about the price they'd paid for those early marriages, or the divorces that had followed. But during one of their phone conversations, he told her more about the war and some of the things he'd seen. Hearing his horror, she asked why he'd joined the National Guard, and he admitted it had been mostly money.

"There wasn't some other way you could have moonlighted?" she asked.

It took him a while to answer. "Yeah, I could have found something. I suppose I wanted to get away, too. I liked the camaraderie you build with the other members of your unit. The sense that maybe you're doing something worthwhile."

"Do you think you did?" she asked softly.

"No." His voice was harsher than she'd ever heard him. "Look at the headlines. We didn't change a damn thing over there. We tried, but we didn't understand them and they didn't understand us. I made friends, but I never knew if it was pretense. God, all I wanted was to come home."

"I'm sorry," she whispered. "So sorry."

"Yeah." He was quiet for a moment. "My best friend over there lost a leg. I suppose I felt guilty I came home whole."

"Did you?"

He laughed, if gruffly. "Maybe not."

"The soldiers we send are so young," Molly said. "Kids."

"This once the Humvee I was in drove over an IED." He paused. "You know what…?"

"An improvised explosive device."

"Yeah. Cut right through the armor. Turned it to shrapnel. Killed the guy sitting next to me. He was eighteen years old."

"Eighteen." She grappled with that. "How old were you?"

"By then I was a real man. In my twenties."

She was smiling, although she didn't know how she could, as sad as she felt. "A father figure."

"Something like that." And she heard his smile, too. "I've never talked about any of this with someone who wasn't there. No, that isn't true. I tried with Lexa, when I came home that first time. She didn't want to hear it."

"Listening, isn't that one of the most important things we can do for each other?"

It was hard to interpret his silences, but she relaxed when he answered. "I'm starting to think so."

Today was a rare, almost warm day, weird considering Thursday was Thanksgiving. The holiday hung over Molly, who had come to think of it as D-day for Cait. Or D-week, anyway. She was nine weeks right now. She had to make a decision.

I will not think about that today.

Molly had picked up deli sandwiches and met Richard at the riverfront park. She felt almost daring, sneaking away from school to meet him in person. The "in person" part made her a little giddy, which she wouldn't have wanted anyone to know.

He got out of his Ward Electrical van when she pulled in next to him. Despite the sunshine, he put on a parka over his dark green uniform shirt, and she tucked gloves in the pocket of her own parka. He'd brought the coffee—plain and dark for him, a frothy latte for her. She bent and inhaled the steam before smiling at him.

"This was a good idea."

"You say that now, but you may be shivering in a half hour."

"If I am, we can sit in the car," she pointed out reasonably.

They walked past the playground, where a young mother was pushing a toddler on a swing, then across short, damp grass to one of the benches that overlooked the river. It was running high and brown with snowmelt from higher in the mountains, but was still some feet below flood stage.

Molly laid out their food between them and accepted her cup, taking an appreciative sip. "This is so much better than a brown bag lunch at my desk."

He made a sound of agreement. "Or a burger in the van."

"Fast food's not good for you."

Richard laughed. "I do try to go a little easier on the grease than I used to."

"I suppose not having anyone else to cook for cuts down on the incentive."

"You could say that." He sighed and stretched out his legs, stacking one booted foot on the other. "I've been trying a little harder since Trevor arrived, but he's walked out on so damn many meals, it's a little discouraging."

"Still?"

He sipped his coffee before answering. "Not as often."

"That's good." She hesitated. "Isn't it?"

"Yeah. It's good. Sometimes I think he's mellowed toward me, then something happens and it's like a lit fuse. I don't know what to think."

"Does he talk to his mother at all?"

"Not according to her." He unwrapped his sandwich.

"Do you talk to her often?" Belatedly, she thought, *Not my business.*

"No." His gaze fixed on the river, face unreadable. "We don't have much to say to each other." About the time Molly was wondering if she'd been warned off, he spoke again. "You and your ex?"

"Heavens, no! I haven't talked to him in years beyond

saying 'yes, Cait is here' and passing on the phone. And not even that in a long time."

"Years?" He glanced at her, some lines having deepened on his forehead. Not a frown, but…something. "You said he doesn't see much of Cait, but I wondered if you'd told him…"

"No. Absolutely not," she said strongly. "He has no interest in her whatsoever."

"I don't get that."

"I don't, either." She was shredding her own multigrain roll, so that seeds pattered onto the paper wrapping that lay open on her lap. "The ironic thing is, he was hot to have more children. His pressure was one of the things that damaged our marriage." Wow, did she want to tell him this?

"You didn't want a brother or sister for Cait?"

"It wasn't that. I did agree to try, but I was in grad school and the timing was lousy. We already had problems, and some of the pressure was coming from his parents. As it was he didn't have much time for Cait."

"His parents?"

"He's an attorney. Did I tell you that?" When he shook his head, she smiled wryly. "Family law firm. Colt is the third generation to make partner. No surprise there. Believe it or not, he's Colton Callahan the Third. He suddenly decided—or his parents decided, I'm not sure which—that it was time we hatched a Colton Callahan the Fourth."

"Good God," Richard muttered. "Caitlyn Callahan wasn't good enough?"

"Apparently not. After all, she was only a Caitlyn the First. His parents weren't what you'd call warm. They never made me feel as if I measured up. For one thing, in their world the wife didn't work. She entertained for her husband, she served on the boards of charities, she put on fundraisers for appropriate causes. College was fine, good. Graduate school unnecessary."

"And you stuck to your guns."

His approving smile turned her to mush. "I did."

"Wasn't Colton in law school at the same time you were in grad school?"

"No, I was an undergrad when we met, but he was already in his second year of law school. Not thrilled when I got pregnant."

"I don't suppose you were, either."

"No, of course not. But…" She looked down, evading the warmth in his eyes. "Once I felt her move, I was a goner."

"So you ended up divorced before you could get pregnant again."

Decision time. Did she really want to get this personal?

"It wasn't that simple," she said, stalling.

When he reached out and removed her sandwich from her hands, she realized she was mangling it. He rewrapped it, his eyes never leaving her face. "In what way?"

"I had endometriosis. Increasingly painful menstrual periods. It turned out the scarring was so severe, it would be difficult to impossible for me to get pregnant."

His face hardened. "Tell me the son of a bitch didn't leave you because you didn't get pregnant on demand."

"I think it contributed, but that wasn't the whole story. We didn't have much marriage by then." Colt hadn't taken well her rejection of his sexual advances when she hurt too much. She'd needed pampering and sympathy he never thought to give. Didn't care enough to give, Molly had come to believe. Their marriage, their family, increasingly became for show, while at home they hardly spoke. "I've suspected for a long time that I never would have married him if we'd waited."

"If you hadn't gotten pregnant."

She nodded.

"Ditto for me." He wadded the wrapping for his own sandwich and tossed it from hand to hand. "I think Alexa got pregnant on purpose."

"What?" Molly gaped at him.

"I never asked her. I mean, she was having my kid. I didn't want to stir hard feelings we'd never be able to bury. But I knew. She was unhappy about me going away for college. She'd wanted me to stay close—the community college or Western Washington. I wasn't breaking up with her—we talked vaguely about me coming home some weekends, you know how it is—but I was desperate to go away. I'd been recruited by half a dozen West Coast schools, and I chose UC Berkeley. I could hardly wait to go. Reality is, I wouldn't have come home much. Not with airfare from California. Lexa knew that. She was taking the pill."

"And you trusted her."

"Yeah. I trusted her."

Neither said anything. The silence was oddly comfortable, even companionable. Molly reached for her sandwich again and began eating this time.

"That's why you're antiabortion for Cait, isn't it? Because you know what it's like not to be able to get pregnant when you want to," Richard finally said.

His insight surprised her. Why not tell him the whole truth? That she couldn't get pregnant again, ever? That she'd had a hysterectomy? Because it was too much. He didn't need to know. *I will not live vicariously through my daughter to that extent.*

"I can't deny there's some truth in that," she conceded. "But I've been doing my best to wall off how I felt then from Cait's situation. Cait's too young to have a baby. I know that. Yes, I feel squeamish about her having an abortion, but my own history isn't the only reason."

"No." He sounded thoughtful. "Squeamish is a good word. Who wouldn't be?"

"I think she's going to refuse to have one."

"That's what Trevor says, too."

"Really? She is talking to him, then?"

He gave a rough laugh. "Who knows? But yeah, some. He says he offered to marry her."

"Oh, my God."

"Boggles the mind, doesn't it?"

"He's really willing?"

"He's scared to death."

"If it's any comfort to him, right now, I'd withhold permission. But she turns sixteen in April, and I think that's the age of consent in this state." She made a mental note to check. Surely, please God, Cait wouldn't do anything that dumb.

Like you did?

Richard set his now-empty coffee cup on the ground and shoved both hands in his pockets. His rueful gaze met hers. "Do you ever wish you could think about something besides your kid?"

Molly's half laugh felt surprisingly good. "Frequently."

"Were we as self-absorbed at their age?"

"Um…yes?"

He laughed. "Probably. But my parents weren't nearly as sympathetic."

"Did they oppose you getting married?"

She could see that he was really thinking back. "I don't know. Yes and no, I guess. Neither of them were college educated…they'd gotten married young, so the concept didn't seem out of line to them. My father might even have been happy I had no choice but to go to work with him."

"Do you wish you hadn't?"

His chest rose and fell with a long breath and he let his head fall back. "I don't see what else I could have done. I couldn't force her to have an abortion. One way or the other, I'd have had to help support her once she had Trevor. How could I have left for college and done that?"

"You might have been able to work and take classes, too," Molly suggested tentatively.

"Not on an athletic scholarship. Or, at least, I couldn't have worked enough hours. I could have taken classes locally—but then she'd have been home alone all the time with a little kid and I'd have missed living with my son. So the answer is no. I thought in circles until I was dizzy back then, and ended up where I started."

"No regrets?"

"Oh, I had 'em, but I've tried to get past them. I did go back to college after Lexa and the kids went to California. I finally had the time." He slid Molly a look she couldn't interpret. "But I did it only for myself. By then I'd built Ward Electrical into something I couldn't walk away from."

"What would you have walked toward?"

"Engineering. I dreamed big." His mouth quirked. "Dams, bridges. I do mean big. I went ahead and got my degree in structural engineering."

"So now you know how to build those dams. I'm glad you were able to do it," she heard herself say.

His gaze seemed suddenly intense. "Why? Does that raise me a notch on the social scale?"

"What?" She stared at him. "That's a jerk thing to say! I meant I was glad for your sake. Because it meant something to you." She started to gather their lunch leavings. "I'd better get back to school."

"No." His hand shot out to grip hers. "Molly. I'm sorry."

"It doesn't matter."

"It does." His chagrin kept her from wrenching her hand away. "It's me. I wondered whether you looked down on me. A guy who works with his hands, who didn't get an education."

"But you did."

"You didn't know that."

She was suddenly so close to him, it was hard to breathe. She wrenched her gaze from those bitter chocolate eyes and looked down at his hand holding hers. That didn't seem to help. He had wonderful hands, so big they dwarfed hers, long-fingered, calloused, sinewy. "I'm not a snob. You own a thriving business. I suspect you make two or three times the money I do. I was a high school teacher, for goodness' sakes! Now I plan in-service days for classified staff. I decide when a student's grades disqualify him for the football team. I made the earth-shattering decision to replace two urinals in the boys' restroom this summer. All of that makes me superior *how?*"

"It's not about you. I guess something's been simmering. By high school a part of me had started looking down on my dad. Me, I was going to be someone. Look how all the colleges wanted me. Whatever I did, I'd be changing lives. Having to swallow my pride and accept that I'd live a life no different than Dad's, that stung. I didn't realize how much it still does." He paused, his eyes never leaving her face. "I'm sorry," he said again, his voice husky.

Molly offered a shaky smile. "It really is okay. We all have our triggers."

His gaze lowered to her mouth. "You trigger all kinds of things in me."

Her pulse bounded. "Yes," she whispered, and his mouth settled on hers.

MAYBE THIS WASN'T THE time or the place or the mood, but, damn, he couldn't help himself. She was there, her mouth soft and tremulous, her eyes dilating.

"Yes," she whispered, and he was kissing her without making a conscious decision. The first touch of her lips was cold, but they warmed quickly and felt every bit as lush as he'd dreamed. That first faint tremble was the sexiest thing he'd ever felt. He wanted to dive deep, but somehow knew better. This was a woman to savor. He nibbled on her full bottom lip, touched the tip of his tongue to the dip in her upper lip. He brushed his mouth back and forth, licked the seam of her lips, nuzzled his nose against hers until she smiled, and he felt that down to the soles of his feet.

Finally, finally, her lips parted and he slid his tongue inside, meeting hers. She tasted of coffee and cheese, milk and her, an indefinable taste that was something like a peach. She was holding herself completely still, but she sighed, and then a sound like a moan vibrated her throat. Richard's control broke, and he wrapped his hand around the back of her neck to position her better. Somehow they weren't holding hands anymore, either; his squeezed her waist and hers both came up to clutch his shoulders. He kissed her with devastating hunger, and felt equal yearning from her. She sucked on his tongue, and he shuddered. If they were anywhere else…

That kiss might have gone on forever if voices hadn't intruded. With a groan he lifted his head to look down at Molly's face, tipped up to his. Her eyes were closed, her lashes long and thick, forming crescents on that creamy skin. He'd mussed her hair plenty, wiping out any pretence of Ms. Cool and Collected Vice Principal. She was a woman, aroused from the way she was breathing and from the dazed look in her gorgeous, smoky gray eyes once she opened them.

"You're beautiful," he whispered, kneading her neck and loving the thick textured silk of her hair tangling his fingers.

Her eyes searched his. Then a smile that was almost mischievous curled her mouth. "You're sexy."

He grinned, probably foolishly. "Seems like we're on the same page."

Molly gave a throaty chuckle. "And, oh, if our children ever flipped to this page."

"Oh, hell." It was next best thing to a splash of that snowmelt river water. "You had to say that."

She sighed. "It was nice to forget them for a minute, wasn't it."

"Nice?"

Molly laughed at his outrage. "Okay, better than nice. I didn't know if you really wanted to kiss me."

"I've wanted to kiss you since that first meeting in your office, when I hated you."

All trace of the smile vanished; there was something hugely vulnerable in the way she looked at him now. "Really?"

"Did I hate you?"

"Want to kiss me."

"Yeah." His voice was pure grit. He bent forward enough to rest his forehead against hers. "I still do. But we seem to have company."

"Company?" She stiffened, pulled back, turned her head. "Oh, thank God."

"Thank God?"

"What if it had been students from the high school?"

"That might not have been the best," Richard admitted. "Do they make it over here to the river from school?"

"I'm sure they do. We have closed campus for freshmen and sophomores, but the juniors and seniors can head out for lunch."

He hadn't felt this good in he couldn't remember how long. Years. Maybe never. "We'll make out somewhere different next time," he said, smiling at her wickedly.

She snorted. "In your dreams."

"Oh, I've been dreaming."

They'd started toward the parking lot, passing a pair of incurious mothers paying more attention to their offspring than to the other people at the park. Molly's hand slipped into his. "I've been dreaming, too," she said softly.

He almost said, *I want you.* He did. Desperately. But

he had a bad feeling he knew what she'd say, what she'd make him admit—their kids had to come first right now. Richard had no idea how his seriously screwed-up son would respond to his dad suddenly having a sex life. A relationship. Oh, yeah, and with his pregnant girlfriend's mother.

Richard hadn't forgotten the way Cait had reacted the time she'd come home and found him alone there with her mother. The spoiled brat in her had come out. God knows, he thought, their lives were complicated enough right now, the way their kids had tangled them all into a knot.

No, he wouldn't say anything that blunt, but he was damned if two selfish brats would make him wait indefinitely to go after the first woman he'd seriously wanted in years.

"We'll work it out," he said easily.

A choked laugh escaped her. "But not necessarily well."

They'd reached their cars. He stopped her, taking her other hand, too, so she had to face him. He smiled, kissed her lightly, then not so lightly. They were both breathing raggedly. "I think it'll go fine. I wish to hell it could right this minute," he murmured.

Obviously not yet firing on all cylinders, she blinked bemusedly at him.

"Our time will come, Molly Callahan."

She could have said, *I'm not sure.* Or stiffened and stepped back with a *Maybe.* Or even a suspicious, *Time for exactly what?* And, *Do you plan to use a condom?* She didn't say any of those things. She gave him an astonishingly sweet smile. "Okay," was all she said.

And, damn, his body surged at the sight of that smile. His fingers tightened on hers. He groaned.

Molly grinned. "Go back to work," she said, then pecked him on the cheek and got in her car.

Leaving him with an aching erection and absolute faith that he would soon see every magnificent inch of her body bared. He would be able to touch and stroke and knead, kiss and suckle and lick.

He planted his hands on the side of his van, bent his head and groaned again.

CHAPTER ELEVEN

CAIT CHOSE THE BREAKFAST table for her great announcement. Filling her travel mug with coffee, Molly had just looked down and noticed, to her exasperation, that she'd slipped on navy-colored flats even though she wore black slacks. They probably weren't that noticeable—but it would bug her all day. She'd want to hide behind her desk instead of getting out in the halls and classrooms. And, oh, heavens, she had that meeting about possible revisions in the plan for snow days.

"I'm not getting an abortion."

There'd been such confusion with the first snowfall, all of two inches, with some buses completing full routes and others...

She turned in slow motion to stare at her daughter, who sat at the table with a bowl of cereal, as yet untouched.

"What?"

"You heard me."

So many emotions rose in her, contradictory, painful and joyous, she choked. Was barely able to speak. "Cait..."

The slightly pointy chin set defiantly. "You said it was up to me."

"Yes, but... Do you really understand what this will mean for you?" Molly shut her eyes for a moment. "Did you have to pick the worst time for us to talk about this? I can't be late today."

"There's nothing to say." Her hair fell forward, hiding her face as she bent over her cereal. "I'll tell Trevor."

Molly couldn't seem to move. "Oh, honey."

Cait looked again at her mother. Her eyes burned with some inner light. "I can't do it, okay? I just can't. Even if it means...I don't know what."

"I don't know what, either. That's the part we need to talk out, you know."

"Yeah. Okay. I guess." She grabbed a napkin and dabbed carefully beneath her eyes. "You know your shoes don't go?" she said, sniffing.

Molly sighed. "I just noticed. Let me change and then we'd better get moving. If you want a ride."

"It's cold. I don't want to walk."

That, apparently, was that. Cait didn't want to talk any more about it during the short drive to the high school. Molly's thoughts were all but turning backflips. Had she somehow influenced Cait to decide against abortion, which—*now, be honest with yourself*—was really the most sensible decision for a girl her age? Was it really any better that her daughter was going to bear a child and *give it away?* And what about the practicalities in the meantime? Cait should be able to make it through first semester without her pregnancy being noticeable. She was unlikely to show at all before, say, mid-January at the soonest. She could keep dancing until then, too. But then what? Alternative school? *Could I homeschool her?* Molly asked herself wildly. Do we need or want to hide her pregnancy from the world? Is it really anything to be ashamed of?

Cait leaped out almost before the car came to a stop.

She was hurrying away when Molly called after her. "If you want a lift home, you know where to find me."

Cait flapped one hand that said, *Like I don't know, Mom? And do you really have to embarrass me by yelling after me in the parking lot?*

Molly collected her briefcase from the backseat, locked the car and walked in a different direction, toward the admin building. The only thing she knew for sure was that she wanted to talk to Richard.

And was afraid of what he'd say. Especially after he'd understood why she had personal issues with the abortion option.

She was opening the door when she spotted a group of senior boys getting out of a Camry with macho tires bigger than the manufacturer had recommended. Trevor.

He didn't see her. She didn't see Cait lying in wait. But Molly watched him laughing at something one of the other boys had said. They wrestled with each other in that rough-and-tumble way boys did.

Molly wondered when he'd laugh again.

"YOU DON'T MIND ME having invited Richard and Trevor for Thanksgiving?" Molly stabbed a fork into the potatoes to see if they were done.

"No." Cait was dumping cranberry sauce into a small, cut crystal dish. "It's cool you did. I mean, what would they have done?"

"Richard said probably go out. I gather he's never done the whole turkey and stuffing thing."

"It's okay having them here. Mom, I can mash if you want to check the turkey."

The doorbell rang, and Cait went to let the Wards in while Molly opened the oven and tugged at the drum-

stick. It almost came loose in her hand. The thermom-
eter had popped, too. Definitely done. She grabbed two
hot pads and lifted the roasting pan from the oven to
the cutting board she'd laid on the counter.

"Smells great," Richard said, smiling at her from the
doorway. He looked good in dark slacks and a charcoal-
gray V-neck sweater with the sleeves pushed up on
strong forearms. Dark hair curled in the V of the
sweater. No midday shadow on his jaw; he'd shaved
and his hair, brushed back from his face, was still damp.

Molly controlled with difficulty an internal melt-
down, returning his smile. "Welcome."

From behind his father, Trevor eyed the turkey like
a wolf might its freshly killed prey. Molly had a feeling
she wouldn't have as many leftovers as she'd envisioned.

"Anything I can do?" Richard asked.

"Um…maybe carve, once I get the stuffing out. Cait,
why don't you turn on the broccoli. I think we'll be
ready by the time it's done."

They all ended up helping—Trevor mashed while
Cait heated rolls, Molly carried the yams to the table and
lit candles. For once, they were eating at the mahogany
dining room table she and Cait seldom used. Cait had
set it with their good china, too, a wedding gift Molly
had kept and still loved.

Once they sat down, Richard said a quiet grace, and
they began to dish up.

"I'm sorry Brianna decided not to come," Molly commented, adding green salad to her plate then passing the
bowl on to Trevor, who sat to her right.

Richard looked up from the dressing he was ladling
onto his plate. "I am, too. She says she'll come for

Christmas, though. Apparently Alexa has made plans." His gaze flicked to his son. "With friends."

Something dark crossed Trevor's face. Molly saw muscles in Richard's jaw spasm. When he didn't say anything, she did. "I suppose it seems strange, the idea of not spending Christmas with your mother."

"I don't want to spend Christmas with her." His voice was guttural. Too late, he tried to hide a tremor in the hand that held his fork.

"I'm sorry," she said quietly. "I shouldn't have said that."

He looked at her. "You don't know."

"No. I don't."

"I suppose you had the perfect, happy family." His voice was ugly with sarcasm.

"No, she didn't, and you don't have to be so awful!" Caitlyn exclaimed.

Molly blinked.

Trevor's head swung toward Cait. "I wasn't…"

"You were! Mom grew up in foster homes, okay? She didn't *have* a mom to be mad at."

Molly's heart swelled. She couldn't have spoken to save her life.

A tide of red rose from Trevor's neck to his cheeks. "I'm sorry, Ms. Callahan."

Oh, help. I have to say something. After a deep breath, she managed, "It's okay, Trevor. There have been times in my life when I was jealous of people who had regular families." She made sure her gaze held his. "There've also been times when I've realized 'regular' from the outside isn't necessarily better than what I had."

He nodded and bent his head to his plate.

Molly reached out and squeezed Cait's hand. The gesture was quick; she didn't even look at her, and made no effort to prolong the moment. But she had to say thank you.

Then her eyes met Richard's and she saw a tangle of emotion in his dark eyes as complex as what she felt. But he smiled, and she saw he meant it.

"I'm glad you decided to play basketball," Molly said, cutting turkey on her plate.

Trevor mumbled something.

"What?"

"Some of the guys aren't that glad."

"Because you're beating one of them out for a position."

"Yeah." He took a bite, chewed and swallowed. "They've been a team. You know? I haven't even been practicing, and now here I am." He shrugged.

"Is it definite you'll be starting Tuesday?" his father asked.

"That's what Coach says."

"Do you mind if I come? Or would you rather I didn't?" Richard's tone was careful, neutral.

Once again Trevor shrugged. "It's an away game."

"Not that far."

"I don't mind."

"Good." Richard smiled. "What about you, Molly? Do you go to games?"

"All home ones."

"Do you want to come with me?"

Both the kids stared at them. Molly glanced at her daughter. "Cait, do you plan to go?"

"If I do, I'll take the bus."

"Do you mind...?"

"Why would I?"

They both knew why. Having your mom attending all official social events wouldn't thrill any teenager.

But Molly smiled at both Richard and Trevor. "Then yes. I'd love to see Trevor play. And it would be fabulous if the team could beat Snohomish right out of the gate. We *always* lose to them."

"That's what Coach says." Trevor reached with new enthusiasm for the bowl of dressing. "They can't be that good."

"It's a way bigger high school than ours."

"The team's okay," he said. "I think we have a good chance." He stole a look at Cait. "It's too bad you're not a cheerleader."

Wow. Would she have made it through the season? Basketball ended in early February—assuming West Fork didn't make it to the playoffs. Which they usually didn't, but they'd come close last year. Trevor might make the difference. That would extend the season well into Cait's fifth month of pregnancy. No, Molly realized, it was lucky Cait hadn't succumbed to her friends' pleas and gone out for the squad.

"I like dance better," Cait said, but subdued.

After a moment of silence—they were probably *all* calculating how pregnant she'd be—Trevor spoke. "You'll come to the game, anyway, won't you?"

Her chin was high, but her eyes showed vulnerability. "What difference does it make? You have friends."

"I don't have a girlfriend."

"Really? That's not how it looked to me at Halloween."

He gave a hunted glance at Molly and Richard. "I was mad."

"You mean, pawing Ashley was for *my* benefit?" Any vulnerability had been replaced by sparks.

"Yeah." He sounded and looked freaked. "Kind of. I mean, maybe."

"Does *she* know that?"

"Well, not exactly. I didn't *say*... And it's not like we, you know..."

Before Cait could get her mouth opened, Molly lifted a hand. "Whoa. Can you two continue this somewhere else? Some other time? It's way more than I want to know. And probably more than Trevor's father wants to know, either." Although she couldn't be sure of that. What was inducing panic in her was the realization that Trevor might actually still like Cait. Love her? No, they were too young. Ridiculously young. But...think of the complications if they resumed their relationship. *Imagined* they really were in love. Talked about a future.

No, no, no.

Cait snorted, an indelicate sound. Trevor looked embarrassingly relieved. Richard, Molly saw with narrowed eyes, was amused. *His* kid wasn't fifteen years old. Although surely the last thing he'd want was his kid losing the chance to go to college, just as he had.

Somehow or other, conversation found less dangerous paths, and the meal ended more pleasantly than it had begun. They all agreed to wait a little before they had pie. Richard offered to help clean up and gave his son the evil eye until he offered, too.

"If you'll help me, why don't we let these two off the hook? The kitchen isn't big enough for four," said Molly.

"Sure," Cait said. "Let's go upstairs. You can tell me why Ashley Jantz hasn't run you down with her Corvette."

Richard turned to Molly. "A kid drives a Corvette?"

"Daddy is a big-time contractor and loaded."

"Jantz?" He stared at his son. "You've been messing with Gordon Jantz's daughter?"

"I wasn't messing with her!"

"Yes, you were," muttered Cait.

"Aargh!"

"Shoo," Molly told them, flapping her hands.

They went. The argument rose in volume until it was finally cut off upstairs by the bedroom door.

"He's in deep shit," Richard remarked, picking up the turkey platter and serving bowl.

"Good," Molly snapped.

"What?" He followed her to the kitchen.

Fired up herself, she set the pile of plates on the counter and faced him. "You don't *want* our children to have a big romance at this point, do you? Why don't you think *that* one through?"

He did, with commendable speed. "You're right. I don't. *I* want to have a romance with *you,* and something tells me the two relationships aren't compatible."

"You think?" She huffed and went back for more dishes.

He did the same. "Molly, I never said I wanted them to get back together. God. What I'd like is to see my son behave honorably. Support Cait. Not make sure she sees him with his hands all over some other girl only because he wants to hurt her feelings. That's all I meant."

Her shoulders sagged as she dropped a handful of silverware in the sink. "I'm sorry. I do see that. Listening to them, I had this horrible vision of them running off to get married, drugged by young love."

"Is that what you did?" he asked gently, and the next

moment he'd set down his own load and put his hands on her shoulders. When he turned her to face him, his eyes were warm and understanding.

"Yes." Why was she nearly hyperventilating? "No. Oh, I suppose I thought I was in love. Colt was older, sexy, charismatic…. But mostly, I was pregnant. And I wanted a family."

It was as simple as that, she realized in a kind of horror. She had so desperately wanted something she'd lost. Even though she'd had a huge crush, for want of a better word, on Colt, she wasn't thinking marriage and forever…until she got pregnant. And then, suddenly, there it was—a shimmering possibility. And she'd grabbed at it. A dream.

Studying Richard's face with sudden intensity, Molly couldn't help wondering. She'd said to him, *I've been dreaming, too.* Was that what this was? Whatever she felt for him? A fantasy, and not real at all? An image of them all as a family?

"What are you thinking?" he asked, searching her face with equal intensity.

"I'm panicking," she whispered.

He tugged her closer. "Don't. Not about us. Damn it, Molly! We have lives separate from our kids. We have a *right* to have lives of our own. Don't mix all of this into one stew."

But she couldn't help seeing with extraordinary clarity that Cait's and Trevor's problems were too interconnected to separate from anything she and Richard tried to build. Unless he was talking about sex and only sex. An affair they could somehow keep separate from their children.

How could they? This was a small town. Sneaking

around seemed sordid. She realized she'd hate it if he suggested a night away at a motel or something like that.

But I want him, she all but wailed. *I do. Why can't I have him?*

Maybe…maybe they'd have to wait, at least until Trevor had left home. They were adults. It wouldn't kill them to wait a few months.

Yes, but what if Trevor didn't leave for college until next September? That was *ten* months away. Worse yet, what if he went to college locally, maybe even continued to live with his dad?

No matter what, by then I will be grieving the loss of Cait's child, Molly thought bleakly. *And along with this baby, everything else I've ever lost, or known I couldn't have.*

I am pathetic.

What had he said? *We'll work it out.* Her rejoinder: *But not necessarily well.*

But maybe their time would come. Or maybe with time she'd realize she didn't want this—whatever it was—to amount to anything.

Right now, though, she gazed into those extraordinarily dark eyes and feared, terribly, that she'd fallen in love with this man, and that their time *wouldn't* come, because too much was in their way. And, dear God, she felt selfish even thinking that, when she'd just renewed her resolve that Cait would come first.

RICHARD HAD NEVER SEEN SO many conflicting emotions on one person's face. It scared the crap out of him. What was she thinking? What could be making Molly look so heartbroken?

A feeling of desperation drove him to step forward

and pull her into his arms. Before she could object, he kissed her, and not gently. It was a full-out, open mouth assault on her senses. Triumph filled him when, after a stunned moment, she wrapped her arms around him and kissed him back. Her breasts felt so damn good against his chest, her thighs against his. Her height coupled with her heels meant he didn't have to bend far to devour her mouth. His erection pressed against her where it felt the best. Groaning, he grabbed her hips to move her against him. The vibration in her throat sounded like a purr. She was doing some rubbing of her own. In another second, he was going to lift her onto the counter and pull that sweater up. He wanted to see her breasts more than he wanted the sun to rise tomorrow. To bury his face between them, to lick, taste, suckle....

"No." She went utterly still in his arms. "This is crazy."

His body throbbed painfully. His hands squeezed her hips. He didn't know if he *could* stop. Knew he didn't want to, even as he also knew she was right.

"The kids could come downstairs anytime," he remembered. He was hoarse with regret.

"That's not what I mean, but it's true. They could. Richard." She swallowed. "This is too complicated. We need to think."

Think? His brain cells had melted down a good long time ago. Restoring function didn't happen that fast.

"Please. Let's...let's clean the kitchen and not give them any reason to be suspicious."

That was too much. "Why should we be ashamed of having a relationship?"

"I'm not ashamed. But I know where my focus needs to be."

He'd never expected to be jealous of how much a woman loved her child. For a minute he thought, *And the kid's a spoiled brat besides,* then *was* ashamed of himself. It wasn't even true. Caitlyn was confused, scared, in turmoil. Spoiled? This was a girl whose own father couldn't be bothered to give her even an occasional day of his time, who apparently didn't believe she counted because she wasn't male and therefore worthy of being a Callahan the Fourth. Trevor and Bree at least knew both their parents loved them, even if they'd had to live with the consequences of their family splitting.

Yeah, so what was Trevor's excuse?

Richard nodded to Molly and turned to go back to the dining room. They worked after that in near total silence, some of the ease between them gone. His body still ached, and he realized he felt a whole lot of other things, too. He was hurt, because she had a cooler head than he did and, apparently, more reservations. Or was less powerfully drawn to him. And yes, jealousy lingered and he was uncomfortable with that. There was resentment because these two kids had turned all of their lives into high drama and were determined to stay in the spotlight. And he was still scared by that expression he'd caught on Molly's face.

They all got through pie, which Cait had again baked, and he and Trevor made their excuses shortly thereafter. Richard couldn't tell what had happened between Trev and Cait upstairs. They weren't yelling at each other when they came down, but they weren't talking easily, either, and they sure weren't holding hands or giving each other lovelorn looks.

No, the only lovelorn looks would have been from him, if he hadn't had to stifle them.

"Good dinner," he said, once he'd pulled away from the curb.

"Yeah." Trev sounded preoccupied.

"Trevor." Richard waited until he was sure he had his son's attention. "Don't you think it's time you told me what happened with your mom?"

"No!" Trevor jerked back, coming up against the passenger door. "Why would I?"

"A better question is why *won't* you?"

"Oh, come on." His lip curled. "You know what Mom's like."

"I'm not so sure I do." Richard accelerated slightly to make a green light.

"What's that supposed to mean?"

"Do you realize how long it's been since I've actually seen your mother face-to-face?" Silence. "I was thinking about it the other day. Six or seven years, give or take a few months. And before that all we had were brief meetings in the airport when we handed you off." He'd hated those flights made to pick up or return his children. "It's been a lot longer than that since we had a meaningful conversation. Ten, eleven years, at least. I *don't* know your mother anymore."

There was a long, long silence. Richard waited it out. Trevor was a smart kid. Let him think it through.

"You know what I'm talking about," he finally muttered.

"I don't have the slightest idea what you're talking about," Richard said wearily.

Shrug.

They'd reached home. Richard reached up to press

the button on the remote control and pulled into the garage. Trevor shot out of the pickup and raced into the house before Richard so much as set the emergency brake.

Another highly successful, father-son moment, he thought with renewed frustration and depression.

MOLLY HAD CONSENTED to drive to Snohomish with him for Tuesday night's game, which was something. Richard was determined not to press her for anything but conversation. They kept it light during the forty-minute drive, although he knew she was sneaking glances at him, probably trying to nail down his mood.

She looked good tonight. Really good. He'd felt a rush of hunger when he picked her up. She wore a turtleneck, tighter jeans than usual and athletic shoes. She had her hair in a ponytail, which made her look ridiculously young and left tiny tendrils of softer hair at her temples and nape. Once they arrived, watching the sway of her hips as she climbed the bleachers ahead of him came close to killing him.

He'd seen Trevor play only a few times. Last year he'd flown down to Sacramento when the team played in a three-day-long tournament and had felt such pride, he'd had a hard time not jumping to his feet and bragging to everyone in the stands, "That's my kid. Mine."

He felt the same tonight. Trevor might have what it took to make it to the pros. Richard had been good, good enough to be wanted by some top college programs. But he'd known in his heart that he was done growing, which left him too short to be a forward on a professional level, and he wasn't quick enough to be a guard.

Trevor was different. For all his grace and athleticism, it was obvious that he *wasn't* done growing. His feet still looked too big for his body; he had that lankiness a kid has when his body is unfinished. Like Molly, Lexa had been tall for a woman, so Trevor got it from both parents. Richard was willing to bet he'd end up two or three inches taller than his old man. And if he didn't…he *was* quick. And he had a hell of an outside shot.

When the team first began warming up, he casually sent up a shot from so far away, Richard, and probably everyone else in the stands and on the court, had stared in disbelief. The perfect arc ended with the ball swishing through the net. Trevor paid no attention to the resultant silence followed by murmurs.

Molly had leaned close to Richard and murmured, "Show-off."

"Yeah." He'd laughed. "I think that's exactly why he did that. He's putting a scare into the other team."

The game was intense from the first drive down the court. A Snohomish player put up a shot and Trevor sprang up and smacked it away from the hoop. One of his teammates snatched the ball, passed it to the West Fork guard and ten players tore the other direction down the court.

At halftime West Fork led by two points. The team was outclassed by Snohomish—except for Trevor. He was everywhere, as strong at defense as he was at offense. His slam dunk was primitive and powerful, his outside shot a thing of beauty. Richard could only watch in awe.

Molly, he discovered, was a vocal supporter. She yelled encouragement, she moaned disappointment, she laughed, she clapped, she stuck two fingers in her mouth and let out an earsplitting whistle that had Trevor looking up from a time-out huddle and grinning right at her.

That grin socked Richard in the chest. It was delighted, triumphant, filled with a young male's vanity and a boy's mischief. He hadn't seen that grin in a long time.

"Oh," she said finally, sagging to the creaking bleacher seat. "I don't know if I'll survive the game, never mind the season. Oh, Cait!" She waved at her daughter, who was bounding up the bleachers to them. "He's amazing."

"Did you *see* him, Mom?" Her face was alight. "I knew he was supposed to be good, but…wow."

"I've seen him play, and I didn't know he was that good," Richard said. "We could end up with recruiters from every major basketball powerhouse in the nation knocking on our door."

"Will they even see him play?" Molly asked. "He'd have been better staying in L.A. if he wanted to get noticed, wouldn't he?"

"Probably, but I think he'll get noticed no matter what." He was giddy. *That's* my *kid*.

He could tell Molly was laughing at him the rest of the game, when she wasn't on her feet screaming her own delight. Trevor had been dominant in the first half; he ran away with the second. He stole the ball, took it down court himself, dunked, did layups, took wild outside shots. But he wasn't all hot dog, he also played team ball. Perfect passes, so smooth they looked effortless, had West Fork defeating last year's league champions by fourteen points.

When the final buzzer went off, Molly jumped up and down and hugged Richard. "We killed them! We killed them."

Grinning, he lifted her in his arms and stole a kiss. "Yeah, we did."

The whole West Fork contingent was jumping up and down. The bleachers thundered and groaned.

They went outside to wait by the bus for the players to come out of the dressing room. It was so cold, they all hunched in their parkas and breathed in dragon puffs but stayed warm from excitement. When the boys swaggered out, the applause was loud and long. Molly loosed another whistle, which had all the boys grinning this time. Richard saw Cait roll her eyes—oh, God, her mother was making a spectacle of herself—but she was smiling at the same time, and her cheeks were pink.

They got pinker when Trevor stopped to put an arm around her and murmur something in her ear. That silenced Molly and Richard both. He remembered what she'd said Thursday. No, he definitely did not want Trevor imagining himself in love with Caitlyn—the mother of his child.

Disaster that way lies.

Was Trevor smart enough to understand what he'd be giving up if he did something stupid now?

Richard almost groaned. The kid was seventeen. Of course he wasn't. Good God, he wasn't smart enough to use a damn condom.

Maybe, it occurred to Richard, the easing of tension between the Callahans and the Wards hadn't been such a good idea after all. Maybe it would have been better if they'd stayed enemies.

Maybe Molly was right, and they should do some serious thinking before they *all* got in over their heads.

CHAPTER TWELVE

NINE O'CLOCK ON THE NOSE, the phone rang. Molly didn't have to look at the number on the screen to know it was Richard's. In line with her decision to keep some distance from him, she hadn't answered last night. Tonight, she told herself she didn't want to cut him off entirely. Being cautious didn't mean she couldn't talk to him sometimes, or be friendly at games.

And she already missed him, after only one day without talking to him. *Oh, I'm in such trouble.*

"Hey," he said. "Wondered if you were planning to go to the game tomorrow night."

She glanced at the school calendar, always kept handy. Friday, November 30. Home game, West Fork vs. LS. As if she hadn't known.

"I told you I never miss a home game." She was smiling because it felt so good to hear his voice.

"Can I pick you and Cait up?"

"I…" Her mouth opened and closed. "Actually, Cait's going with a friend. And sleeping over." Tomorrow night was going to be the big night, when she was going tell her best friend, Sabrina, about the pregnancy.

"You, then?" Richard said quietly.

"Yes," she heard herself say. "I'd like that." They'd have fun at the game, and then…then he'd bring her home. To a house the two of them would have to themselves. For an entire night.

I won't invite him in. I don't dare invite him in.

They agreed on a time. Neither made any effort to prolong the conversation, even though a part of Molly wanted to, and she suspected he did, too. She felt so high school lately—eager for the sound of one voice, hungry for any tidbit about his life.

In love.

Huge mistake.

No, they could make it work. But later. Much, much later.

THE GYMNASIUM WAS standing-room only the next night. West Fork stomped Lake Stevens. Embarrassed them. Made up for every humiliation in the past ten years. It was Trevor, of course, but not entirely. He made his teammates better, and they all played like champions, even the boys coming off the bench. The second string stretched the lead further, and the crowd rejoiced. Coach Bowman was near tears when Molly saw him after the game.

"It's the Promised Land," he told her, and she felt obliged to pat him on the shoulder and remind him that the season had barely begun.

"Snohomish," he was murmuring as he wandered away, seemingly in a daze. "Lake Stevens."

"I'm glad Trevor has made somebody happy," Richard said, gazing after him quizzically.

"He made a lot of people happy tonight."

"That's not the same."

"Now, Coach Loomis—" she nodded toward where the beefy football coach stood by the locker room doors

"—is no doubt grinding his teeth because his team had a lousy season, and now he's seeing the might-have-been."

"The ghosts of Christmas past?"

"Something like that."

He only laughed, his mood obviously as ebullient as everyone else's. As he escorted her from the gym with his hand coming to rest now and again at the small of her back, Molly wondered if it had occurred to him that they could have a night to themselves. Well, not entirely; presumably Trevor would wonder where Dad was if he didn't come home. Unless…

"Trevor is staying the night at a teammate's house," he announced abruptly, the minute they were alone in his pickup. "A bunch of them are, I guess. At Josh somebody's?"

"Loomis."

"No. Tell me the kid's not…?"

"Sorry. He is. Poor Coach got to watch his son triumph in company with Trevor, while the football team he coaches sucked this year."

Richard's low chuckle sent ripples of pleasure all the way to her toes. "Did this Josh play football, too?"

"Adding insult to injury…no. He played wide receiver until this year, but as a senior he wanted to concentrate on his favorite sport. Basketball."

They'd joined a line of cars and trucks creeping toward the exit from the parking lot.

"Oh, man."

Molly's laugh turned into giggles she had trouble stopping. Maybe because she had bubbles fizzing in her bloodstream. "I feel so mean! He's such a nice man."

"He did get to see his kid help stomp two rival high schools," Richard pointed out.

"There is that."

They were both quiet for a minute that felt too long. Long enough that Molly sneaked a peek at his face in profile, only to have him turn at the same moment and meet her eyes. They stared at each other for a long time before she gulped and wrenched her gaze away.

"Trevor seems to have turned a corner." *That's it— be upbeat, supportive, a fellow parent. Not a woman.*

"Yes and no." Richard's hands flexed on the steering wheel. "Sometimes I think so, but then we butt heads again. He still won't tell me why he's so angry at Alexa."

"And you really have no idea."

"As I told him—not a clue." He was frowning now. They'd almost reached the street. "I keep thinking it might be the divorce. Maybe he was fonder of Davis than I realized."

"But then why…?"

"He may be angry at me because I'm not Davis."

Molly blinked. What an awful thing even to wonder, for a man who loved his children as much as Richard did. "Do you have any reason to believe that?" she asked tentatively.

He sighed and rotated his shoulders as if to ease tight muscles. "He did choose not to spend this summer with me."

"But you said it was the job."

Richard accelerated and she realized they'd finally escaped the parking lot. Which meant they'd be at her house in less than ten minutes.

I've already made up my mind.

Have you really?

"He told me it was the job. He may not have wanted to hurt my feelings."

Molly thought about that, and was shaking her head almost immediately. "No," she told him with conviction. "I don't believe it. His anger is too personal. Too aimed at you. Although the divorce might tie in somehow. Maybe he's mad because you didn't stay married to his mom. He could blame you for the, er, succession of stepfathers that presumably meant moving, new schools, et cetera, et cetera."

Richard seemed to consider that. "Maybe. He had to be upset that he wouldn't be able to finish out high school in the same place, with the same friends, same teammates."

"I'm surprised his coach didn't throw himself on a sword."

"God." There was that low chuckle again, husky enough to feel like calloused fingertips. "I hadn't thought about it. Maybe he did. I don't follow the L.A. news."

"Was Trevor mad at his mom after her last divorce?"

Richard frowned. "Not mad. Confused, maybe. He was…let me think. Eleven, maybe? Not heartbroken, I know that. I think Bree might have been fonder of Scott."

"Do you know *why* her last two marriages broke up?" *So not my business,* Molly realized belatedly. English teacher—*belated* could be another word for *too late*.

Richard's glance struck her as cautious. "No," he said after a minute. "After Scott, she said she wasn't in love with him anymore."

She could hear the *but*. He knew more. Suspected more. *Really* not her business.

Isn't it, when I'm thinking about sleeping with him?

The English teacher pointed out how imprecise she

was being. She was definitely not planning on doing any "sleeping" with Richard Ward. Well, unless he spent the entire night.

She must have made a sound, because his head turned. She discovered he'd pulled up to the curb in front of her house.

"Alexa got bored easily," he said, and Molly realized he'd assumed she was upset—piqued? angry? something?—because he'd quit talking.

"You don't have to tell me."

"No, it's okay. Alexa needs to be in love." He shook his head. His hands were still on the steering wheel, but not squeezing the way they did when he felt something powerful. Loose, relaxed. "Actually, that's not it. What she needs is to have a man passionately in love with *her*. If her husband gets too focused on work, family, whatever, she's lost. She pouts, she teases, she tries to get him under her thumb again, then failing all else she finds someone else who fills the bill."

Molly felt an unhappy cramping in her chest. "That's what she did with you."

"Yeah." He was watching her now, his eyes shadowed but his mouth quirked on one side. "It was tiresome. I was trying to build the business to take care of her and the kids. Dad hadn't retired yet. I had to be sure he wouldn't erase any gains I'd made if I got sent to Iraq. I was signing contracts, working my butt off, hiring, supervising and firing until I was sure we had some solid employees, coaching Trev's Little League team." He shook his head. "And the truth is…"

"You weren't in love with her anymore."

He never took his eyes off her. "I'm not sure I ever

was, except in a high school kind of way. But I'm a man who takes his commitments seriously."

"His responsibilities," she whispered, remembering his reaction when she'd suggested he didn't.

"Yeah. I never looked at another woman. Wouldn't have. I was building a life for my family. That wasn't enough for Lexa." He sounded impatient, shook his head. "The point is, she's never in it for the long haul, at least until she finds a guy who will worship and adore her above all else, until they both shall die."

"You don't think that's possible?"

"Yeah." Even in the diffused lighting, she saw his jaw spasm. His voice was rough. "I do."

She was melting down. Utterly. Completely.

"To hell with Alexa," he murmured. "Molly, are you going to invite me in?"

There wasn't any decision at all.

"Yes." She tried to smile, felt her lips wobble. "Please, Richard."

"I thought you'd never ask." His hand slid beneath her hair, and he kissed her.

HE COULD HAVE MADE LOVE to her in the pickup, no problem. He wanted to. He hadn't been so horny since he was sixteen. Damn, but he hated letting go of Molly long enough for them both to get out.

Richard had the presence of mind to hit the button on his remote locking the truck and met her on the sidewalk. He was reaching for her when some headlights swept over them. They were standing out on a city street at only ten-thirty on a Friday night. There would likely be a fair amount of traffic. In fact, some of her neighbors had probably been to the game, too.

"Josh doesn't live near here, does he?" Richard asked hoarsely.

"No, and Sabrina doesn't, either. We should be safe unless one of them gets homesick in the middle of the night."

He'd have been amused by the idea if his body hadn't been seized by such urgency. "You got your key?"

"I'm hunting." She mumbled a swearword he guessed she didn't say at work as she rooted through the giant leather satchel she called a purse. He steered her up the walk as she searched. *Get inside before you start ripping her clothes off.* There's a plan.

She found the key and got it in the lock. The interior was dark but for a lamp left on in the living room. Richard shut the door, locked it and turned Molly to face him. Her purse fell from her hand and thudded to the floor.

"I want you," he said, voice pure gravel. "Do you know what you look like in these jeans?" He spread his hand on her butt, squeezing.

"Fat?"

"Lush. Sexy. Stick figures don't do it for me."

"Thank heavens." She sighed, and then their mouths met.

He tried to take it slow. This was their first time, after all. Slow didn't seem to be a viable gear. Fortunately, she didn't seem to care.

Richard kissed her deep and long. One hand roved while the other kept her tight against him. She seemed to be cooperating with that goal, since her arms latched around his neck and she matched every roll of his hips with one of her own.

Man, he wanted to take her up against the door, but

what if her daughter decided to stop by the house for a forgotten item?

"Bed," he growled.

"Upstairs."

He grinned wolfishly. "You walk up ahead of me." He could relive the fantasy that had tormented him during both basketball games, after watching Molly ascend the bleachers. Only this time, it would have a happy ending.

She eyed him with caution if not suspicion, then started upstairs. Richard followed close behind. What he'd have *really* liked was if she were naked. He stroked her ass, eased his hand up to her waist and finally stopped her halfway up so he could press against her body. He nuzzled her neck.

"I don't know if I'm going to make it."

She shot him a flirtatious, laughing glance, wriggled her hips. "What a shame that would be."

He'd have loved to sweep her up in his arms, but Molly wasn't a small woman and they could end up hurt. While he weighed risk and benefit, she bolted, and he went after her. By the time he made it into the bedroom behind her, she'd freed her hair from the ponytail, letting it fall down around her shoulders. Something about the movement, almost innocent, no more than a woman letting her hair down, turned him on more than an impromptu striptease would have.

"I love your hair," he told her, and plunged his fingers into it. He already knew how it felt, silky but not soft, thick and strong. He stroked, letting it run through his fingers. He didn't kiss her, because he might not have been able to stop, and he wanted to look at her.

"Lift your arms," he said roughly, and when she did he peeled her sweater over her head. The sight of her in a peach-colored, lace-edged satin bra that barely confined gorgeous breasts was enough to make him feel as if he'd taken a blow to the belly. A sound escaped him. Something raw, ragged. As if in a dream, he lifted his hands and cupped her, ran the pads of his thumbs over her nipples.

Molly moaned and arched her back, thrusting her breasts more fully into his hands. He lifted them, squeezed, bent his head and nuzzled the bared curves. And then he reached behind her and unfastened the clasp. With slow, deliberate movements, he caressed her shoulders—she had beautiful shoulders—easing the narrow straps off, until the bra slid down and dropped to their feet. He didn't watch it go. He was enthralled with her breasts. The skin was as creamy as he'd imagined, her nipples a beautiful, dusky color, the areola as generous in size as her breasts were.

Her head was bent as she watched him look at her and then touch her. Richard knew he was groaning. His big hands couldn't completely enclose her. He'd never seen anything sexier than her firm nipples peeking from between his fingers.

Suddenly he'd had enough. He did pick her up only to lay her on the bed, where her hair spread across a dark red, textured cover. It was a perfect backdrop for all that skin. A redhead's skin. He unsnapped her jeans and peeled them and peach-colored panties over her amazing hips and mile-long legs. He hung up at the shoes, and she laughed at him as he fumbled at the laces and finally yanked one shoe off after getting frustrated at a knot he'd created. Then socks, and he tossed the jeans over his shoulder.

"You have the most beautiful body I've ever seen," he said, with utter sincerity.

As he stared, she blushed, which delighted him. Even her breasts turned pink.

Richard shed his own shirt, kicked off his shoes and went on one knee above her on the bed. Now he kissed her, first her parted lips, deep and drugging, before stringing more kisses down her long, white throat and then to his target. He licked, nibbled and suckled. He damn well wallowed in those breasts, and in the small sounds she made and the way her hips rose from the bed.

Somehow she'd come to be kneading his shoulders, testing the contours of his chest and the muscles in his back, and finally she rubbed her palm up and down over the long bulge beneath his zipper. That was the breaking point for him. He'd never taken his pants off so fast in his life. Then they were kissing, arms around each other, moving against each other, tangling their legs, rolling so first he was on top, then her. And, oh, man, the sight of her above him almost blew his fuse.

He swore and said, "Condom," in a voice that wasn't his.

Molly went still. "Well, you don't really have to..."

"Live what you teach." He rolled her over and reached a long arm to his jeans on the floor. He'd stuffed several condoms in his back pocket, hoping for the best.

Praying.

He dropped the extras on the bedside table, tore open one—and surrendered it when Molly grabbed it from him.

"I've always wanted to do this."

"What? You've never?"

"I was too shy the few chances I would have had. And on the pill after Cait was born. Until…"

He didn't want her thinking about her son of a bitch of an ex, who'd pushed her despite her pain and her career ambitions to provide his Colton the Fourth. Richard reared up and drew her nipple into his mouth, suckling hard.

She gasped, moaned and gripped his head to hold him to her breast. Only when he let loose did she remember what she held in her hand and what she wanted to do with it.

She took her sweet time, too, unrolling the condom over him with strong fingers that teased and tormented as they went. He was paying her back before she was done, his own fingers playing in the dark red curls at the juncture of her thighs, then slipping below into the damp folds between her legs.

They came together in pure pleasure and need. Being inside her felt better than anything he could remember. He was past thinking, all sensation. The feel of those hips between his hands, her breasts pressing against his chest, the sight of her bared throat and parted lips, the color on her cheeks and the dark fire of her hair. He hadn't made love to a woman in too long, and guessed it had been longer for her, but nothing about this felt awkward. They moved as if they'd practiced until they found perfection.

He held on until she cried out and he felt her deep spasms, then ground himself against her and let himself go. He did manage to twist as he collapsed so that all his weight wasn't on her, but she half rolled with him so they stayed connected. Her hair was tickling his face, but Richard didn't care. When he could force his eyelids up, he gazed cross-eyed at the strand that lay across his nose. Beautiful.

He had to clear his throat before he could pull up any speech. "That was amazing." He mulled that over. No, he decided. "You're amazing, Molly Callahan."

"Who knew?" she mumbled into his shoulder.

"Knew what?" He was smiling, one of those stupid, unstoppable smiles that, thank God, she couldn't see.

"That I was amazing." She sounded genuinely bemused. But then she tilted her head back so she *could* see him. "That sex could be so good."

"I already knew you were amazing. I didn't know sex could be so good." He adjusted her in his arms, loving the feel of all that lush flesh against his harder length.

Molly was quiet for a minute. Her "Do you mean that?" surprised him.

He gently stroked the hair from her face so he could see at least the curve of one cheek and one eye. "Which part?"

"That...that it was good. Better than usual." She moaned. "Forget I asked. That's pitiful."

He shook with his laugh. "No, it's not. It's sweet. It's vulnerable."

She punched his arm, but wasn't in a position to put much force behind it.

Richard turned his face so his mouth was closer to her ear. "It's natural," he whispered. "And yes, I mean it."

"But you're gorgeous. You must have women throwing themselves at you all the time."

He started to deny it, but knew that wouldn't be completely honest. Yeah, on a regular basis he had women hinting that they could be interested. The trouble is, he wasn't. "I'm not that kind of guy," he finally said. "Wasn't even in high school."

"Oh."

"You?"

She shook her head. "By nineteen, I was dating Colt. Married before my twenty-first birthday. A single mother after we parted ways. Anyway, I have to care. Spontaneous sex with a stranger doesn't appeal to me much." But then she lifted her head and grinned at him. "Although that day in front of the grocery store? When I ran into you and Trevor?"

"Yeah?"

"The idea did cross my mind."

He laughed and kissed her. Not much talking happened after that.

CHAPTER THIRTEEN

"You want to talk about it?" It was the next morning. Sitting on a stool at the breakfast bar, Molly pushed aside the paperwork she'd been reading about new state-mandated in-service training for para-eds and looked at her daughter.

Cait had dragged in from her overnight at Sabrina's, taken her bag upstairs and then come down to the kitchen. Even her "hi" had been subdued. She shrugged and opened the refrigerator, stared at the contents without moving and finally shut it without removing anything. "It was okay," she said.

Molly only waited.

"Sabrina was really blown away. I mean, she'd heard the rumors but she didn't believe them. She's freaked that I'm going to have the baby."

"She didn't succeed in tempting you to change your mind?"

Fury flashed on Cait's face. "What side are you on anyway?"

"Yours," Molly said simply. "You know that."

Cait sniffed. "I guess I do." She hesitated, gnawing on her lip. "I've really been a bitch, haven't I?"

"Yeah." Molly smiled at her daughter. "You have."

The teenager giggled, then with startling suddenness burst into tears. Molly didn't have time to slide off the stool. Cait threw herself at her mother, burying her face against Molly's shoulder. She cried, Molly rocked in that timeless, instinctive motion and held her, her own eyes burning. She'd have given anything, *anything,* to save her child from this pain.

"I love you," she whispered. "Whatever decision you make, whatever comes of it. I love you."

Eventually the sobs subsided, and finally Cait withdrew. Her face was blotchy, swollen, wet. "Oh, God. I have to blow my nose."

Molly kissed her cheek, wet as it was, and got her a paper towel. She watched as Cait blew and mopped herself up. She ended up splashing cold water on her face at the sink and drying it on the dish towel. Then they looked at each other.

"*Have* you changed your mind?" Molly asked.

"I want to." Emotion washed over her daughter's face. "But I can't. Mom, I just can't!"

Molly nodded. "Then you've made the right decision for you. A hard one, but right."

"Nobody will ever look at me the same, will they?"

What could she do but be honest? "No. But here's something to think about. Yes, you have two and a half more years in high school. I know that sounds like forever now. But when you leave for college, this will be behind you. You can tell close friends about your pregnancy or not. That'll be entirely up to you."

"So even if the rest of high school sucks, it won't last forever." Cait pulled off a smile that filled Molly with pride.

"Right." *Oh, heavens. Don't let yourself cry.* "And I know this sounds horribly trite, but it's also true. The people worth caring about will stand by you. They'll still be your friends."

"Easy to say," she muttered.

"I know it is. I know."

They were silent for a minute. If it weren't for Richard, Molly thought, she'd consider starting a job search. She and Cait could move next summer. Cait could start over in a place where no one knew she was anything but a beautiful, smart, transfer student.

Richard or no Richard, was that what she should do? Molly had to ask herself. Or would Cait be a better person for making this decision and living with the consequences rather than escaping at least some of them?

I don't know.

Something else to think about, it occurred to her. What with Facebook and other social media, the world was shrinking. Could Cait ever truly have a fresh start, or would her history follow her?

While her mother was thinking, Cait went back to the refrigerator. "I'm starved. Sabrina's family eats this really gross cereal. It's like something you'd feed a horse."

Molly had heard the complaint before. "How about a grilled cheese sandwich?"

"Ooh. That sounds good." Cait rummaged in the fridge. "Do you want one, too? I'll make them."

"Sure."

"It was a really good game last night, wasn't it?" Cait said, plopping the block of cheddar cheese on the counter.

"You bet. Now, Coach Loomis, he wasn't as happy."

Cait actually giggled. "I saw him. He was *green*."

"Well, it doesn't help that his own kid rejected his sport in favor of basketball."

"Josh's choice."

"That doesn't mean his dad can't suffer."

Cait paused in the act of buttering a slice of bread. There was a suspended moment before she resumed movement. "Like you will, you mean?"

"No, that's not what I mean. Parents always suffer when their kids do. But we also have egos. When you excel, I'm glad for you, but I enjoy the reflected glory, too. How can I help it?"

"What about reflected shame?" she asked bitterly.

"Cait, look at me for a minute."

Her daughter turned from the stove.

"You made a mistake. I wish it hadn't happened, that you hadn't gotten pregnant now, at your age. But I'm also incredibly proud of you. You made a really difficult decision, a brave one. And the courage you showed making it and sticking to your guns also reflects on me. I'm proud for you, but for me, too, because I can take some of the credit for the person you've become. That's how parents think."

Cait's face momentarily crumpled before she whirled back to the stove, pancake turner in hand. "I love you, Mom."

"I know." Molly smiled at her back, the sting of all that pride and grief inside her. "I always knew."

Her daughter glanced over her shoulder with wrinkled nose. "Because you're so-o smart."

Molly laughed. "You used to think I was."

"Maybe I still do," Cait said, very softly.

It was one of those moments that made every travail of being a parent worthwhile.

IN THE FOLLOWING WEEK, Molly enjoyed every minute of this new, gentler relationship. She didn't kid herself, though, that it would survive if Cait learned her mom was sneaking around to have sex with the last man on earth of whom she'd approve.

Molly was torn between two opposing lines of thought. The first was: why in hell were two single adults trying to hide a perfectly legitimate romantic—or was it only sexual?—relationship from their kids? The second was: *dear God, please don't let us be caught.*

She felt more alive than she had in years. If it was just sex, she could be consoled by the knowledge that it was fabulous sex. She had never in her life had anything that could be labeled a "quickie," but she'd now had a couple of those, and they really did spice up the day. Twice she and Richard had met at her house at lunchtime— her house being safer because Cait was stuck at school thanks to the closed campus rule, while Trevor wasn't.

The first time, they'd barely made it inside the door. Her blouse ended up torn. The only clothes of hers that came off were her tights and panties. Richard only unzipped his pants and shoved his boxers down. He took her against the wall.

On their second lunch date, they did get as far as the sofa, and she protected her wardrobe by hastily unfastening a few buttons.

After both occasions, the afternoon had passed with her basking in a physical glow that definitely reduced her stress levels as she fenced with bureaucracy, a janitor who got caught stealing and parents irate over an incident they deemed to be bullying.

The thing was, Molly was pretty sure the relationship was romantic, too, because even when they'd had frantic, passionate sex at lunchtime, she and Richard also talked on the phone come evening for up to an hour. One of them called the other almost every night. For the first time, Molly had become grateful that Cait vanished to her bedroom fairly early every evening. The behavior was normal for her; she might be working on school assignments, but mostly she seemed to be online with friends, on the phone with someone or listening to music. Sometimes all three at once. That left Molly free to talk to Richard.

They never seemed to run out of things to talk about. Occasionally it was their kids, often tidbits of news or philosophical debates. She argued with him for a good hour one night about whether someone who had chosen to join the military then had the right to claim conscientious objector status when deployed to a war of which said person disapproved. Intriguingly, Molly had taken the "no" stance, Richard the "yes." It reminded her of the heady days in college before she became a married student with a baby. She loved learning how this man thought, and it was obvious he felt the same about her.

What they didn't do was talk about their relationship. They were in limbo and both knew it. Cait's and Trevor's problems had to come first. That he agreed with her was one of the things Molly loved about him.

And yes, *love* was the right word. Although she didn't think so, it was possible Richard was mostly interested in the sex. But she had fallen in love. Really in love, in a way she'd never been in her life. What she'd felt for Colt was more of a crush. It was part of the same excitement of being out on her own for the first time, knowing how many possibilities there were, imagining a future. The two of them would never have lasted if they hadn't trapped themselves with a pregnancy.

Which she couldn't regret, because then she wouldn't

have Cait. But maybe…maybe she had another chance. She hadn't thought she would, not once childbearing became impossible for her. And then once the years passed. By the time she'd turned thirty-five, it was obvious the good guys were all taken. On her occasional dates, she usually figured out fairly quickly why *this* guy wasn't.

What she hadn't figured out yet was why *Richard* hadn't let himself get snapped up postdivorce. He'd been single for something like ten years now. Two of those years had been spent serving in Iraq, but still. Either Alexa had burned him badly, or the way he'd gotten trapped into marriage and responsibility in the first place had left him disinclined to burden himself that way again.

But she kept remembering the way he'd said, "Our time will come, Molly." He couldn't have meant only for sex, could he?

"BREE TOLD YOU THAT?" Richard adjusted the phone while he juggled cold cuts and French rolls between fridge and counter. "Yeah, he's doing a lot better."

He'd been surprised by the call from his ex-wife. He and she had hardly talked in years, not since the kids had gotten old enough their parents didn't have to discuss visitation and travel arrangements. He hadn't missed talking to Lexa. On the other hand, he couldn't blame her for feeling anxious about Trevor and needing reassurance. It was to her credit that she was still worrying, even if she had dumped their son on Richard.

"What happened?" she asked.

He hesitated. If anyone told her about the pregnancy, it should be Trev. He was almost a man; if he didn't want his mother to know, Richard thought that was his right. Whether he'd told Brianna or not, Richard couldn't guess.

"I really don't know," he said. "He's begun to take responsibility, that's all. Thinking about consequences." Something about your baby growing in a woman's belly did that to a man, if he had any decency to start with.

"So you think he's gotten over whatever upset him?"

A tentative note in her voice raised Richard's antennae. It gave him an inkling that Lexa did have an idea what set Trevor off. That she'd lied to him.

Yeah, why should that surprise me?

Suddenly he was pissed. "And what could that have been?"

"I don't know!" The little girl voice became shrill, defensive. Nothing was ever Alexa's fault. "I told you I didn't!"

"Yeah, you did."

Evidently not hearing his dry tone, she continued. "It must have had something to do with Davis and me. But why would that bother him?"

"I don't know," he admitted. "Are you seeing anyone?" he asked, hoping she wouldn't take his interest as personal.

The small silence was answer enough. "As it happens, I am," she said finally. "What, are you worried about me leaving Bree home alone when I go out?"

He was more worried if she *wasn't* going out. He'd always wondered how many men she'd brought into the kids' lives in between husbands. "Brianna's fourteen. I think she can take care of herself."

"I suppose you're living like a monk."

Richard couldn't help grinning at her snottiness. It

was damn hard not to say, *As it happens, I'm not. I screwed a woman blind against a wall the other day. Or was I the one who went blind? Either way...never did that before.* But, oh, damn, he wanted to do it again. Even if his legs and arms had both been shaking from the strain of holding Molly by the end.

"Probably better if we stayed focused on the kids," he suggested.

She snorted. "Then why did you ask?"

"I thought it might have something to do with Trev's attitude."

More silence, which confirmed his suspicion. What he still didn't get was *why* their son would go off the deep end because his mother split up from yet another husband.

"Listen, I've got to go," he said. "I'll tell Trevor you called. He's, uh, still got a lot of anger. I wouldn't hold my breath waiting for him to get in touch."

He heard sniffles, made himself murmur a few reassuring things and gratefully ended the call. With a little luck, he wouldn't have to talk to her again for months. Maybe years.

It suddenly occurred to him that she might expect to be invited to Trevor's high school graduation. That would be normal.

Trevor's decision, he told himself. And it was way too early to be worrying about something that didn't happen until June of next year. Then he wished he hadn't thought about the month of June at all. That's when Cait's baby was due. Trevor's baby. The baby that probably none of them would ever see, except possibly for Molly, who would likely be at her daughter's side in the delivery room. Wouldn't nursing staff whisk the kid away immediately, when he or she was destined for adoptive parents? Maybe the adoptive parents would even be there, in the delivery room. He found himself breathing hard, remembering the birth of his own children. The shock and joy, even for Trevor, whose conception sure as hell hadn't been planned. The sudden, stunning love.

He gritted his teeth. Why was Cait putting them all through this? He knew where his vote would have gone, if he'd had one. And this wasn't it. If there was anything crueler on earth to do to two kids the ages of her and Trevor, he couldn't think what it was.

And he found himself aching as much for Molly as for anyone. Hearing that baby's first cry, her grandchild's first cry, and knowing she'd never see him again…that would haunt her for the rest of her life.

It might be cowardly of him, but Richard was intensely grateful that he wouldn't have to be there. He and Trev would wait for a phone call and pretend to be glad when it was over, that Cait was all right, that the two teenagers could start looking to the future.

After they got past mourning.

In living color, the film resumed in his head. Trevor's beet-red face all scrunched up, dark matted hair, scrawny long body and flailing limbs. Ten fingers, ten toes. Like almost every other parent, he'd counted. Ugly—newborns were, by any objective standards.

Love.

Richard wanted to be glad this baby would live, whatever the sacrifice on Trevor's and Cait's part—hell, on his and Molly's, too—but he couldn't. He couldn't bring himself to think that letting this child be born and giving it away was the right thing to do.

He wished suddenly that Molly hadn't had a lunch meeting. It wasn't so much sex he wanted right now as to see her. To talk to her. He wanted to have the right to go to her house tonight, ring the doorbell, walk in and kiss her. Maybe cuddle her on the sofa while they watched TV or only talked. That wasn't so unreasonable, was it?

He knew that, if this thing they had lasted, eventually they'd be free to take it anywhere they wanted. But Richard was discovering that he wasn't nearly as patient a man as he'd thought he was.

"YOU WANT TO COME OVER for a bit?" Molly asked. "Cait's spending the evening at the library studying."

"You're sure?"

"Sure she's going? Or that I want you here?"

"Sure it's safe."

She grimaced. "This is so pathetic."

"Yeah, it is." He laughed then. "I'm on my way. And it doesn't matter if she comes home before I leave. She knows we talk, right?"

Molly relaxed. "Yes, I haven't hidden that. She doesn't know how often, but she's heard me on the phone with you a few times."

"Trevor, too, but he doesn't approve. He thinks we should butt out, that he and Cait are dealing."

"Is that a quote?" she asked, amused.

"Direct," he assured her.

She was still laughing when he was gone. She couldn't resist dashing upstairs to brush her hair and make sure she hadn't dribbled pesto down the front of her shirt. And brushing her teeth wouldn't hurt, would it?

The doorbell rang not ten minutes later. Richard

hadn't wasted any time getting here. When she opened the door, he stepped inside and gathered her into his arms, kicking it shut behind him.

"I thought all day about you," he muttered. "This keeping my distance thing isn't working for me."

Alarmed, she drew back. "We have to."

"I know, I know. That doesn't mean I have to like it."

"No. Me, either." She leaned into him. His hands were roving, seemingly sampling the sharpness of shoulder blades, the indented line of vertebrae down her back, the curve of her waist and—no surprise— the plumper contours of her butt. She loved having his hands on her. She loved nestling her head in the crook between his shoulder and neck and inhaling his essence. For the first time all day, she felt…right. "Why today more than usual?" she asked. "Did something happen?"

His hands went still. "Alexa called."

For a moment, she quit breathing, too. Not liking the sharp edge of something that felt like jealousy, Molly reasoned with herself. It was surely natural he'd talk regularly to his ex considering they shared two children, even if it hadn't worked out that way for Colt and her. Plus—if talking to Alexa had set him to craving Molly, that couldn't be a bad thing.

She stepped back, making sure the motion seemed casual. "Any special reason?" she asked, leading the way to the living room.

"Brianna tells her Trev sounds more like himself. Not psycho-off-his-rocker, as my daughter puts it."

Laughing, Molly started to settle on the sofa, then stopped herself before she could sink down. "Do you want tea or coffee? I assume you've eaten."

"I only want you." His eyes were especially dark and hungry. "I had this fantasy all afternoon."

She plopped down. "Cait could come home."

"Sex wasn't the fantasy, although I indulge in that one pretty often, too."

She took his hand and pulled him down beside her. His arm came around her shoulders and he pulled her close. She felt him rubbing his cheek against her hair.

"This was the fantasy," he said softly. "Holding you, talking, maybe watching TV. You know. Normal stuff. But all done with you."

Her heart took a peculiar jump usually triggered by too much caffeine. "Oh."

"I was really glad to hear from you." His voice was husky, and more than her heart zinged.

"I'm glad you could come."

They cuddled in contented silence for a few minutes. "Trevor still isn't calling his mother?" she finally asked.

"Apparently not. The kid holds a grudge."

She smiled and contemplated the little bit of Richard's chest she could see in the V of his shirt. Colt had had a nearly smooth chest. She rather liked Richard's chest hair.

"Kids at school know about Cait yet?" he asked, after a bit.

Molly nodded against his shoulder. "Her friends. She told Sabrina last week, then gradually some others. Which undoubtedly means word has spread. We don't get that many pregnancies at the high school. She says people whisper when she passes."

"Hard on her."

"She's maturing before my eyes." Molly straightened

so she could look at Richard. "She's holding her head up. I'm proud of her."

"I don't blame you. I still wish she wasn't doing it."

"Because Trevor is standing by her?"

"Because giving that baby away is going to stick with them forever."

Me, too. The knowledge was there, an ache in her heart.

"The alternative wasn't so great, either," she pointed out.

"Damn it, you think I don't know that?" He scowled at her.

Molly knew she was flushing. "You should be proud of him, too."

"I am," Richard snapped. "That doesn't mean…"

"You don't have to keep saying it!"

His jaw worked. "No. You're right." His voice had softened.

"I liked it better when we weren't talking at all."

Something sparked in the atmosphere.

"Then let's quit," he said, and kissed her.

All thoughts of their kids left Molly. She loved Richard's kisses—the way he consumed her, but gently, tugging at her lips with his teeth and the suction of his mouth, sliding his tongue against hers in a sensual dance, encouraging her to respond in kind. She sank back against the sofa, and the next thing she knew she was slipping her hands beneath his sweater to the bare skin of his belly and upward, while he had her blouse unbuttoned.

He made a pleased sound when he discovered she'd worn a front-closing bra. One flick of his finger and it opened. Molly groaned when he left her mouth to nuzzle and kiss her breasts.

"We shouldn't…" she whispered, even as her fingers flexed on his chest. His hard, male nipple was a nubbin beneath one palm. She moved her hand experimentally.

"Shh." He suckled, nipped then let his tongue play with her nipple. "We won't take our clothes off. We can pull ourselves together in a hurry."

That sounded reasonable enough for Molly to let her instinctive anxiety go. Cait hadn't been gone that long, anyway. She probably wouldn't be home for a couple of hours.

Molly's hips lifted from the sofa to push against his hand. She groaned when he cupped her and squeezed.

"Wish you were wearing a skirt," he muttered.

Or nothing. Nothing would be even better.

But when he unfastened her slacks and slipped his hand beneath her panties, worry stirred in her again. "Maybe we should go upstairs."

"How do we explain *that* if Cait comes home?"

Oh, God, this felt good. Her knees fell open.

How would she explain to her daughter why Richard was upstairs? He could hide behind her bed if Cait came home and then sneak out later…. No, his truck was at the curb in front of the house. Cait would already know he was here. Of course that wouldn't work.

She whimpered and felt her body tightening. He seemed to know exactly how to touch her, when to let his fingertips ghost over her flesh, when to apply pressure and how much.

"Yes. Richard. Please." She lifted up and ground against his hand.

The sound of a key in the front door lock had her

jolting upright. Richard swore and leaped back, yanking down his sweater. Molly fumbled for her zipper as she heard the door open.

"Hey, Mom."

There were footsteps. More than one set? She got her zipper up and pulled the edges of her blouse together but she couldn't even pretend to have buttoned them when she heard the gasp.

"Mom!" It was pure shock.

"Dad?" Disbelief.

Knowing her face had to be flaming red, Molly turned her head to see the worst. Cait and Trevor stood only a few feet away, gaping at their parents.

Trevor's gaze moved from where Molly clutched her shirt together in a fisted hand to his father's face. Then his face contorted. "You're doing Cait's *mom?*"

Richard rose to his feet. "I'm in love with Cait's mom." His voice was quiet but hard, too.

"I can't believe it." Rage twisting his face, Trevor picked up the coffee table and threw it on its side. Cait screamed and Molly shrank into the corner of the sofa. "You're as bad as Mom," he snarled at his father, and ran out.

Cait tore after him. "Trev?"

The front door opened and in the next second slammed shut, rattling a couple of pictures on the walls. Molly winced.

Cait reappeared, disbelief still in her eyes, but something worse, too. "How could you?" she spat, and then her feet were thundering on the stairs.

Swearing, Richard dropped onto the sofa.

CHAPTER FOURTEEN

"YOU NEED TO GO," Molly said frantically. She struggled with her bra clasp, her hands shaking.

"Molly…"

"Not now. Please." She moved on to her blouse, looked down and saw she'd started to button it askew. She had to start over.

"Goddamn it, Molly, talk to me." Richard sounded so harsh, her head came up. She saw that he looked as shaken as she felt. His dark hair stuck out every which way, and his lips were slightly swollen from their kisses.

With a sinking heart, Molly realized they'd have given themselves away even if they'd miraculously had time to rearrange their clothing and sit a cushion away from each other.

"Oh, dear God," she whispered.

He moved so that their thighs bumped. His hands, steadier than hers, took over buttoning her blouse. She stared at his face as he bent over the task, concentrating.

Her heart cramped when she remembered what he'd said. It hadn't really registered then; she'd been so tangled up in guilt and horror at getting caught. Had Richard meant it when he said he loved her? Or was he only being chivalrous? She cringed at the memory of Trevor asking if his dad was "doing" her.

Yes, Trevor, he is.

Richard smoothed her blouse down, then met her eyes. "This isn't the end of the world," he said gently.

Molly drew a deep breath. "No. Of course it isn't. I'm hideously embarrassed and, wow, completely dreading going upstairs and talking to Cait, but I know we'll get past it." She hesitated. "Trevor, though. He scared me a little."

"I know." Lines had gathered on Richard's forehead. "I haven't seen that level of anger from him in a while."

"No. What did he mean, you're as bad as Mom?"

"I don't know." He groaned, leaned back and closed his eyes. "No, that's not true. I'm wondering…"

When he didn't finish, Molly nudged. "Wondering what?"

He ran a hand over his face.

"I can't remember what I told you about Alexa and me. The end of our marriage. But I know I didn't tell you I walked in on her with another man in our bed."

Instinct had her reaching for him. "Oh, Richard."

He returned the grip of her hand. "That was bad enough, but it got worse. She admitted this guy wasn't the first. I was so busy, she said. I never paid any attention to her. We never did anything fun." He made a hoarse sound. "I was working twelve-, fourteen-hour days, trying to make Dad's business big enough to provide us more than a subsistence living. I guess I wasn't much fun."

"You were something a whole lot better than that," Molly said fiercely.

"I was being responsible," he said, but to her relief his face had relaxed.

"Yes, you were." She bit her lip. "I don't think I loved Colton by the time we split up. So it wasn't the same."

He grimaced. "I didn't love Alexa by then, either. I guess she knew that. But I did love my kids. Losing them was the worst thing that ever happened to me."

"I suppose saying I'm sorry now is silly."

He laughed a little and his eyes focused fully on her. "No. It's nice. But let's not forget how long ago all that happened. And I've got to tell you, I was glad I was unattached when I met you."

"Me, too," she admitted.

His gaze became seeking. "I said I love you."

"I...heard you." Silly to be breathless.

"I do."

Abruptly her eyes filled with tears and she threw herself at him. His arms closed solidly around her. "I love you, too," Molly mumbled into his chest. "I can't help it."

"Why should you?"

"The kids…"

"To hell with the kids," Richard growled. "We should have been honest from the beginning."

"Maybe. I don't know." She wiped the tears away on his sweater, then lifted her head. "You didn't finish earlier. You must think Trevor knows his mom cheated on her last husband."

"I'm thinking worse than that. I'm wondering if he might have gotten an eyeful."

Molly thought about that. Dear God, if so, it would explain why the eyeful Trevor had also gotten tonight had upset him so much.

"Will he talk to you now, do you think?"

The lines deepened on Richard's face again. "He'd damn well better."

Molly nodded, then kissed him. Only once, softly. "You really do need to go."

His arms didn't loosen. "Yeah, okay. We have plenty to talk about, but…later." He bent his head enough to lean his forehead against hers. They stayed like that for a minute, breathing in reassurance from each other. Then he let out a long sigh, squeezed her shoulders and pushed himself to his feet. "Call me later?"

"If I can."

"All right."

She walked him to the door, where they held each other again for a moment, letting go only reluctantly.

"Good luck," he said.

Her smile felt crooked. "Ditto."

TREVOR SHOVED CLOTHES into his duffel bag, ready to go out the window if he heard the garage door open. He'd already searched for the key to the crap car that was supposed to be his, but he couldn't find it. Dad must have stuck it on his own key chain. Trevor wished he knew how to hot-wire a car. If he had time, he could probably figure it out, but he didn't. The last thing he wanted was to be trapped in the garage when Dad came home.

Shit. He so totally couldn't believe this. Ms. Callahan. The vice principal who'd suspended him twice. Cait's mother. And Dad was doing her? This had to be a nightmare.

Packed with as much as he could carry, he let himself out the back of the house and cut across old Mrs. Phipps's yard to the next street over. Then he walked fast, head down, listening for the deep growl of Dad's truck. He made it to the highway out of town without hearing it. Maybe Dad was still at the Callahans'. Would he have stayed to talk to Cait? Trevor felt a strange, hollow sensation beneath his breastbone at the thought of the three of them together. Dad would look for him eventually; he wouldn't want to admit to Mom that he'd lost him. Trevor told himself he was glad that he wasn't out scouring the streets now.

Headlights hit Trevor walking along the shoulder. He turned to see several cars accelerating toward him. The light must have changed back in town. Still walking, but now backward, he stuck out his thumb.

They all passed. He turned, only to see brake lights flare. The last car was slowing, pulling over onto the shoulder.

Trevor broke into a jog.

"HE'S GONE," RICHARD SAID. The phone to his ear, he was pacing the downstairs, tension making it impossible for him to quit moving.

"What do you mean, *gone?*" Molly asked. "You mean he hasn't made it home yet?"

"No, I mean he's packed and taken off." A sound tore its way from his throat. "He didn't take everything, but he's got his laptop. I had some money in the checkbook on my desk, too. He helped himself."

"But…where would he go?"

"I don't know." Nothing new in that, he realized dismally. All the gains he and Trevor had made, erased.

"He must have called a friend."

"I don't know," Richard repeated.

"Did he have enough money to buy a bus ticket to California?"

"I don't know," he said again. She was trying to help. *Don't yell at her.* Closing his eyes, he tried to think.

"He'd probably hitch, anyway. Goddamn it. But I don't think he'd head for California. He's not even speaking to his mother."

"No, but he must have friends."

"Yeah. He's making some here, too." He could start calling around...

"Who all live with parents."

"You've tried his cell phone?"

"Turned off. I left a message." A clumsy one. He should have rehearsed what he wanted to say, but hadn't had the foresight to do that. He thought he'd said the right things, though.

Uh-huh. Saying the right things had gotten him so far with Trevor up until now.

"I'm so sorry, Richard. This is my fault," Molly said unhappily.

That arrested his attention. "Your fault how?"

"I shouldn't have invited you over."

"I shouldn't have made a move on you. If it's any-body's, it's my fault."

"We could argue about it all night, you know."

He let loose a ragged laugh. "Yeah. How'd it go with Cait?"

"Not as terribly as I expected. I apologized for being dishonest with her, but not for dating you."

Dating wasn't exactly the word for what the kids had caught them—almost—doing, but he'd go along with it.

"Good for you."

"I told her that we wanted to focus on her and Trevor, but...but we'd fallen in love without planning to."

"*Can* you plan to fall in love?" Richard asked, amused despite the worry churning in his gut.

"You know what I mean," Molly scolded.

"Yeah. I know." *God, God. What do I do now?*

"Richard?"

"Uh-huh?"

"Do you want me to ask Cait if she has any idea where Trevor would have gone?"

He blinked. "Good idea. Otherwise…damn. I don't know where to start."

"You know, he probably went to a friend's to cool off."

"Would he have packed as much as he could carry if that's all he had in mind?"

They went back and forth a few more times, but, truth was, neither of them had any insight into his son's current, convoluted thinking. Who knew what was eating at Trevor? Richard suspected that he'd walked in on some strange man "doing" his mom—but why had that triggered rage at his father, too?

Molly called back twenty minutes later to say that Cait would make a few phone calls and was going to "think about it."

"Tell her thanks," Richard said.

He called Bree and told her Trevor had taken off, and if he contacted her would she please let him know. She said she would. He tried eventually to go to bed, but sleep eluded him. His eyes were gritty come morning, his movements slow and heavy, foreboding hanging heavy over him.

He went into the office where he pretended to be working on the computer. There was no way in hell he'd actually accomplish anything or could manage real human interaction.

He phoned Molly midmorning. When she took the call, the first thing she said was, "No word?"

"Nothing. I assume you'd have let me know if he'd showed up for class."

"He's absent." She hesitated. "Cait's talking to some of his friends."

"Will the coach throw him off the team if he doesn't show for practice this afternoon?" One of those unpleasant thoughts that had come to him during the night.

"No. He won't be happy, but all Trevor will get is a warning. He may get benched for the Friday game, though."

"He deserves to be," Richard said grimly.

"Missing practice is one thing, though. If he doesn't show for the game…"

Richard swore. "I can't believe he's throwing his future away because he discovered his father isn't a monk." Regretting the way his voice had risen, he glanced at his closed office door. It wouldn't shock him if his receptionist, Jeanne, had her ear to the other side. She did like to gossip.

"It hasn't even been a day yet," Molly said gently. "Don't write him off so quick."

"I wouldn't do that." He managed a wry smile. "Thanks, Molly."

After hanging up, he wished he'd ended the call by saying "I love you." He knew this wasn't the time to have that talk with her, the one where he found out whether she was thinking about a future with him. But he wished they'd already had it. He'd like to know they were a solid team, instead of being torn in different directions by their respective kids. He felt pretty confident that Caitlyn had not given her mom a thumbs-up and said, "You go, Mom." She was used to having her mother to herself, to being the center of attention, and no way would she like losing the spotlight. Especially when she was in the middle of the performance of her life.

And I'm being a jackass, he thought, but couldn't take it back. In her own way, Cait was being gutsy. *Is she spoiled, or am I jealous because Cait does hold center stage in Molly's eyes?* Lousy thought.

Hell, being thirty-seven didn't guarantee complete maturity.

The rest of the day was hellish, the night more so. He left another message on Trevor's phone. This time all he said was, "I love you, and I wasn't open with you. That was wrong."

What he was thinking was, *You're still my little boy. Ten fingers, ten toes. Please come home.*

SPRAWLED ON THE BEANBAG chair, Trevor was tempted to delete his father's voice mail without hearing what he had to say, but in the end he couldn't resist listening. After the second one, he muttered some words.

Cait had left two messages, too. Hers was the last one.

"You're a jerk for running out on me. How come *I* had to talk to them and you didn't? It wasn't *your* mother that was half-naked."

He snorted. *You want to bet? Been there, done that.*

"I wish you'd call me." Now she sounded sad. "We're all really scared, Trevor. Even your dad. You promised…" She broke off. He could hear the deep breath she drew. "Just…will you call me, at least?"

Shit. Hell. Damn. He thought some other words, too, then groaned and hit Send. He *had* promised to stick with her through this.

She answered on the first ring. "Trevor?" It came out shocked.

"Yeah, it's me. You guilted me into calling."

"I didn't mean…"

"Yeah, you did."

She sniffed. "Maybe."

He found he was smiling, and was glad he was alone. The guys whose apartment he was crashing at were all out. Two of them had classes at the community college and the third, Alonzo, worked at a gym. It was actually Alonzo whom Trevor knew; he'd graduated from West Fork and had been hanging out with some of his teammates who were still seniors. He'd been surprised when Trevor showed up asking if he could stay for a day or two, but had been cool with it.

"You okay?" Trevor asked.

"Yeah. Mom and I talked, and…wow, I so wish I hadn't found out about your dad like that, but she really likes him. I mean, he's an okay guy, isn't he?"

"Yeah." Trevor's mouth twisted. "I'm still mixed-up about him, but…yeah."

"Where are you?"

"I'm in Everett. You know Alonzo Baker? I'm at his place."

"Oh. Um, I hear Coach Bowman is really steamed."

He winced.

"I wish you'd come home."

"Uh." He hadn't made up his mind until right then, but…shit, what were his choices? "I guess I will."

"Really?"

"Yeah. I meant to keep going to L.A., but that was stupid." He paused. "Have you seen my dad?"

"No, but he and Mom keep talking. He's totally pan-icked."

Part of him thought, *Good,* but he was also embar-rassed. He'd acted like a little kid, completely uncool. And it wasn't because he'd thought his father never got any, although probably that's what they all believed. It was because... He shifted uneasily.

"How will you get home?" Cait asked practically.

"I can either wait until Alonzo can bring me or go out and hitch."

"There's probably a bus."

Maybe, but he didn't want to try to figure that out. He didn't say anything.

"I wish I had a license. But I know your dad would come and get you."

"I'll think about it," Trevor said.

"Okay." She was quiet for a moment, then said in a rush, "I'm glad you called. I was really freaked."

"Yeah. I'm sorry the way I ditched you."

"You should be." That was more tart. More *her.*

After she was gone, he wondered if she'd tell her mom who'd tell his dad where he was and that he was thinking of coming home. Probably, he concluded. He stared down at the blank screen on his phone.

What was he waiting for? He knew what he was going to do. *So do it, all right?* His hand shook a little as he scrolled to his father's last call and pushed Send.

THE HOUSE WAS A TYPICAL student-crash-house dump a few blocks from the community college in north Ever-ett. Richard had taken a year's worth of classes here to get the basics covered on his way to his own four-year degree. Finding the place hadn't been a problem.

He'd coasted to a stop at the curb and set the brake when the front door opened and Trevor came out, duffel slung over one shoulder, the strap for his laptop case over the other. He loped across the lawn and opened the passenger door.

"Hey."

Richard nodded.

His kid shoved his possessions behind the seat, then got in and slammed the door.

They hadn't said much on the phone.

I shouldn't have taken off like that.

No, you shouldn't.

Richard's offer to pick him up had been accepted. Now what?

"We need to talk," he said finally.

"Here?"

"You hungry?"

Trevor agreed that he was. Of course. Richard remembered at that age his own enormous capacity for food—and he hadn't still been growing.

He'd passed a Subway on the way, and drove back to it. Once they had their sandwiches, they sat in a booth off to one side.

Richard decided to quit messing around and get down to brass tacks. "What happened with your mother?"

Trevor had started to unwrap his sandwich, but he stopped. One of his hands curled into a fist. For a minute Richard thought he wasn't going to answer, but finally he met his father's eyes.

"She was still married to Davis, and I walked in on her naked. With this guy." His voice cracked on the last. "He's an assistant coach at my high school. Way younger than Mom. Like, twenty-five?"

Damn you, Alexa. "She met him at your games."
Richard didn't even make it a question.

Trevor twitched. "Yeah."

"That's it?"

"No, that's not it!" Trevor's voice rose to a roar.
Heads turned on the other side of the restaurant. Even
though his eyes were wild, he noticed and subsided.
"She gave me this whole spiel about how Davis doesn't
care about her anymore, and she's *lonely.*" He spat that
out. "And I said was she serious about Coach Magnoni
and she said she didn't know. She didn't know," he repeated in bewilderment and anger. "She was ruining
her marriage and everything else, *and she didn't know.*"

Richard looked down at his own sandwich, untouched. How could he begin to explain Alexa's behavior while still preserving her in her son's eyes? Was
that even possible?

But Trevor didn't wait for him. "I figured out it wasn't
the first time. A couple months before I came home and
this other guy was just leaving. Mom looked, I don't
know, rattled, because I wasn't supposed to be home yet.
I thought, *weird,* and let it go. I asked her and she didn't
want to admit it but she finally did. So then I asked if
she'd been screwing Davis while she was still married to
Scott and she didn't exactly say yes but I could tell she
was." He stared at Richard, the betrayal he was feeling
stark in his dark eyes. "That's what happened to you,
too, isn't it? Mom screwed around on you."

He'd lied, if only by omission, enough to this boy
who was becoming a man. Who was only eight months
younger than Richard had been when his girlfriend told
him she was pregnant.

"That's what happened," he said.

"She's a slut!"

"Trevor…"

"Why did you let her have me and Bree?" The hurt roughened Trevor's voice. "When you *knew*?"

So that's what this had all been about. Richard wished he'd figured it out sooner. Forced a discussion.

"Because she was a good mother," he said heavily. "She *is* a good mother. Did you ever have the slightest doubt about that?"

"Yeah, when I walked in and saw *my* coach humping her!"

Now Richard winced.

"And then you…" Trevor broke off.

"I'm sorry about that. Sorrier than I can tell you. But it is *not* the same thing." He made sure Trev saw how serious he was. "Neither Molly nor I are married. Although I hope we will be."

That set Trevor back. Dark thoughts flickered through his eyes. "You really want…?" he finally asked, hesitating to put it into words.

"I do," Richard said firmly.

"Wow."

"Why wow? Well, except I know you and Molly didn't get off to a very good start…."

"You think?" Trevor sneered.

Richard raised his eyebrows. "Whose fault was that?"

"Mine. Isn't everything my fault?" Sarcasm mixed with grief in a murky brew.

"No." For the first time Richard let himself relax. He leaned back in the booth and smiled. "You don't have that big an ego. Of course it's not. Some of it is your mother's fault. Some your idiot assistant coach's. Some mine," he admitted.

"I hate her," Trevor mumbled, and Richard under-stood he wasn't talking about Molly.

He told his son some of what he'd figured out about Alexa. "She keeps thinking a man will fill all her needs, and it isn't possible. So when he fails her, she starts looking again. I didn't understand it then, and I still don't. But I hold with my belief that she was a damn good mother."

"Didn't you want us?" Hurt made Trevor sound like the little boy he wasn't anymore.

"More than anything on earth. But after your mother and I split up, I was expecting to get sent to Iraq."

"You did," Trevor said slowly. "Not that much later, right?"

Richard nodded. "Less than a year later. If I hadn't had that hanging over me, I might have asked at least for joint custody. But I didn't see how I could." He took a drink of his bottled water. "By the time I got back, she'd remarried. You guys seemed happy. Settled. I was damn near a stranger to Bree at that point, and even you and I had to get reacquainted. And I had the possibility of another tour to contend with." He shrugged. "When she moved you to California, I felt like a giant sinkhole had opened in the middle of my life. I fell in it every time I so much as thought about you. But you two were doing well. When I saw you, you seemed happy. You both got good grades. Scott was okay with you. I didn't see what I could do."

Trevor was nodding. "I guess I can see that." He gri-maced. "And then came Davis."

"And then came Davis."

"He was okay. But…wouldn't you think it would have

hit him that if Mom would sleep with him when she was married to someone else, she'd do it again?"

"He might have thought they really fell in love. She probably told him what a big mistake the marriage to Scott had been."

"I'm glad she didn't have more kids."

Richard winced. "There are plenty of modern families like that. Half brothers and sisters from several different fathers. Or mothers."

Trevor's eyes widened. "You and Ms. Callahan—Molly—aren't going to have a baby, are you?"

He groaned and scrubbed a hand over his face. "No. No, she's not pregnant. And no, I can't imagine. I think we're both done with the child rearing years."

Trevor expelled a rush of air with a whoosh. "Man, that would have been too much."

Richard let himself smile crookedly. "Because I was such a lousy father?"

His son grinned. "You got it."

In concert, they reached for their sandwiches.

CHAPTER FIFTEEN

WHAT DID YOU BUY A pregnant teenage girl for Christmas?

Molly had started her shopping, of course. Despite the recent turmoil, she wasn't that disorganized. She'd bought gift certificates, books, DVDs, all online. Cait had suggested a CD for Trevor, which took care of shopping for him. She'd even bought a book for Richard, an inadequate gift but the only one she could think of.

But her own daughter was different. So far, everything Molly had bought for Cait was impersonal. And, darn it, she was down to only two weeks before Christmas, so she'd decided to brave the crowds and hit the mall.

Molly drifted through Nordstrom, undecided. Not clothes, that was for sure. While Cait would need maternity clothes in the not-too-distant future, those wouldn't exactly be fun for a teenager. Thrift stores? Maybe. Molly thought about dusting off the sewing machine she so rarely used. This whole thing was hard enough on a kid Cait's age without her being stuck in completely untrendy clothes for four months or more. Was it possible to replicate current teen styles with a belly panel?

Nothing related to dance. Although continuing to dance would be good for her mental and physical health. At least leotards stretched, probably to infinity.

Molly gave a last pained look at the teen department and turned away.

Jewelry? Maybe some bath and body stuff. She ought to head out into the mall, look for some specialty stores.

Her feet came to a stop and she suddenly had trouble breathing. Oh, why hadn't she been more careful? Not five feet in front of her was a table displaying one-piece cotton sleepers for babies. These were in classic baby colors: mint green, soft yellow, delicate pink, summer-sky blue. The blue ones had sailboats embroidered on the breast; the soft yellow had puppies.

Somehow her feet *had* moved, and she was standing right in front of the table fingering a buttery-soft sleeper. She lifted her gaze to see other display tables and racks. Small undershirts, T-shirts, corduroy overalls and miniature denim pants with cargo pockets. Socks... oh, God, so tiny.

Her chest hurt. Her throat burned. Bewildered, she realized how close she was to crumpling to her knees and sobbing. *What's happening to me?*

But she knew, she knew. *I'm falling apart, that's what.*

Molly had shopped children's clothing departments hundreds of times since she'd discovered she would never have another baby. The decision not to even look at the baby stuff hadn't been consciously made, but she had adhered to it religiously except for the few times she'd had to suck it up and buy a shower present. It had been years since she'd been required to do that, although the time would come again when Cait's friends got married and had babies.

When I have grandchildren, she'd always thought.

She lifted a fleece "sack" with arms and a hood to

her face and gently rubbed her cheek against it. It was
red, perfect for the season, cozy, unisex. Tears leaked
out now and she turned away when a couple of young
women passed carrying bags stuffed full of purchases.
One of the two was pregnant and she gave a cry of delight and pounced on some holiday-themed T-shirts.

"Oh, I missed those!"

"Your little button won't be born until the first of
February," her friend pointed out practically.

"Yes, but…"

They eventually departed, neither paying any attention to the woman paralyzed in the midst of racks of
tiny, soft, evocative baby clothes.

I could buy one outfit, she thought. *To send him or
her away in.*

Her rib cage contracted in agony as she imagined it.

If Cait was keeping her baby, they could find out
soon—maybe now—whether it was a boy or girl. They
could be dreaming, planning. Looking at cribs and mo-
biles and comforters. A stroller, of course, they'd have
to have one. Molly hadn't kept any of those things, not
once she had the surgery. Even though money had been
tight then, she hadn't been able to bear having a garage
sale. On a day she'd felt strong, she had packed it all up
and taken it to a thrift store. That had been almost as
terrible a day as the one when the doctor told her she
had to have the hysterectomy.

Now as she stood there with her heart breaking,
Molly realized she wouldn't be doing any Christmas
shopping today. She had to get out of here before she
really did break down in tears.

She turned and made herself walk away. *Keep your
eyes on the housewares—that department always has*

beautiful displays. It's...safe. She'd almost escaped from the baby department when she saw the teddy bears with embroidered eyes and noses, plump bellies and plush fur.

A broken sound escaped her.

This isn't only Cait's baby. It's Trevor's, too, and Richard's. And mine. Mine! How can we let this baby go?

She was almost running by the time she reached the double glass exit doors that would let her escape to the parking lot.

RICHARD HAD TALKED TO Molly a couple of times since the big blowup, but they didn't try to get together.

"Let's give the kids time to adjust," she had suggested, and he couldn't argue. The fact that Trevor was home again and Cait apparently hadn't thrown a major hissy fit were steps in the right direction. He shouldn't let himself get greedy.

Now, if Molly had said anything about postponing their relationship beyond a week or so, then he'd have argued. Damn it, he wanted them to spend Christmas together, as a family! But his patience was eroding faster than he'd expected. Within days of not seeing her, he was already suffering withdrawal symptoms.

Richard had driven Trevor to school the morning after his return, even though he knew that it wasn't necessary. Molly came out of her office when he spoke briefly to the school secretary, who handed Trevor a pass. She wore one of her suits, the jacket of which nipped in enough at the waist to emphasize her magnificent breasts. Richard doubted she was aware of the effect.

Her cheeks were a little bit pink when she smiled at Trevor. She was undoubtedly remembering the last time she'd seen him—and he'd seen her. "I'm glad you're back," she told him. "Does Coach Bowman know?"

Dark color had risen into his cheeks, too, and he shuffled his feet and seemed to have acquired a few twitches. "Uh, yeah. Dad called him last night."

"And?"

"He's benching me Friday."

"I'll bet he hates to do that."

"Yeah." Trevor flashed her a grin. "He's really mad at me. He says he'll be even madder if we lose."

"I hope there won't be a repeat."

"There won't be, Ms. Callahan." Richard was proud of the way his son looked her in the eye despite his embarrassment.

"Good. You'd better hurry if you're going to beat the bell," she said.

She'd walked Richard out to the parking lot, giving him a chance to tell her more than he had last night on the phone about what Trevor had said.

"Poor Trevor." She'd sighed. "And then for him to catch us…."

"Yeah. He gets the difference between us and what his mother was doing, but…"

That's when she suggested they cool it for a few days. He didn't like the idea, but knew it was smart. He needed to concentrate on Trevor. On making what understanding they'd arrived at solid.

He risked everything, though, that evening after dinner. "I think you ought to call your mother."

Trevor's chair scraped the floor as he reared back. "What?"

"You heard me. I don't mean this instant." Seeing the rebellion on his face, Richard continued. "Listen to me for a minute. I know how you feel. I know you're angry, and I know you may never feel quite the same about her. But the fact is, she's still your mother. She loves you, and you love her." He let what he'd said settle. "She was scared when I had to tell her you'd taken off on your own. You don't need to see her until you're ready, but it wouldn't hurt to say, 'Sleeping with other men when you were married was really lousy. Sleeping with my coach, letting me catch you in bed with him, that stinks. But you're my mom, and I love you.'"

He waited.

Trevor's dark eyes were unhappy. "I'll think about it," he said after a minute.

Richard smiled at him. "That's all I ask." He stood up to clear the table, and as he circled it he squeezed his son's shoulder. "You scared me, too."

Trev stood and collected some dirty dishes. "It wasn't cool, the way I took off." He took a deep breath. "I'm sorry."

What crossed Richard's mind was something of a surprise. It was the knowledge that, while Alexa had definitely screwed up, she'd also done a lot of things right by their kids. He wasn't sure he'd told her that often enough.

MOLLY MADE HERSELF TAKE two full days to think about what she was going to ask of her daughter. Before she opened her mouth, she had to be sure she was proposing this for the right reasons. That she wasn't letting this yearning pull her into something horribly wrong for Cait. *Or,* Molly thought, *for me.*

Was she really prepared at her age to start all over with a newborn baby? Handle the sleepless nights, the cost of day care, the stress of juggling work and child rearing? *Remember what it was like,* she kept reminding herself. The never-ending exhaustion, the sense of living on a knife-edge, always wondering when you were going to make a horrible mistake that would traumatize your child forever. Did she have the needed patience anymore? The energy?

If she said to Caitlyn, *I want to raise your baby as my own,* she had to be able and willing to follow through. She couldn't expect any more from Cait than she would have if she herself had unexpectedly gotten pregnant and had a baby. The deal would be that Cait got her life back, that she'd become a regular teenager again. She wouldn't nurse the baby; she wouldn't give up any of her activities to babysit. Her baby would become a little sister or brother. That would be the deal.

Molly thought about talking to Richard about this, but she needed first to decide whether this was really something she wanted to do. That she was committed to doing. He'd said he loved her, but that didn't mean he was thinking about marriage. In ten years, he hadn't remarried. She couldn't make any assumptions, and saying, *So, do you want to be a daddy while I'm being mommy?* would be a big—gigantic—assumption.

Decide, she told herself. Talk to Cait. *Then* talk to Richard.

One thing she couldn't predict was how Cait would react. Would she be thrilled? Grateful? Horrified? Feel like her mother was trying to steal her baby from her?

And what about Trevor? Would this be too weird for him? In his eyes, would it be better if the child disappeared so that he could imagine some kind of ideal family? Or would he be okay with, well, maybe even seeing the baby from time to time?

And would they tell the baby that Big Sister Cait was really his or her biological mother?

Yes. Molly had no trouble with that answer. She couldn't live with the lies, otherwise. Families came in all shapes and sizes. What was wrong with being matter-of-fact about what happened? Saying, *We all loved you, and I wanted to be your mommy?*

Nothing, that's what.

A part of her knew that she'd really made the decision when she stood in the baby department at Nordstrom. Maybe, secretly, she'd made it long before that.

Acknowledging her certainty, she realized how sweaty-palmed nervous she was about talking to Cait. About saying, *I want your baby.*

CAIT'S EYES WERE red-rimmed when she came home from dance on Wednesday. When Molly asked what was wrong, she cried, "I don't want to talk about it," and stormed upstairs to her bedroom.

Okay, today's not the day for the big scene, Molly thought. She was relieved enough for an excuse to put it off that she felt like a coward.

When Cait came downstairs for dinner, though, she opened up. "Ms. Arden heard I'm pregnant. She says if I'm going to keep taking classes, I have to bring a note from the doctor giving permission."

Molly set down the serving spoon. "Oh, honey."

"It's not like I'm playing football! Or...or wanting to bungee jump or do flips off my skateboard!"

"She's a businesswoman. As much as she loves you,

she has to be cautious. If you were to miscarry at the dance school, she needs to know she isn't legally liable."

"Like that would be a bad thing," Cait said disagreeably.

Molly felt her spine become rigid. "Is that really how you feel?"

The fifteen-year-old gave her a desperate look. "You know it isn't!" Her breath hitched. "Just sometimes…"

Molly took her hand. "I know. I do."

"Yeah." Cait gave a forlorn smile. "I guess you do. But…it's not the same."

Oh, God, she thought. Maybe this *is* the day. The moment. Anxiety seized her, and all the words she'd rehearsed jumbled in her head.

"Why are you looking like that?" Cait's eyes widened. "You're freaking me out."

Molly spared a glance for the stir-fry dinner she'd spent the past forty-five minutes preparing, but which neither of them had yet dished up, never mind started eating.

"I've been thinking," she began, and her daughter stared. Molly finally said it. "Your baby is family. I'd like to keep her and raise her as my own. Or…or him. Whichever it is."

"What?"

It was like a dive out the door of a small airplane, something Molly had never had the slightest desire to do. The hum of the engine was receding, she was falling and her parachute was not opening.

CAIT DID NOT REACT WELL initially. On the positive side, she didn't come out with guns blazing. She went with the wounded, shocked, staggering-for-cover persona.

Molly toughed it out. She hadn't really expected her daughter to fall into her arms with a "Thank you, thank you, thank you, Mommy." And be fair, she told herself, the idea wasn't the everyday thing moms suggested. Especially since it rapidly became clear that Cait thought Mom was too *old* to raise a baby. Apparently she fell solidly in the grandmother camp.

"I'm only thirty-five," Molly pointed out, with what she thought was commendable evenness of temper. "These days, lots of women aren't starting their families until they're my age. If I were to remarry *and* hadn't had a hysterectomy, I might well consider having a baby."

Cait was flabbergasted at that. "You mean…you and *Richard?*"

"It's not an option," Molly reminded her. "I can't have a baby." And, damn it, saying the words still hurt.

"Oh, my God." Darling Cait had already said that three or four times. Molly thought maybe she was actually praying. It was pretty insulting, when you got right down to it.

But Cait *did* listen, and asked some good questions, and puckered her brow and brooded when Molly in turn asked how *she'd* feel about having the baby stay part of the family but not be hers.

"You mean I couldn't take her if, like, I got married when I'm twenty-one and wanted her."

For some reason they were talking about this baby as though it was a girl. Instinct or convenience? There was something to be said about languages that offered a gender-neutral pronoun.

"That's what I mean," Molly said. "I think if we do this, we should make it an official adoption. You and Trevor relinquish parental rights, I adopt. Otherwise, for me to do even simple things like approving medical care or filling out permission forms would be a challenge."

"Wow." She'd said that several times, too.

"I don't expect you to give me an answer tonight." *But, oh, I wish you would.* "It's not like we don't have plenty of time. I did want you to start thinking."

Caitlyn lasered her with a challenging stare, blue eyes to gray. "What if I say no?"

Molly rubbed herself over the breastbone, trying to quell panic and pain. Heartburn. The real kind.

"Then I would have to accept it. I'd be disappointed—" to say the least "—but I'd also understand. I know this would be…strange for you."

"You mean, weird."

"Possibly." She let out a breath. "Of course it would be. For all of us. At first."

"Everyone would *know.*"

"Everyone already knows." One thing she couldn't do was let Cait delude herself. "Just because the baby disappears doesn't mean your classmates will forget."

Cait ducked her head. "I thought… I mean, I guess I was thinking…" she mumbled after a minute.

"That when you showed up at school next September, slim and baby-free, you could pretend the whole thing never happened?" That sounded cruel, it occurred to Molly belatedly.

Am I being cruel? Was she in essence insuring that Cait would be haunted forevermore by her one mistake? *Should I instead be looking for that new job, trying to give her a fresh start her junior year?*

Cait did do the wounded look exceedingly well. Big eyes, tremulous lower lip. "That's harsh."

"I'm sorry," Molly said on a rush of contrition. "It was."

"But maybe kind of true."

She held her breath.

And that was when Cait said it. "Probably my answer is yes, but… *Can* I think about it?"

"Of course you can." Molly's smile felt a little tremulous, too. "No matter what…"

"You love me." Caitlyn tumbled around the table and into her mommy's arms. "Yeah, I know."

And yes, the swelling of love was so profound, Molly knew she would survive if ultimately the answer was no. Because Cait was her baby. Her first, and, Molly had always believed, her only.

But now…maybe not her only.

"WHAT?" BLOWN AWAY, Trevor stopped dead in the middle of the sidewalk. A cold wind cut through his sweatshirt, but he ignored the discomfort.

He was walking Cait to dance, something he hardly ever got to do anymore since he had practice right after school most days. For some reason Coach had canceled today, though, so he'd hurried to catch her. He was spending a lot of time with her, even though they were more like friends right now than boyfriend/girlfriend. Sometimes he thought he wanted her to be his girlfriend again, but then he'd have second thoughts because… well, she hadn't liked sex, at least with him, and he *was* the one who'd screwed up so badly and she was having to pay the price. And then there was the fact that their parents had a thing going, and if Dad and Ms. Callahan got married… Wow. He and Cait would be like brother and sister. And how weird would that be?

But this…was she *serious?*

"You heard me," Cait said.

"Come on, hurry up, I'm *cold.*"

"Wimp." She wore a parka—pink, of course, and it had a faux-fur-lined hood, really girlie but he had to admit he liked the way it framed her face.

"I don't feel any need to show I'm manly by freezing to death." She trotted off down the sidewalk, a bright spot of color on a gray day when the trees were bare of leaves, dark and skeletal. Pretty.

He followed her, catching up quickly with his longer legs. "Your mom wants to keep the baby." He couldn't get his head around it.

"And you feel the need to repeat me…why?" Cait shot him an annoyed look that he sensed was cover for something. He couldn't tell what.

"How do you feel about it?" he asked slowly.

Her steps slowed. "I'm not sure yet."

"But?"

"I think it's a good idea."

Okay, *now* he was freaking. "I thought there was no way you were keeping this baby."

"I wouldn't be keeping it. Mom said if we do it, we should make it official. You and me both give up our rights, the way we would if an adoption agency took the baby away. And Mom would adopt it."

"But it would still be right there."

She whirled. "I know!" she yelled, face red. "What do you think, I'm stupid?"

If the label fit.

She growled and stalked away again.

"Talk to me," Trevor said, trailing her.

"I'm trying." She said it so softly, he barely heard her.

Now he broke into a jog so that he could catch up and get in front of her. Then he walked backward so he could see her. "I know, I know. I'm sorry. It's just… The baby would still be here."

"That's the point," Cait said huffily.

He couldn't get past the basic concept. He'd been counting on the baby vanishing from their lives. Not that he'd forget he *had* a kid out there somewhere, but that wouldn't be the same. "But it…"

Her eyes narrowed. "Are you talking about the baby?"

"What?"

"When you say *it*."

"What am I supposed to call it?" He was yelling now. Losing it. *It*.

"Our baby," she informed him, all pissy, "is a little girl or boy. Not an *it*." She flounced up the steps to the dance school, although he hadn't even realized they'd arrived. "Goodbye," she said, yanking open the big door, and left him.

Stuck on the idea that his baby—a little girl or boy, oh, God—might stay in his life. Forever.

He stood where he was for a long time, freezing but unable to move.

"WHAT DID YOU SAY?" In the act of opening containers from the local Thai restaurant, Richard gaped at his son.

"Ms. Callahan is going to adopt the baby." Trevor looked dazed.

"Who told you that?"

"Cait. Who else?"

Shock, incredulity, anger, disbelief… *Let me count the ways*. "And this was Molly's idea? Or was it Cait's?"

He had to nail it down. Not get sucked in by some dumb teenage scheme.

"Molly's. I mean, Ms. Callahan's. Cait told me her mom said that's what she wants. She asked if she could keep the baby."

In that moment, Richard figured out what emotion was paramount. Hurt. He'd talked to Molly the day before yesterday, and she hadn't said a word about this. Hadn't even hinted she was thinking it. Never mind asking. "What do you think?"

Well, this was one way for her to make it plain she wasn't envisioning a future with him. Apparently for her, "I love you" meant hot sex when their respective kids weren't around.

Which would be pretty much never once she started all over with a baby.

He shoved back his chair and stood. "You eat. I'll be back later."

Trev jumped up, too, looking alarmed. "You're going over there to see her?"

"To *see* her? Hell, no. I need to hear this from her. Not thirdhand."

"Are you mad?" Trevor's voice probably hadn't cracked like that since he was about thirteen.

Good going. Scare your kid, why don't you? Richard didn't care. He grabbed his car keys and wallet from the kitchen counter and kept going into the garage.

Ten minutes later—maybe less, he'd violated some speed limits on the way here—he was ringing Molly Callahan's doorbell.

Cait opened the door, her expression an echo of Trevor's. "Wait," she said urgently. "He wasn't sup-

posed to *tell* you. It's not like we've made up our minds.
I was just…"

Richard pushed right past her. He pitched his voice
to be heard as far as her bedroom upstairs. "Molly?"
Call it a bellow.

She appeared from the kitchen, wiping her hands on
a hand towel. "Richard?" she said in surprise.

"Tell me," he said. "Tell me you aren't planning to
torture us for the rest of our natural lives."

She went so still, she might have been turned into
a statue. Only her eyes were alive, shimmering with
emotion, taking in the fury that seemed to be consum-
ing him.

And then even her eyes were shielded. She resumed
drying her hands and looked at him with calm profes-
sionalism. *Ms. Callahan,* although barefoot and having
shed her jacket. "I take it you're not a fan of the idea,"
she said coolly.

A part of him was aware that Cait hadn't moved.
Cold air was coming in the open door. He advanced on
Molly, the muscles in his jaw painfully flexed.

"You couldn't talk to me about this?"

"I thought I should be clear in my own mind whether
I wanted to do it." She raised her eyebrows, managing
icy disdain. "Perhaps mistakenly I believed Cait and I
were most impacted by this decision."

The blow was deadly. It was all he could do not to
hunch forward in a much-too-late attempt to protect his
vulnerable midsection. His belly. His heart.

"That tells me where I rated in your planning, doesn't
it?" He said that quietly, so quietly he hoped Cait didn't
hear. But then he made sure his voice hardened. "Even
if you don't give a damn about me, make some effort to

think about your daughter and my son, will you? And a little less about yourself?"

Her face had bleached pale. That was her main reaction, along with the fact that she'd gone back to being a statue.

He gave her a last, scathing look, turned and walked out.

If he had to stop a block from her house to pull himself together…well, it was dark, and no one would know.

CHAPTER SIXTEEN

"THERE'S NOTHING TO SAY," Molly insisted, and tried to escape into her bedroom.

She hadn't wanted to talk to Cait about Richard last night, and she wasn't going to tonight, either. There *wasn't* anything to say. He'd made his opinion really clear. And he'd done it in a way that left her quite certain there was no going back, even if she'd been willing to give up the idea of raising Cait's baby in favor of a future with him. A future they hadn't even discussed, that might or might not have been a possibility.

Her daughter had been trailing her through the house like a yapping dog going for the mailman's leg. "Mom, you should talk to him, even if you won't to me."

Molly finally stopped at the bathroom door and turned, feeling almost frozen inside. "You saw him. You heard what he said. If you were me, would *you* call him? And what would you say?"

"Well…I don't know." Cait faltered. "But I think you hurt his feelings."

"*I* hurt *his* feelings?" Oh, that was funny, considering what he'd done to her. She felt as if he'd stuck several particularly well-aimed skewers in her.

Tell me you aren't planning to torture us for the rest of our natural lives.

Dear God, was that really how it seemed to him?

That she wanted to keep the baby even though its very presence would forever be a torment to Cait, Trevor and Richard?

She hadn't slept last night. She didn't know how she'd be able to tonight, either, but she was desperate to be alone.

"He was wrong," Cait said urgently. "Trevor and I talked about it today. We both like the idea of you keeping the baby."

That made Molly blink, not a pleasant sensation when she felt as if she had sand on her eyeballs. "Trevor likes the idea," she repeated slowly. Carefully.

Cait's flush was a giveaway. "Maybe not *like*. But he's getting used to it, Mom. He is."

Her thoughts had slowed down, too. Her brain felt grainy and thick. "You weren't so sure *you* liked the idea."

"But I do." Cait nibbled on her lower lip before going on in a burst. "I hated the idea of giving the baby away. This is, well, it's scary, too, but in a different way. But once I thought about it, I knew it was right. You'll love the baby, and I always wanted a sister or brother. Plus, I never knew how much you wanted another baby. I can tell you really do want her, and it makes me feel…I don't know, like I'm giving you a gift. And that feels good."

A sob escaped Molly. It came from nowhere. She hadn't even felt it rising to her throat. She covered her mouth with her hand and stared over it with blurry vision.

"Oh, Mom!" Cait flung herself at her mother.

Molly gave in to the tears and wrapped her arms around her daughter, who held her as tightly. She became aware that Cait was swaying on her feet, instinctively rocking her mother. That made Molly cry harder, and laugh, too. *My fifteen-year-old daughter is comforting me as if I were a distraught child.* The realization of the astonishing role reversal blazed through her.

"I love you," Molly blubbered, laughed again, then cried some more. Cait had begun to giggle, too, although Molly caught a glimpse of her wet face and knew she was also crying.

It was a completely ridiculous scene, and wonderful, too. It had to be five minutes before Molly pulled herself together enough to straighten.

"I have to blow my nose." More like, *I ab doo bo by dose.*

They both went into the bathroom, both blew, both mopped and washed their faces and giggled a little more at the absurdity and the marvel of *sharing* so completely.

And finally they sat on Molly's bed, limber Cait cross-legged at the foot and Molly leaning back against a heap of pillows at the head. They looked at each other.

"What did Trevor really say?" Molly asked.

Cait's face was blotchy and Molly suspected hers was worse. She had a redhead's skin. Plus her eyes were way puffier than her daughter's.

"When I first told him yesterday, he was freaked. That's when he told his dad. But I guess he thought about it, and he's really okay with the idea. If...well, we were both thinking maybe you and his dad might get married, and if you did Trevor would have to get used to thinking about the baby as, like, a sister or brother. But if you don't, he won't see the baby any more than if she was adopted by someone else. Unless, well, we stay, um, friends. You know."

Molly wasn't sure she wanted to know. She'd been

trying not to think about Cait and Trevor's relationship. They'd obviously grown close. But were they sleeping together again? She'd decided not to ask. It was a little late to worry about an unwanted pregnancy, wasn't it? Not to mention a little late to worry about any impact on her own relationship with Trevor's father.

She made a noise that could be taken as vague agreement.

"The thing is…Mr. Ward said he was in love with you." Cait looked strangely stern. "Are you in love with *him?*"

Molly couldn't do anything but nod. She hurt too much.

"Then…you should have talked to him. Why didn't you?"

Why hadn't she? These past weeks, they'd talked about everything else under the sun. What if he had made the same decision? Asked Cait and Trevor if he could keep the baby and raise it, without once having mentioned to her that the possibility had even crossed his mind?

Her heart cramped. *I would have been hurt, of course. Worse than that—I'd have felt rejected. Ignored. As if I was inconsequential to him.*

Which, she realized, was exactly what he'd felt.

Cait was watching her. "So?"

"So what?"

"Are you going to go see him and explain?"

Those knife blades were still embedded in her. She needed to pull them out, but was afraid of how much she'd bleed.

"No." Her voice was dull. "I'm not."

"Why?"

"You heard him."

"He was mad." Cait frowned. "I've said really awful things to you when I was mad, and you forgive me. Because you love me no matter what. That's what you always say. Don't you love him enough to forgive him?"

"This is different."

"Because you think he doesn't want the baby?"

Molly laughed, and it wasn't a nice sound. "Think?"

"Because you might have to choose between him and the baby," Cait said slowly.

The words stole Molly's breath. Was that why she hadn't talked to Richard about what she was thinking? Because she'd *known* he wouldn't want to keep this baby? Because…she'd been afraid that, if he forced the choice, she would choose him?

Oh, God, she thought—*I would have. I would have chosen him.*

So…why hadn't she?

Because…I never let myself acknowledge that the choice might have to be made. No, she'd told herself that he was an uncertain factor in her planning. After all, he hadn't asked her to marry him, had he? Now, feeling as if she'd been stabbed again, and this time she'd rammed the blade into her own belly, Molly faced a truth. Of course he was going to ask her to marry him. He wasn't a man to say "I love you" and not mean it wholeheartedly, with all that followed. *She* was the one who'd put off having that conversation. Because… She wasn't absolutely sure. Maybe because she'd wanted to present him with a *fait accompli.* Had she thought once it was done, he'd hide his reluctance and accept her decision, because he loved her?

Yes. Dear God, yes, she thought, misery gripping her. That's exactly what she hoped.

"Mom?"

"He shut the door, Cait."

"Mom, talk to him!"

She heard his voice. His cruelty. *Even if you don't give a damn about me, make some effort to think about your daughter and my son, will you? And a little less about yourself?*

"No," she said. "No."

"So, what'd you say to her?" Trevor leaned against the doorjamb, blocking the exit from the kitchen.

Hateful things. Richard's gut knotted when he remembered. The look on Molly's face… A look *he'd* put there. Eyes closed, he squeezed the bridge of his nose until the cartilage creaked. "I was angry."

"Why?" Trev sounded genuinely puzzled. "I mean, I wasn't sure I liked the idea, but now that I've thought about it I think it might be good. Instead of always wondering, you know, Cait and I won't have to. Because he'll be part of our family." He hesitated. "I guess you didn't want another kid."

Richard was ashamed that he hadn't even thought it out that thoroughly. It had honestly never occurred to him that keeping the baby, for either him or Molly, was an option. No, in general he wouldn't have said he wanted to start a new family. But if he'd married Molly, in the normal course of events, and she'd desperately wanted a baby—would he have been willing?

Maybe, he thought, then had to suppress a groan. Yeah, probably. He guessed there'd been a fear factor for him. He'd loved his kids desperately, and had lost them. He wasn't sure he could survive a loss like that again.

But he'd just suffered one, anyway, and it was his own fault. He hadn't known he could love a woman as much as he did Molly. He didn't even know why her, why now. It was, that's all. And he'd gone over to her house and told her she was so selfish, to get what she wanted she was willing to hurt everyone else, including her own daughter.

His stomach heaved and he turned away from Trevor to face the kitchen sink. In case.

"I said unforgivable things," he said dully.

"Cait said maybe she could talk her mom into getting another job and moving away, so you don't have to see the baby."

Bracing his hands on the counter, Richard swallowed back another surge of nausea. "No," he managed to say. "I don't want that."

"But you hate the idea. And…you might run into her sometimes. Wow. What if I want to spend time with my kid?"

My kid. Trevor had moved from terror and rebellion to a full sense of responsibility and even emotional acceptance, while his father… *God. While I told Molly— in Cait's hearing—that keeping our grandchild would torture all of us.*

How could I say that? Mean it, even for one, enraged minute?

Richard didn't know.

"This really sucks!" Trevor paced across the kitchen and back, his steps agitated. "Things were good. It's me that messed them up. Again."

"No." *God help me.* "I did that all by myself."

"If I hadn't told you. If Ms. Callahan had come to you herself."

"If she'd come to me and said, 'I've decided to keep the baby, and Cait and Trevor have agreed'?" Richard shook his head. "It wouldn't have made any difference, Trevor. I thought..." Damn, this was hard to say. His throat and tongue weren't cooperating. "I thought we had an understanding. We weren't engaged yet..."

"Because of me," his son said desperately.

"Partly," he conceded. "Partly we just hadn't gotten there yet. But we *had* gotten far enough that, if she felt the same about me as I do about her, she should have talked to me. And that's the bottom line. She wouldn't have cut me out like this if she had been thinking marriage. Seems I was kidding myself."

Trev stared at him with wide, shocked eyes. "But... shouldn't you *talk* to her?"

Richard grunted and ran a hand over his face. "I think I've done enough talking," he said, and held up a hand when Trevor's mouth opened. "Then and now."

He stepped into the utility room, started the washing machine and began dumping dirty clothes in heedlessly.

Irritatingly enough, the door opened behind him. "Uh, Dad?"

His shoulders tensed. Teeth gritted, he stuffed a pair of jeans in. Shit, he'd forgotten to put the laundry soap in first.

"I was wondering."

"What?" Richard snapped.

"Well, I know I took off not that long ago. So maybe I haven't earned driving privileges again."

If he'd been capable of humor, this would be funny. "But you want your car back."

"Well…yeah."

He closed his eyes again. The washer began churning. Still no soap. White briefs spun by, tangled in a denim pant leg. Richard sighed. "All right. Fine." He pulled his keys out of his pocket and tossed them to his kid. "You know which one it is. Screw up again and I'll be taking it back."

"Awesome!" Trevor declared with enthusiasm. Keys rattled. "Did you keep up the insurance?"

Richard's shoulders shook. Okay, a sense of humor *was* buried deep in there somewhere. Not dead after all. "Yes," he said. "You're good to go."

"Awesome," Trevor repeated, and went.

Richard stood staring at the clothes swirling in the washer—still no soap—and wondered if he'd always been this lonely.

"WE HAVE TO GET THEM BACK together," Cait said passionately. "But Mom is so-o stubborn."

"Dad is, too." Trevor took a slurp of his milk shake. He'd called her the minute he left and she'd come running out of her house as he was pulling up. He was always hungry, but tonight even she decided some French fries and a root beer float would be good, so they'd gone to Tastee's. He almost wished now they had left town, maybe driven to Marysville or someplace, because everyone working the counter went to their school. And they'd all looked funny at Trevor and at Cait especially, and now were whispering and sneaking looks toward their table.

Cait, he saw, wasn't paying any attention. First he thought she hadn't noticed, but then he realized that she was probably already used to people whispering about her. He didn't get it that much, but it must happen to her every day now that the word was out. There was probably even an element of meanness in it, with her mom being Vice Principal for discipline.

"Don't worry about them," she said suddenly, jerking her head toward the cretins behind the counter. She stared a challenge at them, and they hurried to look busy.

"I still can't tell you're pregnant," Trevor said.

She shrugged and picked up a French fry. "I'm having trouble with the snaps on my jeans. I've had to ditch a couple pairs of skinny jeans."

"Oh." While he ate, he made a cautious survey of what he could see of her, sitting on the other side of the table. She had really great breasts—too big, she'd told him in disgust, for a ballerina. She might get by with them in modern dance, but probably not. Would they get even bigger as the pregnancy went along…?

Trevor frowned. He did like Cait. A lot. But the more he thought about it, the weirder the idea of the two of them together seemed. Given the baby, and their parents. He'd pretty much resolved to stay friends, at least until… He didn't know. Maybe when they were both in college. If the chance came.

"Forget me," she said impatiently. "What about Mom and your dad?"

"I don't know." He vented his frustration on the wrapping he was wadding in his hands. "They're being stupid."

"Maybe." Cait bent her head. "But, see, my father really did a number on Mom. She hasn't had a serious guy friend since."

"You've never said anything about your dad."

She jerked her shoulders. "I haven't even seen him in…I don't know, like four years? He pays child support because he's an attorney, and wouldn't it look bad if the authorities had to track him down as a deadbeat dad. I think he wanted a boy."

She told him stuff then, about how her father was Colton Callahan the Third, and how once he'd remarried and had a son—Colton the Fourth, believe it or not— he'd lost interest in her. "I guess I didn't cut it. Unless they'd named me Colton, and I doubt Mom would have gone for that."

"He sounds like an…" *Don't say it. The guy is her father.*

"I don't like to think about him," she said quickly. "And he's not the point, anyway. Only that Mom maybe had a hard time trusting that your father really wanted *her*. You know?"

Trevor leaned back in the booth, thinking. "It might be the same for my dad. Mom really messed with him. She's…um…I've told you about her."

Except for Dad, Cait was the only one he'd told. About walking in on her and his coach, about the things she'd admitted to and even about Trevor's realization that she'd probably screwed around on his dad, too. "I used to think it was weird he hadn't married again. If he ever got close, I never knew." He grimaced. "Not that I probably would have. I mean, we talked, but we'd go four or five months at a time without seeing each other."

"So they're both afraid to trust each other."

This was uneasy territory for Trevor. Only girls talked about relationships and things like trust. He shifted in his seat. "I guess," he said finally. "It might be something like that."

"If your dad won't call, do you think he'd do something like send her flowers and an apology? Write a note?"

"He's being really stubborn."

Frowning fiercely, Cait scooped up a gob of the melting ice cream and sucked it up. "Well, then," she announced, "we have to trick them."

Alarmed, Trevor stared at her. "What do you mean?"

She told him.

WHEN THE DOORBELL RANG, Molly was sitting at the breakfast bar immersed in the never-ending paperwork—state employees apparently did nothing but issue reams more of it. She sighed, rubbed her eyes and got to her feet.

She opened the front door to see a huge bouquet of flowers. A gorgeous bouquet, held at eye level. Lilies and roses and Queen Anne's lace. She breathed in the scent of the Asian lilies and realized that a gawky kid was holding the arrangement out to her.

"For Molly Callahan."

"Thank you. Who…?" she asked, accepting it.

"There's a card." He bounded down the steps, cut across the lawn and jumped into a white delivery van.

"Well." Molly bumped the door shut with her hip.

"Who is it, Mom?" asked Cait, who was sitting on the living room sofa painting her toenails.

Molly detoured into the living room. "Somebody sent flowers."

"Wow." Cait took a wide-eyed look, blew on her toes and carefully set her feet on the floor. "Those must have cost a bunch." Then she cackled. "That's a pun. Get it?"

"I get it."

"Who are they from?"

"I don't know." Molly set the enormous arrangement in the center of the coffee table and extracted a small white envelope clipped to the cream-colored ceramic vase. With Cait watching avidly, Molly opened it.

The dark scrawl was unfamiliar, but then she'd never seen more than Richard's signature. And this was signed "Love, Richard."

I'm sorry. I didn't mean it.

And then the "love" part.

"Can I see?" Cait waggled an impatient hand.

Numb, Molly handed over the small card.

"That's really nice," Cait said after a minute. "Are you going to call him?" Inexplicably, she sounded nervous, or as if she didn't really want her mother to call. Despite all the lecturing about how she should talk to Richard, was it possible Cait was happy the two of them had broken up?

It was possible, Molly admitted. Teenagers were, by their very nature, selfish. Then she winced. Not her favorite word right now.

"I don't know," she said. "It *was* nice of him, though. They smell glorious."

"I wonder how much they did cost."

"What? You want to be sure he wasn't stingy?"

"No. I just… Um, I've never gotten flowers, so I didn't have any idea. That's all."

Molly's eyes narrowed. Something was going on. Cait was a lousy liar. But Molly couldn't imagine what she could have to do with the floral arrangement. The handwriting definitely wasn't hers. It was distinctly masculine. And why would Cait do something like this anyway? It didn't make sense.

"Well, we might as well enjoy them. I suppose I could write him a thank-you note."

"That would be polite," her never-prim daughter said primly.

Had she and Trevor bludgeoned Richard into sending flowers? Cait, at least, could be annoyingly persistent. So maybe.

I didn't mean it.

The words stuck with her for the rest of the evening and were still on her mind when she went to bed. Which part hadn't he meant? That she'd be tormenting all of them if she kept the baby? That she was selfish?

Did it matter now?

It was an exceedingly handsome apology. She was surprised by it, on several levels. As furious as he'd been, she hadn't expected an apology at all. And flowers didn't seem to be his style. He'd been kind, thoughtful, passionate, even tender, but never romantic.

So I'm obsessing about it. Sue me. No one had ever sent her flowers before. Colt had brought home a small bouquet a few times, when they were first married, but they were the kind you picked up at the grocery store or a stand in a vacant lot right before Valentine's Day. Either he wasn't romantic, either, or she didn't bring that out in men.

Probably the latter. Delicate, pretty, petite women stirred those kinds of feelings in men, not hefty Amazons.

The next day she wrote and mailed a quick note. *Thank you for the lovely apology. Accepted.* She hesitated for a long time over the salutation, but finally added, *Love, Molly.* She told herself it was appropriate considering he'd signed his note with "love."

That very evening she had to attend the school board meeting to be available to discuss concerns about union demands for improved benefits for classified employees. The meeting droned on, mostly focused on changes in the elementary school gifted program. By the time she walked in the door, she was dragging. She bet she wasn't the only person there to resent the huge waste of time this close to the holidays.

"Cait?"

No answer. Which probably only meant her beloved daughter had earbuds deafening her to anything but some kind of alternative rock. But when Molly went upstairs, she found Cait's bedroom empty. She frowned, but it was only nine-thirty. Their unofficial curfew for school nights was ten, unless something special—and previously discussed—was happening. Molly went back downstairs and put the teakettle on.

The doorbell surprised her. Had Cait lost her key? Molly hurried to the front of the house and opened the door.

Richard loomed on her porch. Surprise robbed her of breath. He looked so good—every cliché of tall, dark and handsome. He must have changed after work, and now wore jeans, a heavy sweater and down vest, increasing his bulk. His expression, though, was closed, his dark eyebrows drawn together.

"Richard?"

"I'm here for Trevor," he said. "He left me a message saying something was wrong with his car."

"But...he's not here. Neither is Cait." Illogically, she craned her neck to look past him. The only vehicle at the curb for fifty feet either way was Richard's pickup. "I don't know where they are," she added.

"Cait didn't say?"

"No, I had a school board meeting this evening." She saw the visible puff of his breath and realized how cold it was tonight. "Please, come in," she said, stepping back.

He did, and shut the door behind him. His presence became even more overwhelming in the close confines of the entry.

Rattled, Molly tried to focus. "When I got home, Cait wasn't here. I didn't see a note."

"Can you check?" he asked.

"I thought I had, but I'll look again."

The teakettle whistled, and she jumped. "Excuse me." It was no surprise when he followed her to the kitchen and watched as she poured her tea. Wondering if she should offer him a cup, she stole a glance at his face and decided. *No.* He wasn't here to chat with her.

There was no note affixed to the refrigerator with a magnet or on the breakfast bar. "Wait! My phone." On the way back to the entry, her eye was caught by the arrangement of roses and lilies. She saw that Richard was eyeing the flowers. "By the way, thank you."

"Thank you?" There was something strange in his voice, but she was in the act of digging her cell phone out of her purse.

"I set it to vibrate while I was in the meeting," Molly explained.

No messages, but one text had arrived.

Mom we had an accident. Okay but at ER.

Heart pounding, she held out her phone to Richard, who looked at it and swore.

"If this was Trevor's fault, I swear I'm yanking the car again." His dark eyes met hers. "Damn it, Cait's pregnant, and he couldn't drive more carefully than this? Listen, I'll run up there and call you when I know something."

"I'm going, too." She shoved her feet in shoes and grabbed a parka. "Hold on, let me make sure I turned off the stove." When she got back, she asked, "Would you rather I take my own car?"

"Don't be ridiculous," he said brusquely.

He waited while she locked up, and then opened the passenger side of his truck for her. The drive to the hospital was short and silent until he was pulling into a parking slot near the emergency room entrance.

"What were you thanking me for?" he asked. He set the brake.

"The flowers." She'd spoken into the sudden silence after he had turned off the engine. When he didn't say anything immediately, her heart stuttered. "I thought… That is…"

"That I sent them?" he said slowly.

"There was a card." Oh, Lord, this was embarrassing. She knew her cheeks were heating, hoped he couldn't tell in the diffused lighting of the parking lot.

"Let's go in," he said.

His stride was so long, she had to hustle to keep up. She heard the beep as the doors locked behind them. "I must have a secret admirer," she said lightly and probably unconvincingly. Who would have done this?

Richard didn't respond. The glass doors slid open and they walked in. Molly frantically searched the waiting room, but didn't see either Cait or Trevor. Half a dozen people sat waiting—an exhausted-looking mother with two children, one held slumped against her shoulder, a man with a hand wrapped in a bloody bandage, a young Hispanic couple, the woman wearing one of those paper masks.

She and Richard went straight to the reception desk.

"Caitlyn Callahan?" Molly said, hearing her voice high and desperate. "I'm her mother."

Richard's hand settled, warm and reassuring, on her back. "Or Trevor Ward. I'm his father."

The woman peered at her computer monitor and then leafed through several file folders that were in a graduated wooden rack. "I'm sorry," she said. "I don't see either name. Are you sure they came here?"

Molly couldn't seem to get a word out.

"No. No, we assumed. Excuse us," Richard said.

He steered Molly away, to a quiet corner. "I tried calling him and he didn't answer."

"Let me try Cait. I don't know why I didn't." As she was lifting the phone out of her purse, it vibrated. New text.

Mom were okay didn't go to ER sorry if i scared you.

Looking over her shoulder, Richard growled. "All right, what the hell is going on?"

Molly was feeling shaky. "I could be wrong, but...I think we've been set up."

CHAPTER SEVENTEEN

"SET UP?" RICHARD ECHOED.

"Give me a minute." Molly sounded grim.

He watched as she typed a text on her phone. She turned it so he could see what she'd written before she touched Send.

Did you pay for half the flowers?

He liked that she bothered with the question mark.

When he suggested going out to the pickup, she shook her head. "Wait."

The response came no more than a minute or two later.

Ummm yes you mad

She typed:

Yes

No punctuation this time.

"Please take me home."

She didn't say a word on the way. Richard used the time to think.

Trevor's car still wasn't outside Molly's house. This

time, Richard pulled to the curb, set the brake and looked at her. "May I come in?"

She didn't seem to want to meet his eyes, but finally gave an awkward shrug. "Fine. I suppose we'd better talk about this."

"Cait?" she called, the minute she'd opened the front door.

No answer.

"She's past her curfew," Molly muttered.

Richard grunted a laugh. "If only that was the worst thing she ever did."

Molly huffed. "Do you want a cup of something?"

No, but he said, "Please." It gave him an excuse to stay longer. As he leaned against the counter in the kitchen and watched her refill the teakettle and put it back on the stove, he felt something inside himself relax. This felt…normal. Plus, he loved the sight of Molly, even if she was stomping around and emitting occasional sounds that sounded like compressed steam.

"Hey," he finally said in amusement. "They're good kids. They were trying to help."

"They don't understand."

Okay, his relaxed pose was more pretense than reality. Tension coiled in his gut. "Do you?" he asked after a minute.

Molly gave him a quick glance. Her eyes weren't soft; they stormed with emotion. "I suppose I do owe you an explanation."

"I owe you one, too."

The kettle let out a first squawk, and she occupied herself pouring two cups of tea. She added sugar then handed him his cup. Taking a saucer, he presumed for the tea bags, she led the way to the dining room table.

He understood that she needed the formality of sitting across from each other instead of more comfortably on the sofa.

He sat and put down his cup. "Me first, I think."

Molly bit her lip, then nodded. Head slightly bent, she seemed to be concentrating on the unnecessary act of stirring her tea.

"I was angry," Richard said abruptly. "Mostly, I was hurt that you hadn't talked to me. It doesn't say anything good about me, but I think I wanted to hurt you."

She still didn't meet his eyes. "You did."

He nodded. God. Maybe he'd been right, what he'd said to Trevor. Maybe there was no going back.

"I still don't understand," he said finally. "Why didn't you tell me what you were thinking, Molly?"

She did look at him now, and there was such desperation in her eyes, Richard felt a lurch in his chest. He never wanted to see her so unhappy.

"I've thought about nothing else since," she admitted. "First, you have to realize I *wasn't* thinking about keeping the baby. Not until a couple days before I asked Cait. Not consciously, anyway."

He nodded.

She took a deep breath, then told him how she'd been Christmas shopping and had found herself surrounded by baby clothes in a department store. "It was… excruciating," she said softly. "I told you about the endometriosis."

"Yes."

"What I didn't tell you is that I had to have a hysterectomy."

Hell. He'd noticed the scar, thin and obviously not

recent, and not asked about it. He guessed he'd vaguely thought she'd lost her appendix.

"There I was," she continued, "not even twenty-five, and I could never have another baby. It hit me really hard." Her gaze searched his, burrowed beneath his skin. "I mourned as if I'd had a late-term miscarriage. I hadn't known how deep the assumption had been that I'd have more children."

Richard couldn't help himself. He reached across the table for her hand. She returned the clasp, he thought unconsciously.

"Eventually I told myself I'd moved past it. But I think now I hadn't. I'd only buried the feelings. I told myself how ridiculous it was. I was lucky to have a wonderful daughter. I certainly didn't want any more children with Colt by then. Cait was enough for me."

"But she wasn't."

Molly frowned. "I don't think it's really that. It's… something more primal. I don't know how else to explain it. I wasn't a woman anymore. My arms *ached* to hold a baby." The ache was in her voice, too.

Richard tightened his hand.

"I found myself staring at other people's babies. Even…" Shame colored her cheeks. "Once, I was shopping and saw this really tiny baby in a stroller. The mother had her back turned, talking to a sales clerk, and I couldn't take my eyes off the baby. He was wearing a blue cap, so I knew he was a little boy. I wanted that baby." Her mouth quirked and she met his gaze, uncertainty in hers. He could see what she was thinking. *Have I horrified you?* "I wasn't quite crazy enough to consider stealing a baby, you understand. It was part of my mourning, I guess."

"I wish you'd told me." His voice came out hoarse.

"Told you what?" she asked, looking perplexed.

"All of this. How much impact the subject of babies had on you. That you'd had the hysterectomy. That another pregnancy wasn't unlikely, it was impossible." He wanted like he'd never wanted anything to be holding her, but knew it was too soon.

If it ever happened. If she could forgive him.

"What you must have felt when we discussed abortion as a possibility," he concluded.

Her eyes were suddenly bright with tears. "I didn't know you initially. And later, well, I thought I'd come to terms with all of it. I tried so hard not to influence Caitlyn too much."

"It would have killed you if she'd had that abortion."

"I don't know," she whispered. "The terrible thing is, I still think that might have been best for her. I know she's carrying the baby to term because of me. Because she imagines I was heroic for not having an abortion when I got pregnant in college."

"Look at me, Molly." When she did, Richard said, "Trevor is standing beside Cait because of me. Because he thinks *I* was heroic for marrying his mother. For not demanding she have an abortion. Is that a bad thing? He's acting like a decent human being because I did, or, at least, that's how he sees it. It's ironic that Cait's pregnancy has been his salvation. He had to face responsibility and he grew up."

"So… You're saying it's not so bad that Cait made the choice she did because of my influence."

"That's what I'm saying. Don't feel guilty, Molly."

Her fingers trembled in his. "Thank you."

"I was wrong, the things I said." He had to get this out, but she was already shaking her head.

"No. You were right. I was selfish."

"No."

"Yes. Listen to me. Please." Her voice shook. She wrenched her hand free.

"All right," he said, pitching his voice to be soothing. "I'm listening."

"Keeping the baby may be the right thing. In fact—" her chin tilted "—I think it's too late for me to tell Cait and Trevor that I can't. Won't."

He nodded, but wasn't sure she even saw. Her focus was inward.

"The thing is, I made the offer for the wrong reasons. Because I wanted—*needed*—this baby. Because I broke down looking at size newborn sleepers. I wasn't being noble, or reasonable. It was all about me." Finally, her frantic gaze connected with his. Her chest heaved. She had to be damn close to breaking down again.

As far as he was concerned, everything she'd said was nonsense. She'd been right; he'd been wrong. Keeping this baby—family—was best for all of them. But he didn't put any of that into words yet.

Instead, he said, "That doesn't explain why you didn't say anything to me. Why you sprang it on me that way."

"I was going to tell you. It didn't occur to me that Trevor..." Her gaze slid away. "It should have, of course."

"Why, Molly?" He wrapped his hand around the now-cool mug of tea. The fingers of his other hand flexed against his thigh.

"I made excuses." She gave a self-deprecating smile that trembled. She seemed unconscious of the fact that she was now crying. Teardrops clung to her dark auburn eyelashes. "I convinced myself that there wasn't any point in talking to you until I was sure what I wanted to do. But I've realized since that I knew you wouldn't want the baby. I thought…I suppose I thought I could have my cake and eat it, too." She made a face. "Horrible saying." The tears now formed rivulets down her cheeks. She licked some off her lips but didn't so much as lift a hand to swipe at them. "I didn't know…well, what you meant when you said you loved me. Whether you were thinking about…about marriage or…"

"I was. Of course I was." *I am.*

Molly nodded, looking hopeless. "I wanted you both. And I thought, I *knew,* if I talked to you, you'd say no. And then…and then I'd never have another baby. I would have lost *this* baby. Cait's baby. And I'd be plunged back into mourning, and I didn't know if I could help being so mad at you it would ruin everything."

Somewhere in the middle of that speech, Richard had gone completely still. He'd have sworn even his heart quit beating as he absorbed the real meaning.

If he'd said, no, I love you, I want to marry you but I can't start another family, she'd have let Cait's baby go. Despite everything she'd told him, despite a need so primal even she admitted she didn't understand it, *she would have chosen him.*

"God, I love you," he said, shoving back his chair and rising to his feet.

Staring up at him in disbelief, her face tear-soaked, Molly stood, too. They reached for each other, stumbled into each other's arms. She pressed her face against his neck, and he turned his mouth against her hair.

"How could you think…?" he mumbled. "I was an

idiot, but I'm so damned in love with you, of course I would have listened! Of course I would have."

"I didn't think..." She wept.

"I love you." He kept saying it, and finally she did, too. He rocked her and felt tears burn his own eyes. His down vest might need to go to the dry cleaners when she was done with it, but he'd never felt happiness so painful as he did when she sobbed out her fear against him, while she held on to him as tightly as she could.

It was a long time before her body began to relax against his. She hiccuped and laughed and snuffled and hiccuped again and finally mumbled, "I think I'd better do some cleanup." *Hic.*

"Maybe I should scare you," he murmured in her ear, and she giggled.

Another hiccup.

She stepped back. "You won't leave?"

The simple fear in the words caused another spasm beneath his breastbone. He shook his head, and she fled.

By the time she came back, face scrubbed clean but pink and blotchy, eyes puffy and shy, hiccups apparently vanquished, he'd dumped out their untouched tea, dropped the bags in the trash can beneath the sink, rinsed the cups and put them in the dishwasher.

She hovered at the entrance to the kitchen, so much doubt in her expression he went swiftly to her and gripped her hands. "Now what are you worried about?"

"I trapped you into something you don't want."

Richard half laughed and shook his head. "Oh, sweetheart. I have a confession to make, too."

"What?"

"You know I was panicked about the baby thing from the beginning."

She scrunched up her nose. "Weren't we all."

Well, yeah. That was safe to say. His panic might have been the least of all theirs. Cait and Trevor had both been flat-out terrified.

"Can we go sit down?" he asked.

Molly agreed, and this time he led her to the living room and their more familiar seats on the sofa. He chose the corner, let her take the middle cushion. She curled one leg beneath herself and looked at him, waiting.

He took her hand, because he had to be touching her. "There was the déjà vu factor. An unplanned pregnancy ruined my life, or so I'd always told myself. Now it was going to ruin Trevor's, too."

She nodded. Of all people, she understood that.

"I've always waged an internal war. How could I think my life was ruined when that pregnancy, my marriage, our decision to have a second child, also gave me the two people I loved most in the world?"

Deep thought always crinkled her forehead and pursed her lips. "You loved them too much to regret what happened and the choices you made."

"That's what I told myself. But I also think…" He took a deep breath. This was the hard part. "Maybe on some level, I decided *love* was what had ruined my life. I hadn't been able to follow my dreams. I would have been able to if I didn't love my children so much."

Molly's lashes fluttered. "That sort of makes sense."

Richard laughed. "*Sort of* about covers it." The burst of humor died. "None of this was conscious, you understand."

"But it kept you from letting yourself love anyone else."

"As it happened, the issue never arose." He gave a

half smile. "Until you. Falling for you didn't trip the switch, either. No, it was any thought at all about the baby that did it. That baby could not become real to me." He made sure she heard how deadly serious he was. "Because if it did, if I loved that kid, I was screwed. I didn't know how or why, only that I couldn't, didn't dare."

"Oh, Richard." She leaned against him. "My turn. Don't feel guilty. We can't be responsible for our subterranean emotions. How can we be? You can't reason with what you don't know you're feeling."

"Easy excuse."

"But true."

"There's more," he admitted. "This part was more conscious, although it took me a while to get at it. It was fear. I loved Trevor and Brianna, and they were snatched away from me. I didn't want to hurt like that again."

She touched his cheek, her hand cupped and gentle. "We were all afraid of loving this baby and having to say goodbye."

"But you had the guts to realize we didn't have to."

Molly pulled back, her eyes searching his, her expression troubled. "Richard...starting all over when the kids we have are almost college-age isn't going to be easy. I truly can't blame you if you don't want to do it. I meant it when I said I don't want to trap you. You're feeling obligated now. But we won't be happy if this isn't what you wanted at all."

Swallowing didn't seem to reduce the huge lump in his throat. Richard bent forward and pressed his forehead against hers. He breathed in the scent of soap, salty tears and Molly. "I do want it. You, the baby, everything. Please, Molly. I want it all," he managed to whisper.

Her body shook. Not, he saw when he lifted his head, with new tears. With hope, maybe. He needed to think that's what it was.

"Molly, even if I had doubts about starting with a newborn, I still wouldn't hesitate. This is something *you* need. Something that will make you happy, and me?" His voice was stripped to pure intensity. "What I need is for you to be happy."

Her wobbly smile felt to him like the sun coming up, bright and warm. "Do you know what I've always told Cait?"

Richard shook his head.

"By the time she turned thirteen, she was rolling her eyes every time I said it. But the last time, she cried."

Damn. *He* was about ready to cry.

"I always told her that I loved her no matter what. If she failed at something, if she was a brat, if she was mean to me...."

"If she got pregnant," he realized.

She sniffed and nodded. "I kept saying, 'I love you....'"

"No matter what." His heart didn't quite fit in there where it belonged anymore, but that was okay with him. Uncomfortable, but...good, too. "That's how I love you, Molly Callahan. Will you marry me?"

The smile spread, became glorious. "Yes, I will."

"GOD, MOM'S GOING TO kill me," Cait said dismally.

She sat next to Trevor's bed, her back to it. Lounging on his side on the bed, head propped up on his hand, he could only see her face in profile.

Trevor looked at his phone. "It's midnight."

"She is *so* going to kill me."

"She won't. She wants your baby."

Cait turned on him like a tigress. "Don't say that! Mom's not like that. Take it back!"

"Okay, okay." Holding his hands up, he rolled off the bed to his feet. "Look, Dad's not home yet. Which probably means he's still at your house."

Her shoulders slumped. "Waiting for us."

"Yeah. I think I should take you home."

She heaved a sigh. "Oh, fine." She rose to her feet with the grace all her physical movements had.

For the first time, though, Trevor noticed some rounding in front. Not that much, but it was there. A sort of shiver passed through him as he stared.

Our baby.

Cait saw where he was looking. "I'm getting fat."

"No. You're… Wow."

"I'm pregnant." She screwed her face up. "By the time I go back after Christmas break, everyone will be able to tell."

Like they didn't already know? But there was a distinction, he understood. The unseen could be ignored; the visible couldn't.

He only nodded and took her hand, giving it a quick squeeze before he let go. "Let's go."

The drive was too short. Cait huddled in the passenger seat like he was taking her to her doom. He felt a little shaky about facing their parents, too. They were going to be majorly pissed. Maybe this whole thing hadn't been such a good idea. He wanted to be indignant, because it hadn't been his idea, after all, but couldn't. He'd gone along with it, hadn't he? He'd ordered the flowers, written the note.

Dad's pickup was in front. Trevor parked behind it

and looked at the house. He and Dad hadn't gotten a tree yet, but Ms. Callahan and Cait had set theirs up in the front window, and strung outside lights, too. They were on now, weirdly cheerful.

When he and Cait got out and slammed their doors, it sounded way loud, like gunfire. Trevor cringed. They met on the sidewalk, met each other's eyes and turned in concert to face the music. Whatever *that* meant. Why would the music be so bad? Sappy Christmas carols, that's why, he decided, thinking about the crap that was playing everywhere right now.

On the doorstep, Cait got as far as putting her hand on the doorknob before she hesitated, gulped—and finally opened the door. "Mom?"

"In the living room."

At the first sight of their parents, Trevor's anxiety morphed into stomach-clenching dread. Ms. Callahan sat on the sofa, while Dad stood on the far side of the room with his back to the fireplace, his arms crossed. Both looked at Trevor and Cait with these totally expressionless faces. Stern. God, Trevor thought. Had Dad paced the living room all evening? Had they talked *at all?*

"Nice flower arrangement," Dad said.

Trevor swallowed. "Um, yeah."

"I understand you forged my handwriting."

"Um," he said again. He shuffled his feet and looked down at them. "It wasn't that hard. My handwriting's not that different."

"Good to know, before you decide to write yourself a check from my bank account."

Oh, shit. Dad was *really* pissed.

"I suppose I should offer to pay for the flowers," he

said, and Trevor found the guts to look up. His father was grinning at him.

"Man! You were stringing us along," Trevor accused.

Ms. Callahan laughed. "It was irresistible."

"So, you're not mad?" Cait asked in a small voice.

"I'm not mad." Her mother held out her arms. "Come here, brat."

Cait rounded the end of the sofa and half fell on her mom. *Not* graceful. "You always say…"

"No matter what. I know." Weird that she was looking at Dad now, and they both had dippy smiles.

Trevor's eyes narrowed as he studied them. Then he turned to his father. "You said you were sorry."

"I did."

"And…did you…?"

"I did."

Cait lifted her head from her mother's shoulder. "You did what?"

Well, duh. But Dad said, "I asked your mother to marry me."

She tilted her head back and stared into her mom's face. "And you said yes?"

"I said yes." She hugged Cait exuberantly. "And no complaining allowed. You were asking for it."

Trevor exclaimed, "Yes!" and pumped his fist. Dad held up a hand and they exchanged high-fives before Dad drew Trevor into a huge, back-pounding, guy-version of a hug.

"Guess what, kids. We're family now," Ms. Callahan said. No, *Molly* said. Trevor guessed he had to get used to thinking of her that way.

There was one shadow of worry in Cait's eyes. "The baby?"

"Family, too," Dad told her. He was smiling, a half quirk of his mouth. "A gift, Caitlyn." He said it quietly, in a way that brought a lump to Trevor's throat.

Cait lit up. String of Christmas lights bright. "Cool," she declared. "This is so, utterly cool."

"Of course, you *are* two hours past your curfew," Molly remarked thoughtfully, then cackled. Totally *evil,* and kind of funny.

Cait pummeled her, and next thing Trevor knew Dad was sitting on the coffee table holding Molly's hand, and Trevor had sprawled on the sofa beside Cait.

He had this strange sensation, sort of out-of-body. Not looking down on them all, but more…seeing past and present and future, and knowing that as much as he loved his mother, he'd never felt as if either of his stepdads were *family,* not the way this felt. Somehow he knew that, from now on, this was home.

Dad and Molly, Cait and him and their new baby sister or brother. Maybe Bree sometimes—she'd be here next week.

He took a breath, and saw Christmas Day this year and next and next, and he met Cait's eyes and knew she saw the same picture and she was right. Utterly cool.

* * * * *

COMING NEXT MONTH
from Harlequin® SuperRomance®
AVAILABLE OCTOBER 30, 2012

#1812 SUDDENLY YOU
Sarah Mayberry

Harry Porter is happy to be one of the guys. No long-term commitments for him. But a chance encounter with single mother Pippa White leaves him reeling. Before he can explain it, he's inventing excuses to run into her, to stop by her place, to help her...anything to see her one more time!

#1813 AFTER THE STORM
The Texas Firefighters
Amy Knupp

Firefighting is dangerous—Penn Griffin knows that. But when he's injured rescuing Nadia Hamlin from a hurricane, he's stunned to find that his career is over. And even more stunned to realize the intensity of his attraction to the woman he holds responsible....

#1814 THE WEDDING PLAN
Abby Gaines

All Merry Wyatt wants is a temporary marriage to Lucas Calder to make her dying father happy. Her need to put down roots isn't a good match for Lucas's military career, but at least it's not forever. Or is it? Because her father seems to be recovering!

#1815 THE LIFE OF RILEY
Lenora Worth

Socialite Riley Sinclair is pregnant. Even more shocking, her long-absent ex-husband is the father of her child. When he suddenly returns, wanting to restake his claim, Riley realizes she has some explaining to do. Now if only she could resist this man she never stopped loving....

#1816 ABOUT THE BABY
Tracy Wolff

Dr. Kara Steward definitely wants her unborn child. But the baby's father, Dr. Lucas Montgomery? Not so much. It's not that she doesn't care for him. It's more that their lives are incompatible. Or so she thought before he began his campaign to convince her otherwise!

#1817 THE CHRISTMAS INN
Stella MacLean

Being a mystery guest at a country inn is Marnie McLaughlan's favor to her brother. Then she falls for the manager, Luke Harrison. Falling for Luke complicates everything because Marnie knows her very presence could compromise his job. But at Christmas, things have a way of working out....

You can find more information on upcoming Harlequin®
titles, free excerpts and more at www.Harlequin.com.

REQUEST YOUR FREE BOOKS!
2 FREE NOVELS PLUS 2 FREE GIFTS!

Harlequin

Super Romance

Exciting, emotional, unexpected!

Turn the page for a preview of

THE OTHER SIDE OF US

by

Sarah Mayberry,

*coming January 2013
from Harlequin® Superromance®.*

*PLUS, exciting changes are in the works!
Enjoy the same great stories in a longer format
and new look—beginning January 2013!*

HSREXPINTRO2012

Coming January 2013

THE OTHER SIDE OF US
A brand-new novel
from Harlequin® Superromance® author
Sarah Mayberry

*In recovery from a serious accident, Mackenzie Williams
is beating all the doctors' predictions. But she needs
single-minded focus. She doesn't need the distraction
of neighbors—especially good-looking ones
like Oliver Garrett!*

MACKENZIE BREATHED DEEPLY to recover from the work-out. She'd pushed herself too far but she wanted to accelerate her rehabilitation. Still, she needed to lie down to combat the nausea and shaking muscles.

A knock came from the front door. Who on earth would be visiting her on a Thursday morning? Probably a cold-calling salesperson.

She answered, but her pithy rejection died before she'd formed the first words.

The man on her doorstep was definitely not a cold caller. Nothing about this man was cold, from the auburn of his wavy hair to his brown eyes to his sensual mouth. Nothing cold about those broad shoulders, flat belly and lean hips, either.

"Hey," he said in a shiver-inducing baritone. "I'm Oliver Garrett. I moved in next door." His smile was so warm and vibrant it was almost offensive.

"Mackenzie Williams." Oh, no. Her legs were starting to

tremble, indicating they wouldn't hold up long. Any second now, she would embarrass herself in front of this complete and very good-looking stranger.

"It's been years since I was down here." He seemed to settle in for a chat. "It doesn't look as though—"

"I have to go." Her stomach rolled as she shut the door. The last thing she registered was the look of shock on Oliver's face at her abrupt dismissal.

And somehow she knew their neighborly relations would be a lot cooler now!

Will Mackenzie be able to make it up to Oliver for her rude introduction? Stay tuned next month for a continuing excerpt of THE OTHER SIDE OF US by Sarah Mayberry, available January 2013 from Harlequin® Superromance®.

Discover the magic of Christmas with two
holiday stories of love and forgiveness in

CHRISTMAS IN TEXAS

Christmas Baby Blessings

by TINA LEONARD

Capri Snow isn't happy when she discovers
that the Bridesmaids Creek Christmastown Santa is her
almost-ex-husband and cop, Seagal West. But when danger
strikes, Seagal steps in to protect his wife, no matter the cost.

&

The Christmas Rescue

by REBECCA WINTERS

When Texas Ranger Flynn Patterson saves Andrea Sinclair
and her infant child from her stalker ex-husband, he finds
himself in more danger than just losing his heart.

**Bring the magic of Christmas home
this November 2012.**

Available wherever books are sold.